I SEE ME

Library and Archives Canada
Doidge, Meghan Ciana, 1973 —
I See Me/Meghan Ciana Doidge — PAPERBACK EDITION
Cover art by Irene Langholm
Cover design by Elizabeth Mackey
Stock: Jose AS Reyes/Shutterstock
ISBN 978-1-927850-16-9

ORACLE SERIES  BOOK 1

I SEE ME

Meghan Ciana

MEGHAN CIANA DOIDGE

Published by Old Man in the CrossWalk Productions
Vancouver, BC, Canada

www.oldmaninthecrosswalk.com
www.madebymeghan.ca

For Michael
I was blind until I saw you

Author's Note

I See Me is the first book in the Oracle series. This series is set in the same universe as my Dowser Series, and contains spoilers for Dowser 1, 2, and 3.

While it's not necessary to read Dowser 1 through 3 before reading Oracle 1, the ideal reading order is as follows:

- Cupcakes, Trinkets, and Other Deadly Magic (Dowser 1)

- Trinkets, Treasures, and Other Bloody Magic (Dowser 2)

- Treasures, Demons, and Other Black Magic (Dowser 3)

- I See Me (Oracle 1)

- Shadows, Maps, and Other Ancient Magic (Dowser 4)

Other books in both the Oracle and Dowser series to follow.

THE DAY I TURNED NINETEEN, I expected to gain what little freedom I could within the restrictions of my bank account and the hallucinations that had haunted me for the last six years. I expected to drive away from a life that had been dictated by the tragedy of others and shaped by the care of strangers. I expected to be alone.

Actually, I relished the idea of being alone.

Instead, I found fear I thought I'd overcome. Uncertainty I thought I'd painstakingly planned away. And terror that was more real than anything I'd ever hallucinated before.

I'd seen terrible, fantastical, and utterly impossible things ... but not love. Not until I saw him.

CHAPTER ONE

"THERE'S THAT GUY AGAIN." Sprawled facedown over the black vinyl chair, I had a perfect view of West Broadway through the storefront window of Get Inked.

"What guy?" Tyler muttered as he hunched over my bare shoulder with his two-coil tattoo machine. Someone had to come up with a better name for that, other than 'tattoo gun.' Most ink artists hated calling it that.

"That guy ... from the pizza place two days ago. The guy who tried to buy me a slice of pepperoni, like I eat meat."

I didn't point. I wasn't stupid enough to move my shoulder and risk ruining the ink. All Tyler had to do was look up and he'd see the guy drinking a venti Starbucks and leaning against the pockmarked concrete wall of the convenience store across the street. A tall, skinny guy wearing black jeans and a knit hat in an attempt to look like a hipster, but really just hiding stringy, dirty blond hair. I was serious about the 'dirty' part, as in actual dirt. If the guy let his teeth yellow any worse, they'd match his hair. At least he hadn't actually smelled when he sidled up to me a couple of days ago.

"The daisy would look so much cooler with some color," Tyler muttered. He wasn't easy to distract once he had the two-coil in hand. Normally I liked that about him. "Red ... pink?"

"It's a peony."

"What?"

"A peony. And daisies aren't red."

"Fine. I'll stick with the boring black, as usual." Tyler snapped a used cartridge out of his tattoo machine and plugged in a new one. Then he started filling in the edges of my newest design. I'd copied my peony sketch onto transfer paper about two hours ago, and Tyler and I had argued over its placement for another hour. It had taken me three months to get the flower design exactly right — as perfect as I'd seen it in my head — and ready for its permanent place on my shoulder.

I had a tattoo of barbed wire with various things snagged in the spikes running up my left arm. The 'things' were eclectic — keys, spiders ... even a black-and-white Canadian flag. With the addition of the peony, I was getting Tyler to extend the tattoo over my shoulder now. Eventually, it would meet and intermingle about two-thirds of the way across my back with the ivy leaf pattern that ran up my right arm.

"I don't like him," I said. The guy across the street was playing with something, rolling something silver around in his hand. Pedestrians were steadily passing by him in either direction, but he hadn't once bothered to glance up from his phone.

West Broadway was a major artery through this part of the city. It ran all the way from Burnaby up to the University of British Columbia, which was pretty much as west as it got without running into the Pacific Ocean. As was typical for January in Vancouver, the day was gray. Despite the cloud cover, I kept catching flashes of silver when the light hit whatever the guy was fooling around with. It was probably some creepy magic trick with coins or something.

"He tried to talk to me."

"He must be insane then. Who would want to talk to you?"

Tyler was joking, but it wasn't that far from the truth. I could count my friends on one hand. If I included my social-worker-of-the-day, I'd have to use my thumb.

I didn't like people, so I tried to make sure they knew it right away. The moment they saw me, actually. I dyed my pale blond hair black, and wore it cut blunt just above my shoulders. I also wore white-framed tinted glasses over my weirdly pale gray eyes no matter the weather, and covered myself with as much black ink as I could without getting kicked out of the Residence. So nothing on my neck, face, or hands. I couldn't even get the multiple piercings I wanted, so I hadn't bothered with any. Not even in my ears.

That would all change today.

Today was my nineteenth birthday.

The Residence, which was what we nicknamed the group home for older kids, wasn't going to kick me out. Not right away, at least. Not without another place to stay. But I'd be encouraged to move on. Hell, they'd been 'transitioning' me for two years now.

And yeah, I was an orphan. Something that wouldn't even rate mentioning after today. Because no one cared if an adult had parents. As far as I'd seen, most adults tried to pretend they didn't have parents. Except my shrink, who'd tried to invite me for Christmas dinner last year. As if I wanted to be trapped next to a huge turkey carcass with twenty people I didn't know. Twenty strangers who all knew exactly who I was.

I doubt client confidentiality kept anyone's mouth shut about me, ever. I was such a sad case. Cue the tiny violin. Orphaned at birth. Mother killed in a terrible car accident. Her body never identified. Father and extended family unknown. Surname unknown. Never adopted, though a couple of families gave it a good try. And — wait for it — with a diagnosis. The shame. The stigma. Gasp.

Excuse me while I choke on your sympathy.

Two more hours, and I could leave the country if I wanted.

And that was exactly the plan.

I was done with Vancouver. For now, at least. I might even get around to changing my name, if I could ever think of anything better than Rochelle Saintpaul. Yeah, the nurses at St. Paul's Hospital nicknamed me 'little rock,' because I never cried. Flattering, huh? I've seen the nickname in the nurses' handwritten notes in my Ministry of Children and Family Development file. Then, when it came time to fill out my birth certificate, my social-worker-of-the-day figured out that Rochelle meant 'little rock,' and bam, I had an official name.

Whatever. Who wanted to live where it rained every day anyway?

Tyler gave me the peony tattoo as a birthday gift. He was cool like that, though he could easily get a hundred and sixty an hour for his tattoo work. I was pleased with the results. I'd drawn a section of the peony's petals like they were pierced by the barbed wire, so it looked as if the flower was hanging over my shoulder blade by that precarious attachment alone. I could extrapolate that the placement reflected life, or could read something boring and tenuous into it like I was the black peony and the barbed wire was life, but that was hokey as hell.

I wanted it to look that way, end of story. Though obviously I wouldn't be flashing the new tattoo to my shrink or social worker.

And it wouldn't be any of their business in a few more hours anyway.

Cue stupid grin plastered across my face. I was riding high on life today. Again, I wouldn't be mentioning that to anyone who took notes in a thick file folder. Like, never.

I slipped out the back door of Get Inked into the alley to avoid the guy out front, though I hadn't seen him there for over an hour. It wasn't raining yet. The sky was still a light, overall cloud gray as I skirted the metal recycling and garbage bins. Alleys in Kitsilano were cleaner than any alley I'd ever seen east of here. Even the alley behind the Residence, where I'd lived for the last two years in the Downtown Eastside, had to be cleaned every day, and that block had been updated only a couple of years ago. Part of the revitalization of the parts of Vancouver that freaked the tourists out. Picking up garbage was one of the crappy lottery chores a resident could pull as part of their room and board at the Residence every month. I'd been there two years and only gotten stuck with it once, though.

Anyway, the buildings in this part of Kitsilano were a big mixture of old and new. The tattoo parlor occupied an older two-storey block of concrete, but it was freshly painted, clean concrete. Some trendy coffee shop, a florist, and an interior design place filled the brand spanking new multistorey building next door. I couldn't believe the money people blew on things like that. Crap that they just consumed or threw out after a couple of years. Though I secretly lusted after the white orchids in the front window of the florist.

MEGHAN CIANA DOIDGE

The brilliant snow-white blooms were as big as my hand. The plants were planted in pots that looked like they were made out of ash-gray concrete. Little smooth black and white rocks nestled among the moss on top. I hadn't even bothered to check the prices. They probably cost as much as my tattoo would have if Tyler had charged me, and the blooms lasted like all of three weeks or something.

I had to take two buses from the tattoo parlor to get to my next appointment — the much-anticipated social worker appointment of my year — and I was going to be late now. But there was no way I was going to waste any money on a taxi. I had a plan for every cent in my pockets today.

I pulled my mittens out of my bag. I never went anywhere without my hand-painted satchel. I wore it slung across my chest, against my left hip, and filled with my art supplies. The mittens were hand knit in ivory-white cashmere and worn to hell. They'd been a gift from my last social worker three years ago. A gift given when she'd told me she was going on maternity leave and had to transfer my file ... again. No biggie, really. I'd had so many social workers and caregivers — their term — that I didn't bother to count anymore. They were all genuinely nice people who couldn't do more for me than they already did. Guilt gift or not, the mittens rocked, especially because it was actually cold in Vancouver today. It got chilly this time of year when it wasn't raining.

I crossed out of the alley onto West Broadway a couple of blocks away from Get Inked. I didn't think the guy from out front was following me or anything. He was just annoyingly chatty.

And now he was standing next to the bus stop on the corner of Burrard Street.

Great.

"Hey," he called, lifting his paper coffee cup to greet me. Geez, either that was the same coffee he'd been drinking hours ago or the guy was seriously caffeinated.

I forced myself to continue walking toward him. Obnoxious guy or not, I really needed to catch the next 99 B-Line.

"I was just thinking about you," he said. His accent was full-on American, though I didn't know the difference between the States.

"Yeah?" Ignoring his cheesy attempt at a pick-up — if that was what was actually going on — I looked over my shoulder for the bus. I wasn't religious, but I'd been having a good birthday so far and I'd pray for it to continue without this guy chatting me up to whatever God would have me.

"Rochelle, right?" he said. "I'm Hoyt, remember? You heading downtown?"

"Sure," I answered, completely lying.

"Maybe we could grab that slice?"

"Nah, thanks. I'm not big on pizza"

The 44 bus pulled to a stop in front of us, and the other bus stop occupants shuffled into line around Hoyt and me. I went along with the crowd, making a show of digging into my bag for my bus pass.

"Pasta then, or Mexican?" Hoyt was glancing around like he was worried about someone seeing him talking to me.

We shuffled along to the front door. Hoyt stepped up on the first stair and I took the opportunity to peel away from the line.

"Hey!"

"Sorry," I called as I jogged to the back of the bus. "I just remembered I've got somewhere to be."

The 99 B-Line pulled up, and I cut to the front of the line that was forming for it so quickly no one really noticed.

"Cool," Hoyt called after me. "I'll catch up with you later."

I didn't answer. I flashed my pass and made my way to the back of the bus, pushing through the annoying people blocking the aisle.

I noticed that Hoyt hadn't gotten on the 44. He was standing to the far side of the bus stop, texting. He looked up to scan the windows of the 99 as it pulled past him, and I turned my back. I really wasn't interested in exchanging waves — again, if that was what was going on. What someone like Hoyt wanted with me, I had no idea. Nor was I interested in finding out.

My day was unfolding perfectly, as planned. And that never happened.

Even though it was one of those double-length accordion buses, I had to stand because the bus was crazy-full of school kids. Standing was cool. I preferred not to sit by anyone anyway, but the kids were annoying. Sure, they were only a couple of years younger than me, but still. School didn't make them any less oblivious. Predictably, most of them got off two stops later at Granville Street, either to shop or transfer to downtown.

I still didn't sit down. Honestly, I liked the way I had to counter the pull and push of the bus's momentum. With my feet solidly planted, I hung, swaying from one arm. My right hand gripped the chrome bar overhead. I was actually left-hand dominant, but I never used my left hand for such menial tasks. I reserved it for art.

Vancouver — or at least this part of it — sped by outside the wide bus windows but I didn't bother to look. I knew this street and these people more than I wanted to know it or them already. I knew every part of Vancouver that I could get to by bus or SkyTrain. I'd never been anywhere else. Not even on school trips, because I never bothered to track down whoever was currently my official guardian to get permission slips signed. I would just camp out in the school library and read and draw on the days my classes went anywhere.

I should have put on my earphones, but I didn't. So when the hallucination struck, I had nothing to disguise my reaction. Listening to music was a good cover for involuntary spasms. I hadn't had an incident in months, though, so I'd relaxed.

Six years of 'incidents' and you'd think I'd be smarter. I wasn't.

I could still feel the sway of my body as the bus driver tapped on the brakes, as well as my hand gripping the overhead bar far too tightly now. The bones of my hand pressed painfully into the metal. But as the familiar headache rolled up over the back of my head from the top of my spine, I couldn't see anything but white … endless rolling mists of white. The pain settled across my forehead. I tensed every single muscle in my body even while willing myself to relax … even as I silently begged my mind to let it go. Just let it be. Please.

A dark-haired man appeared out of the mist, obscuring my sight.

He was tall. Maybe slightly over six feet. Pale-skinned and wearing a dark suit but no tie. His short black hair was neatly parted and combed. I had no idea who he was, but that didn't stop me from seeing him in my broken mind. I'd been seeing him like this for years now.

I squeezed my eyes shut, though I knew it would do nothing to stop the hallucination as it threatened to overwhelm me. The delusions were always threatening to break me, just as they'd broken me last fall.

The dark aura that radiated from the man was what had first inspired me to favor simple charcoal on paper for my artwork. Each time I offered a new sketch of him for sale in my online Etsy shop, it was purchased within the hour.

Other people wanted to be haunted by my imaginary friends so much that they willingly paid hundreds of dollars per sketch. My shrink would point that out as a silver-lining, but I'd prefer working at McDonald's over delusions, any day.

Today, the man's hair gleamed with the moonlit inky blackness that surrounded him. He was standing by a pile of stones, or maybe by a stone wall? He wasn't ugly, nor did I think he was evil, but he was blackness. Could I call a figment of my imagination evil? He turned his head to look at someone I couldn't yet see.

Oh, God. I didn't want to see.

As he raised his hand to touch the crimson stone amulet he always wore concealed underneath his crisp dress shirts, I dug blindly through my bag, frantically searching for a pencil or a piece of loose charcoal.

I reminded myself of what the world actually looked like right now. Of the chrome bar I was still gripping ... of the aisle in which I was standing ... of the bag I was digging into with my left hand, which was a gift from another Etsy seller — an online friend — who repurposed it out of an old army duffle and painted it with black ivy reminiscent of my arm tattoo. While I was still attempting to not appear frantic, my edging-on-desperate digging through the bag caused the new tattoo on my shoulder to sting.

If I could just hang on to my surroundings ... if I could just ground myself here on the bus, I wouldn't end up screaming on the floor and being dragged to the psych ward ... again.

It had taken me three days to get released into the care of my social worker and my shrink last time. The hallucinations had come and gone for that entire time. They'd continued for a couple of weeks after, actually. I had just gotten very good at hiding them. When I wasn't blindsided as I had been just now.

A woman laughed. The sound of it came from the hallucination, not from the occupants of the bus. Thankfully, I knew the difference now after so many years. That helped me hide my illness from everyone else.

A chill spiraled up my spine to follow the path the headache had taken. Not because the laugh was terrible — it was actually quite musical — but because I knew who was laughing even before the hallucination expanded to reveal her golden curls and jade-green knife. The knife looked like something out of a fantasy movie, but the blond woman almost always wore T-shirt's and jeans when she appeared in my delusions ... except for last fall. Now that he'd seen her, the dark-suited man's gaze was glued to the blond, but whether he was enraptured or enraged, I didn't know.

I didn't want to know. I didn't want to see.

I closed my hand around a piece of charcoal. I felt the grit of it against the skin of my frantic fingers. And that was just enough to help me focus.

The hallucination faded, leaving only a residue of blurry, blank spots in its wake.

I'd headed it off before it could expand in my mind, before it could completely overwhelm me.

I was shaking, clinging to the bar like the lifeline it was so that I wouldn't collapse to the floor. So I didn't show my weakness to the press of people around me. So they wouldn't know how broken I was. How utterly broken.

I'd taken my pill that morning, but just the regular dose. I should have accounted for stress. I never actually felt stressed, as far as I understood the sensation. Not until a second before a hallucination seized me. But my shrink, who was actually a psychologist, kept telling me I had to learn to anticipate the life moments that were stressful to everyone else.

To regular people, she meant.

And anyone else would find aging out of the foster care system that had raised them their entire life stressful.

Well, anyone else without an unknown psychotic disorder. Anyone else who wasn't on meds to keep them focused and calm.

The bus rolled to a stop. I swayed forward and then back, but my feet were grounded. I wasn't going to fall. I wasn't going to falter further.

I looked up to see I was at the Commercial Drive bus stop, which was the best transfer point for the 20 bus. I could barely see through the hazy pain of the migraine that would still try to pull me under if I let it.

Just one more bus.

I was halfway to beginning my life.

I was going to make it the rest of the way today.

I shoved through the press of the crowd trying to enter the bus and stumbled onto the sidewalk.

I wasn't sure how many years I'd been seeing the dark-suited man — at least six — but the blond girl, who was only a few years older than me, was new. Well, newish. I'd been hallucinating her for a little over a year now.

Her hair glowed golden, just as the wicked knife in her hand sparkled green, but I'd never drawn her or him in color.

Real life didn't look like that. Real life was rendered in tints and blurs of gray all around me. The streets, the buildings, and car after car were gray, gray, and gray.

I pulled my charcoal-covered hand out of my bag. I was still gripping the piece that had rescued me from the clutches of the hallucination. I also grabbed the medium-sized sketchbook that I carried with me everywhere. Still trying to get my bearings, I stumbled over to the low cement wall that backed the bus stop. I sat down. I needed to catch a bus up Victoria Drive to get to my social worker's office, but I couldn't manage that right now.

I flipped open the sketchbook to a blank page, ignoring the pages and pages of other drawings it contained. Ignoring buses as they came and went. Ignoring the people staring at me.

Using the charcoal-covered fingers of my left hand, I began to shape the hallucination.

If I could just steal a bit of it ... if I could tie this stolen bit to the page, it wouldn't haunt me. The sketch would free me from the grip of the delusion.

I didn't know why that was — why sketching worked to calm me. It just always had. I'd drawn for weeks after the terrible bout last fall ... weeks and weeks recording and discharging the hallucinations. Weeks of acknowledging them, tying them to paper, and walking away. This is why I sold my work. I released the hallucinations from the confines of my mind into the world through charcoal and paper.

I concentrated on the knife — a jade-colored knife that looked to be hewn out of actual stone — and the way the blond woman held it.

If I could just get the knife right, I could capture the hallucination in the sketchbook, then walk the rest of the way to my appointment.

The walk would give the headache time to abate. My social workers had always made me remove my tinted glasses inside, whether or not I complained about the fluorescent lights in their offices. My eyes were always weird after a hallucination — even paler than usual — which typically made my social workers launch into questions about drugs and other garbage. I didn't need that any day, but especially not today. Today was 'my birthday. Today I would be free … well, as free as my mind would let me be.

If I could just render the shading of the blade's edge perfectly.

CHAPTER TWO

"IT WAS YOUR MOTHER'S," Carol said as she handed me a ratty royal-blue-velvet jewelry box. It was about the length of a sunglass case, but thinner.

"What?" I asked, because I wasn't really listening. I'd signed some papers, retrieved my passport, and was now ready to walk out of this part of my life.

"Held in trust by the ministry."

"Sorry?" I asked. "You kept something of my mother's for nineteen years?"

"It would have been … if you had been adopted …" Carol took off her wire-rimmed glasses and rubbed her eyes. She was a series of shades of brown. Brown eyes, hair, and freckles. Even her sweater, belt, and shoes were brown today, but none of the shades matched. Too much yellow in one, too much orange in the other. Her hair was dull, devoid of shine. Her eyes needed a day off, even though — since it was Monday afternoon now — she'd just had two.

Carol had only been assigned to my file for about a year and a half. Sharon, the social worker who'd given me the mittens, hadn't returned from maternity leave. I'd already forgotten the name of the temp worker who'd been assigned to me in between. Carol didn't really know how to talk to me, about anything. She saw my thick file and it made her sad.

Early on, she'd talked about the possibility of teen adoption. I'd had my name taken off the list the day I turned twelve and was legally able to express my opinion on the matter. I'd had to miss a couple of meetings with Carol, and suffer from a hallucination in front of her, before she let the subject drop.

It was nice that she cared, though. I'd just had more than enough of nice in my life. I wanted more than nice, but I didn't believe that more existed. So I'd take nothing — and no one — on my own terms every day, starting today. Nice just didn't work for me anymore.

"You kept this because you thought I'd lose it?" I asked.

"The ministry —"

I waved off Carol's explanation and snapped open the box to see a gold necklace attached to an antique white rock. The quartz, or whatever it was, was about the size of a nickel and roughly hewn. The chain's links were wide — almost industrial looking — and tarnished. The necklace was attached by gold eyelets that appeared to be drilled right into the stone, but one of them was broken. The metal of it was oddly stretched out, as if some force had pulled the chain apart.

"Did they rip it off her?" I was whispering as I stared at the broken necklace, but I wasn't sure why.

"Excuse me?"

"The paramedics," I said. "Did they rip the necklace off her when they pulled her from the car? Or later at the hospital when she was dying and I was born?"

"I … I …" Carol replaced her glasses and turned back to the thick file on her desk. She always kept my file closed but in sight when we visited. Occasionally, she placed her hand on it when she was discussing something she deemed very important. When she'd taken over the office, she turned the desk so it was against the far wall.

That way she could sit facing the guest chairs without the desk as a physical barrier. The framed inspirational quotes and the fleece throw on the third chair were also meant to add a cozy feeling to the room. Unfortunately for Carol, the item that probably got the most use in her office was the Kleenex box.

She opened my file at the very beginning and began to scan the pages.

"It's not in there," I said. "I've read all that. I'd already know about the necklace if it was in there. There's a note about belongings, but I assumed it meant clothing that had probably been burned after she died, since I hadn't been given anything." I weighted that last part with every ounce of disdain that I could muster over something I'd only learned about moments before — so not much, but more than usual.

"Oh ... I ... you've read this?"

"Yep," I answered. "More than once. It's a bonding exercise. I guess you hadn't gotten around to offering yet."

"Well, I ... that is unorthodox —"

I picked up the necklace. It was as heavy as it looked. "It's broken," I repeated.

"Yes, I saw. I thought about getting it repaired, and cleaned."

For some reason, it incensed me that this woman had seen this piece of me, this piece of my history — maybe even touched it — when I hadn't even known it existed.

"Is the box hers?"

"What? Oh. No, I don't think —"

I stood up and tossed the velvet box on Carol's desk behind her.

She flinched back in her comfy black desk chair. She gripped one of the vinyl arms, then deliberately relaxed her hand when I noticed. Her light coral fingernails were chipped at the very tips. I knew she had a panic button underneath her desk. She'd used it when I was hit with the hallucination that I'd had in her office about a year ago. If she had just let me leave, let me get some fresh air and sketch as I'd requested when I felt it coming on, then she wouldn't have had to use the button. Then I wouldn't have had to suffer the touch of strangers and the questions of the paramedics. I should have left without permission, but I knew that usually resulted in reprimands and restrictions. Also, they kept the front doors barred — literally gated. I had to be buzzed through both the exterior exit and the door between the reception area and the offices if I wanted to leave.

I really hadn't wanted Carol to see me in the grip of a hallucination. Part of me hated her for having seen me so vulnerable. She'd talked about it as a bonding experience afterward. I'd kept my mouth shut.

I coiled the necklace in my palm, then tucked it in the inner zippered pocket of my bag, along with my passport and the big wad of cash I was more than ready to unload. I turned to leave.

"Wait," Carol cried. "What about ... will you be staying at the Residence tonight?"

"Doubt it," I answered as I sauntered out through the door. Social workers always kept their doors open during client meetings to thwart any accusations of abuse. And, of course, so they could call for help. Though as previously noted, they also had a panic button for that. I didn't think any of us foster kids were supposed to know about the panic buttons.

"You need to check in," Carol said as she jumped up from her seat to follow me into the hall. "You need to be careful about stress and ... and ... everything."

I quickly crossed by the other open office doorways. It was almost four o'clock, so most of the offices were empty for the day. At the top of the stairs, the room to my immediate right was painted in what was supposed to be cheerful colors. Kid colors. Egg yolk yellow, deep sky blue, and grass green. The room was filled with a tidy array of toys, low plastic chairs, and a navy blue cushy couch that had seen many better years than this one.

I looked away. I'd always hated that room. I'd met two of three sets of prospective adoptive parents in there. I'd also spent an entire day captive in there — three times — after I'd been voluntarily surrendered to the ministry, but before I'd been assigned my next foster placement. Everyone here was overworked and underpaid, including the foster homes. The rest of us were stuck in the nowhere that was between the two.

But not anymore — not me, not now, or ever again.

"Check in with me," Carol continued. "With your doctor, with your —"

"Shrink." I said. "Yeah, I know. How about we leave the counseling to the experts?"

"I'm a certified —"

"I know to get my white blood count levels checked once a week," I said as I trotted down the stairs with Carol at my heels. "I also know that there will always be a room for me ... if I give you enough notice. I get that you aren't tossing me onto the streets."

I got stalled at the locked glass door inside the front waiting area. This door could only be opened by code, or by remote if the receptionist was around. She wasn't.

Unfortunately, this meant that Carol caught up to me and managed to drag me in for a hug. Being all of five-foot-three had its disadvantages, and overly emotional hugs from chesty people was one of them.

"Right," I said, as I withstood the unwanted human contact without screaming. "Great."

I patted Carol's back.

She didn't let go. "I just loved that picture you drew for me. I'll always cherish it."

"Okay, then."

Carol finally drew back from the hug, but she didn't let go of me. "Oh, no! I bought you something. Special pencil crayons."

Great. I didn't draw in color. "I'll grab them from you later."

"Oh? Okay." The loose promise of a visit got me a smile. She was teary, but not crying.

"Is this your first aging out?"

Carol nodded.

"You're doing great." I really hated to lie, but I really had somewhere to be.

"Really? I was so worried when you were late —"

"Buses, you know."

"I'll miss our monthlies."

I hated it when she called our meetings 'monthlies,' like we menstruated together or something. "Okay, sure, but I've got to go now."

"All right. Be safe, Rochelle," Carol said. "I'll always be here for you. I care about you."

I nodded. This motion caused the migraine I'd just fought off to ping-pong through my head. Carol wasn't being false or anything, but I just needed to go. I needed to think about the necklace, and I had more errands to run. Errands I'd been planning for months. I didn't want to get derailed.

My entire life had been dictated by other people's tragedies and shortcomings, but now I had a future that was just mine. A hallucination, a mushy social worker, and a dead mother's necklace weren't going to slow me down.

"Thanks for everything, Carol." Then I said what I needed to say to get clear of the door, of the building, and of all the many caring-but-overworked-and-under-funded social workers that Carol represented. "I'll call you next week."

"Perfect," Carol said with a teary smile. "Happy birthday, Rochelle."

She even managed to say that — to wish me well on the day of my ill-fated birth — without a hint of irony.

She buzzed me through the door, then through the exterior door with one last wave.

I wasn't going to call Carol next week. I might check in later, just so she didn't send the police looking for me. Though I might be brain-damaged, I was polite. Some might say I was well trained by the system that had raised me.

I thumbed the automatic lock on the secondary security gate that stood two steps in front of the exterior, then slipped through it onto the sidewalk. The ministry was serious about protecting its workers. And with some of the loopy, estranged parents I'd seen raging around here, that wasn't surprising.

The gate clanged closed behind me. The sound made me smile.

I was never going to hear that again.

A bus got me back to Cambie Street within a dozen or so minutes, but then I had to wait for the next SkyTrain to get to my ultimate destination. I actually had enough time that I considered dropping by the Dairy Queen up the hill on West Broadway to see if a friend of mine was working. Then I spotted the jewelry store just a couple of blocks up.

This neighborhood was undergoing gentrification … you know, a cleansing. A bunch of the single-level storefronts had been torn down and replaced with big-brand big-boxes disguised in brick, steel beams, and smooth concrete with upscale apartments above. However, a few holdouts remained to sully the block. The jewelry store was one of them. I'd never actually noticed it before. But then, I hadn't owned a piece of jewelry that had any real worth before.

Even if the stone were only quartz, it would be cool to get the chain fixed. I might be able to mend it myself by squeezing the broken link back around the eyelet that was drilled into the stone with needle-nose pliers. I wasn't sure I had the strength, though. Gold was supposed to be soft, but the links of the necklace were really thick. A jeweler could probably do it properly, and it would hold better.

The dirty windows and door of the place were covered in security bars. The twenty-percent sale sign taped to the inside of the window was seriously sun bleached. The display case was half full of watches. Who wore watches anymore? The other half was filled with what appeared to be hundreds of different wedding bands. I never knew there were so many choices. But then, I'd never even fantasied about getting married.

I had to buzz to be let in, so I did.

Then I waited.

I waited so long that I glanced around for the security camera that I was pretty sure would accompany the buzzer and the bars. It was in the upper right corner of the doorframe.

I removed my tinted glasses and depressed the intercom next to the buzzer button.

"Hi." I spoke into the black box while looking up at the camera. I'm sure I looked ridiculous doing so. "I have a gold necklace that needs to be fixed ... and the money to pay for it."

I didn't mind that most adults found me a little off-putting. That was the point, after all. I couldn't blend in — I know, because I'd tried for years — so I didn't bother. However, most old people could be made to feel really stupid about their prejudice with a simple friendly smile. Though I only bothered smiling in that way when I wanted something, which wasn't often.

The door buzzed, and I grabbed the handle quickly before it could lock on me again.

The store was divided by three rows of waist-high glass cases, with more ringing the walls. It was less dusty inside than I'd imagined it would be. The cash register was at the back, next to a short Formica countertop.

Not bothering to look at anything, I headed back to the counter as the jeweler wandered out of the back office. He wasn't that old. Old enough that he was graying at the temples, but I had friends going gray, so sometimes that didn't mean much. Still, he was old enough to be my father, if he'd been Asian rather than East Indian. Not that I knew for sure my biological dad was full Asian, but I looked to be at least a quarter by my size and the shape of my face. This was why my white blond hair and big, pale eyes — supposedly inherited from my mother — were weird if I didn't keep them covered.

He was young enough that my appearance shouldn't have bothered him.

"Sorry," he said. "I was in the can."

Great. "Okay," I said as I fished the necklace out of the inner pocket of my bag.

"Cool bag," he said. "Did you get that on Etsy?"

"No," I answered — again lying, though I really hated doing so — because I really wasn't into the chatting part of human interaction. "My necklace is broken."

I placed my mother's necklace on the counter, stone first. The heavy linked chain pooled to one side. It was long enough that it would probably fall almost halfway to my belly button if I wore it. By that, I gathered my mother had been tall. I hadn't known that before.

"What's this?" the jeweler asked. But he was speaking to himself, not me, so I didn't bother answering.

He lifted the chain. "Yes, broken, I see, but ..." He stared at the stone, then looked at me. He was acting weird. Concerned, maybe. But then also freaked out around the edges.

He picked up a magnifying glass — one of those ones that jewelers somehow wore in their eye — and looked at the broken link, then closer at the stone.

"Do you know what this is?" he asked. His tone was weirdly harsh, but also excited.

"Quartz?" I said with a shrug. "Can you fix it?"

"Can I fix it ..."

He looked at me instead of the necklace, sizing me up for some reason.

The back of my neck started to itch. I was really aware of the locked door behind me. Could I get out of the store without him letting me out? I hadn't thought of that before coming in. Why would I? I wanted to glance back to check to see if there was a release lever on the door, but I held the guy's gaze instead.

"Where did you get this?"

"It was just handed to me by my social worker. It was my mother's. My dead mother's. But I'm not sure how that's your business."

"You didn't steal it?"

"What? No. Why would I be stupid enough to bring it in here if I ripped it off?"

"To sell it."

"I just want it fixed. Can you fix it or not?"

The guy stared at me for a moment longer. His eyes were really dark brown. Wet seal-pelt brown, but not warm and fuzzy like that image would imply. Slick and nimble seal brown. Tricky ... maybe not to be trusted.

"It's not a quartz," he finally said, returning his gaze to the necklace. "The chain is rose gold, eighteen karat. I'd have to weigh it to be sure, but this is thousands of dollars worth of gold in this market."

He looked at me for a reaction, so I shrugged. He looked at the rough-cut milky stone through the magnifying glass again, turning it in his fingers. "I don't know what idiot just drills gold eyelets into a diamond this size and simply hangs it from a chain."

"Sorry?"

He looked at me. The stone was now hidden in the palm of his hand, which he was practically clutching to his chest.

"Do you know what this is worth? The gold or stone alone? I could sell it —"

"No," I blurted. "Not interested. It was my mother's."

"The stone is almost the size of a nickel," he continued, as if I hadn't spoken. "Depending on clarity, the depth of the damage from the eyelets, and estimating on the low end, it's worth easily fifty grand. And the gold —"

"I don't want to sell it," I said. I was on the verge of yelling. I placed the palms of my hands on the counter to stop myself from snatching the necklace away from him. I didn't like the way he was holding it. I didn't like him holding it at all.

"It was my mother's," I repeated, carefully articulating my words.

"Yes, what a great gift —"

"It isn't a gift. It's an inheritance. Give it back please."

"Yes, exactly —"

"My mother died in a car crash before I was born," I said, getting angry as I heard the suppressed tears in my own voice. I didn't cry, not ever. I wasn't going to cry for this jerk. "Do you get it? She died. Before I was born."

He nodded slowly, like he was just starting to hear me.

"Give it back to me, please."

He passed the necklace back to me. I snatched it from his hand. Not even bothering to put it in my bag, I immediately turned away to cross to the door.

"Wait," he said. "I can fix it for you. And clean it."

"Never mind," I answered without turning back. "Just let me out."

I reached the door and wrapped my right hand around the handle. I was still clutching the necklace in my left.

"You really should wear it," he said, almost pleading now, though he stayed behind the counter. "You don't want to lose it."

"Just let me out. Please." I rattled the door, though I would have preferred not to. I didn't like freaking out in front of anyone. "Please."

He buzzed the door and it unlocked. I yanked it open and leaped out onto the street.

The cool air hit me like a breath of freedom. I bent my head down and hustled back down the hill to the SkyTrain station as fast as I could without running.

Only once I was there, seated in the fast-moving train with the houses and buildings along Cambie Street blurring past outside — only then did I carefully coil the necklace into the inner pocket of my bag.

I zipped the pocket closed.

I tucked the bag securely underneath my arm.

I didn't care what the guy said about the necklace. Didn't care about that money, if he was even telling the truth. But other people would.

I didn't like people wanting things from me. Obviously, I didn't mind selling my sketches, but that was a fair exchange — money for my art. I was an adult. Adults worked to pay for their lives.

I had been lucky that I wasn't an obvious target. I kept my head down, didn't own much in the way of valuables, and people generally left me alone. I wasn't interested in changing that dynamic in any way.

If I minded my own business, other people should as well, but nothing in life tended to be that fair.

CHAPTER THREE

"I'LL GIVE YOU SIX THOUSAND FOR IT," I said.

"Seven thousand, firm," he answered.

"That's way too much, old man." I grinned, just so he knew I was teasing about the 'old man' part.

He chuckled, his belly actually jiggling to accompany this mirth.

I liked Gary. He was nice for an old guy. His buzz-cut hair was gray and his big, gnarled hands had seen hard use — the hard use that had probably bought him this mausoleum of a house in Richmond. And, upon his retirement, the upgraded, insanely expensive RV that currently filled the entire driveway.

We were negotiating for the much less upgraded 1975 Brave Winnebago he had parked on a cement pad at the side of the house. His wife wanted a hot tub there. I figured she'd just be happy to not be staring at the Brave out of her living room windows anymore.

Not that I thought the older RV was an eyesore. To me, it looked like freedom.

The kind of freedom I'd been looking for since I turned sixteen, and started scouring Craigslist and AutoTrader to figure out what kind of RV to save up for. I'd gotten my driver's license pretty much the moment I was eligible. The license had taken some wrangling on my part, and I was seriously lucky my shrink and doctor hadn't pulled it after my last visit to the psych ward. Of course, I'd been rather circumspect about the blinding side effects of hallucinations.

Despite the blip this afternoon, I was certain I had the delusions under control. At the very least, I knew the warning signs and could react quickly — say, pull off the road or park the RV, if needed.

This was my second trip out into middle-of-no-where Richmond. It had taken a SkyTrain and two busses to get here the first time, but I'd figured out a way to skip the second bus on this trip. I didn't mind walking, and I could cut diagonally using the side streets where the bus had to drive in straight lines. The buildings weren't particularly tall around here, so the residential sprawl was massive. The house lots were easily double the size of those closer to downtown Vancouver, though.

It was full dark, around six o'clock when I'd arrived. The sun set early this time of year. I was late, but Gary hadn't cared. The delicious, spicy dinner smells coming from the house behind him when he opened the front door had made my tummy rumble.

I settled my feet. I'd been bouncing around a bit in anticipation. It was a struggle to compose my face. I really, really wanted him to sell this RV to me. He'd kept it in mint condition, with the original orange-striped curtains, brownish-orange carpet, and lime-green countertops. Even the dashboard was burnt orange. You'd think the colors would be completely faded and the fabric threadbare, but they weren't. It was absolutely hideous. I loved every inch of it.

"Six thousand five hundred. That's all I've got."

Gary narrowed his eyes at me and frowned deeply. "I'm not sure. Can your feet reach the pedals?"

I laughed. "You saw me test drive it last time."

"Yup. Nearly shaved ten years off my life watching you pull out in it."

He thrust his hand forward and I eagerly shook it.

I dug into my bag and pulled out the envelope of cash I'd been carrying all day. I opened the stack of hundred-dollar bills and removed five hundreds from it.

Gary sputtered, though probably more over me carrying that much cash than how I'd talked him down five hundred dollars that I'd been completely prepared to pay. I actually had a couple hundred dollars tucked inside my bag in American currency as well.

"I have to buy gas," I said as I handed him six thousand five hundred dollars of my hard-earned, scraped-together-over-the-last-two-years savings. I'd never been so completely excited to part with money in any amount before, let alone this much of it. I'd have to get some new sketches listed quickly if I wanted to eat next week. Thankfully, I wasn't a big eater.

Gary laughed. "You're taking her tonight, then?"

"I'd like to."

"Course, course," he said. "Well ... I should show you how to empty the storage tanks and charge the battery."

"I read the owner's manual and the driver's guide last time."

"Ah, yes you did."

I held my hand out for the keys. He smiled sadly as he dropped them into my open palm.

"There's an Autoplan place over on Number 3 Road," Gary said. "But I'm not sure they'll still be open."

"They are. Until seven," I said. "The insurance guy is kind of expecting us. If you're cool to come with me?"

"Of course, he is." Gary chuckled again. "I'll follow you in my car."

I practically stumbled over my feet to the side door of the RV. The Brave had a single exterior door — right behind the cockpit passenger seat — that opened to the entire interior. There was one bed in the tail section, and the bright lime-green kitchen table could be converted as well. The kitchen and the tiny bathroom occupied the middle of the vehicle. This model didn't come with the drop-down bed over the cockpit, though that had been an option back when it was new.

All I had to do to be exactly where I'd been dreaming of being for the last three years was climb a couple of orange-carpeted steps up into the cockpit between the driver and passenger seats. From there, I could slide in behind the wheel and be off.

Well, right after I got insurance.

I hustled out of the Autoplan place, even more impoverished than I'd been thirty minutes ago, but with my insurance papers safely tucked inside my bag.

The mall parking lot was empty, and the insurance broker's lights winked out behind me as I hustled over to where Gary was tightening the new license plates onto the Brave.

I was glad that Gary had come with me, because it had really smoothed out the transfer of ownership process. He'd slipped out before the insurance guy seriously depleted my savings account further. Apparently, it took four years — not three — to build up a safe driving record and nineteen-year-old's dished out a crazy amount for insurance. I paid for six months upfront without even blinking.

Gary grinned at me as I approached. But then, I was grinning at him like a maniac and practically skipping instead of walking, so I wasn't surprised. He snapped something closed on his Leatherman multi-tool and pocketed the knife. A screwdriver, I guessed.

"All set then?" he asked.

"Just one last thing." I pulled the back off the date sticker the insurance guy had given me and applied it to the blank spot on the license plate. It read July 14. And for me, that spelled six months of freedom. Yes, please, and thank you.

I straightened and offered Gary my hand. I didn't like to touch people, but Gary had been amazing. "Thank you, sir," I said.

He shook my hand and then nodded me toward the Brave without a word.

I crossed between his big Jeep and the RV to climb in the side door.

As I settled into the driver's seat, Gary crossed around to the driver's-side window. I put the keys in the ignition and obligingly hand-cranked the window down when Gary knocked on it.

"I filled her for you," he said, leaning in with his arm on the window ledge. "Tess baked you muffins." He gestured across me toward a basket on the passenger seat. "I'd already figured you'd take the Brave tonight."

"Thank Tess for me?"

"I will. I also put a note in the basket, with our cellphone number, our CB handles, and other things I thought you should know. But, ah, we don't use the CB very much anymore."

"Right." I let him off the uncomfortable hook he was wiggling on. "Because lots of working girls use them at truck stops to solicit customers. I'm good with Google."

Gary cleared his throat and bobbed his head in a nod. "Okay, then. Well, it's still good in case of a traffic jam. The truck and RVs ahead of you will let you know what lane to get into or what bypass to take. I also left instructions on how to change the password for the personal safe, which I'm sure you already saw."

"It's bolted into the floor in one of the lower storage cabinets."

"It isn't foolproof, of course, but you might want to use it for your passport and any valuables you aren't wearing. The sheets are clean, and there's an extra set for the second bed. Tess bought all the plates, glasses, and utensils especially for the Brave. But, well, you know all that already."

"Thank you … again and again." I couldn't stop smiling, even though my face was hurting from it.

"The tires are going to need replacing next year. Sooner if you drive her a lot. Try to get her undercover in the winter, especially in the snow. Don't invite any leaks."

I nodded, though Gary had told me all of this already. I had a good memory but I didn't mind him fussing over me — even if it was really just him fussing over letting go of his Brave.

"Tess and I are going to take a spin down the coast tomorrow, see where we get. It'll be wet, of course, and not all the campgrounds are open."

"That's where I'm headed."

"I thought you might be. Better to do BC in the spring, after the snow has melted in all the pretty places you'll want to see."

"Okay."

He nodded, then did so a second time more deliberately. Finally, he let go of the window and stepped back. "Start her up."

I turned the key in the ignition. The engine tried to turn over a few times and then caught.

"Call the cell if you need us," Gary called.

"Texting seems easier. You need an international data plan. I just bought one myself."

He laughed, thumped the side of the Brave, and turned to walk around to his Jeep without looking back.

I'm not sure why, but as I pulled out of the parking lot and onto the street, I watched in the passenger sideview mirror as he drove off in the opposite direction. I imagined him going home to Tess and their tasty dinner with six thousand dollars in his pocket that he really didn't want, or maybe even need. I had no idea why it mattered to me, but I really hoped some part of him was pleased he'd sold the Brave to me.

I had to force myself to turn left and wind my way back to the highway and into Vancouver, instead of heading straight for the border. I had a couple of suitcases and boxes waiting for me at the Residence. I might toy with the idea of just taking off, but I really wasn't going anywhere without my drawing stuff or an extra supply of pills.

The impulse to just walk away from everything was strong. It felt empowering. And I was still grinning.

Plus, I was going to eventually need food. I always hated the fact I couldn't get away with not eating.

Driving in Vancouver in a twenty-one foot RV was way different from testing it out on the grid-straight roads of Richmond. Navigating to the highway and then heading downtown was totally fine, since it was four lanes wide. I stayed in the far right with the slow traffic. Rush hour had eased off, and technically had been going in the other direction anyway.

The downtown of Vancouver, even in the Downtown Eastside, was filled with alternating one-way streets as well as cars parked on either side of the road. I clutched the massive wheel in my lap — yes, it was one of those, like a bus — and just went slow and steady in as straight a line as I could manage. Driving an RV was a big step up for someone who was more accustomed to helping out busing the other kids around in the Residence's minivan.

I managed to park the Brave in the alley behind the group home without any issue. Thankfully, I wouldn't have to back up when I pulled out. The homeless people who drifted in and out of the area — and who sometimes slept in the alley — were currently spread out among the soup kitchens and church dinners. The garbage and delivery trucks were long gone for the evening. So I shouldn't be bothering anyone. I also wasn't planning on sticking around long.

I'd already said all the goodbyes I was planning to say, which were pretty much none at all. I didn't want to rile anyone up when I wasn't sure where I was going to be in a week — or even a month — from now. We only ever communicated via text message or online anyway. This wouldn't be much different.

I might be back. Though I doubted it.

I had a key to the alley delivery door, and I used it. I'd tucked my portfolio, suitcases, and a couple of boxes behind the supervisor's desk in her office, just off the communal kitchen. Trudy, who'd been the supervisor since the Residence opened, had been away this afternoon at a conference. She hadn't planned on coming back tonight. That worked out just fine for me.

Some other foster kid a year or two from aging out would be sleeping in my bed by the end of the week. The Residence had a long waiting list, and only twenty individual rooms. I think Trudy was actively looking for funding to add four more. It wasn't just about the physical space — the building had lots of rooms — staff and maintenance were pricey.

I was lucky that Trudy had gone to bat for me when I applied. The fact that I ran a somewhat successful Etsy store had impressed her. She'd admired one of my sketches and I'd given it to her for her last birthday. She had it framed and hanging in her office. It depicted the left side profile of the dark-suited man who haunted my delusions. I'd sharply edged the charcoal and then smudged it to carve out his razor-edged cheekbone and his mercilessly straight nose. A section of his amulet could be glimpsed at the edge of his stiff open collar. I never could quite render the markings on the chain exactly as I saw them in my head. It was as if they kept changing every time the dark-suited man appeared to me.

Trudy had mentioned that someone had tried to buy the piece from her last week, and a month before that as well. I told her she should ask an outrageous price and then take a vacation with the proceeds. She hadn't found the idea amusing, though.

I didn't even glance at the sketch as I grabbed my portfolio and suitcases. Once the images were out of my head, I liked to keep them that way.

It only took me two trips to load my stuff into the Brave. I'd organize it later, when I wasn't blocking an entire alley.

I locked everything up behind me. I'd mail the key if I decided to not come back.

I took five art tubes I'd set aside, crossed out of the alley at the east side of the Residence onto West Hastings, and headed down the street to the pharmacy. The post office outlet there was open until 8:00 P.M., so if I hurried, I'd just make it. The tubes contained the latest sales from my Etsy store, Rochelle's Recollections. This series of pictures had been captured throughout last fall, after the hallucinations had really ramped up and practically incapacitated me for those few days in the psych ward. I'd drawn feverishly — perhaps the most I ever had — in an attempt to reorder my mind and dull the delusions.

Some of these sketches featured my dark-suited imaginary friend. They almost always did, which was good in a silver-lining sort of way — as my shrink would point out — because they always sold well. I occasionally caught glimpses of other people. A few times I'd seen and sketched a gorgeous, strawberry blond woman and a stern granny-type with a long braid.

In this current series of sketches, the dark-haired man was facing off with the blond woman in a castle, similar to the echo I'd caught in the bus this afternoon. Despite his formal, but modern-dress, the guy apparently liked to hang around medieval-looking places. Outside of movies and kid's books, I'd never actually seen a castle. And I had no idea why I hallucinated that particular setting. I'd actually walked out of the first Lord of the Rings movie halfway through. I wasn't a fantasy fan in general, but something about seeing castles on screen like that had made me seriously queasy.

In my mind — over the series of days that the images had held me captive — the blond with her flashing green knife had seemed to gain the upper hand over the dark-suited man. But then she'd walked away. It didn't make much sense at the time, and still didn't in the series

I'd produced as a result. I simply deconstructed the scene into simple sketches — bite-sized pieces that I drew to get the pictures out of my head.

My hallucinations never did make any sense. If they hadn't become so incapacitating as I grew older, my shrinks and doctors might have continued to brush them off as an overactive imagination. Early on, they'd encouraged my foster families to keep me active, signing me up for soccer and such.

Then came the pills.

Speaking of which, I had a double prescription to fill. I did pretty well on the clozapine, which I'd started when the hallucinations had ramped up so badly last fall. Once my system had gotten used to it, things really smoothed out. It had taken about three weeks to normalize. I hadn't experienced any of the heavier-duty side effects — like seizures or dizziness — but the meds made me drowsy. That was cool, though, because if I took it before bed it helped me sleep. I also had to get my white blood count checked every week, but that was what medical clinics were there for — especially on a road trip.

Medical insurance was the second reason I'd gotten a BCAA membership — for the year's worth of medical coverage in the States that I could buy through them. The first reason, rather obviously, was I'd just bought an RV more than two decades older than I was. Too bad BCAA didn't do vehicle inspections on Class A motorhomes, but I trusted Gary's mechanic. His checklist was really thorough, and Gary had been obsessive about the Brave's upkeep. The engine certainly looked clean, and was a straightforward design when compared to the minivan. Not that I could identify a spark plug in either case, but I could check the oil.

The clozapine was an antipsychotic, meant to block certain receptors in my brain. I was in a maintenance phase now rather than acute — as I had been last fall — so I took only one of the orally disintegrating pills a day. Before today, it had been months since I'd had a spell like the one that hit me on the bus. I'd sort of tricked my doctor into writing an early refill — on the basis that I'd misplaced my current supply — so I had extra for my trip. Since I'd never lost a bottle before, he readily believed me and hadn't bothered calling Carol. Again, I really wasn't a huge fan of lying, but sometimes it was just the easier route. I wasn't looking forward to filling an antipsychotic prescription in the middle of nowhere, so I figured I'd avoid that as much as possible.

The pharmacist didn't bother to engage me in small talk, and neither did the post office clerk. They knew me and my routine well. The prescription just had to be paid for, and I already had the 'Fragile' stickers on the art tubes.

I still had to figure out how to fill orders from my Etsy shop on the road, but I was certain it wouldn't be an issue. A prepaid cellphone paired with my second-hand laptop would make it easy enough to list new sketches and answer emails.

I was still refining a second grouping of sketches that had been part of my bad stretch last fall. Those hallucinations had been even heavier and more taxing than the first. This series featured — again inexplicably — the curly-haired blond with a samurai sword on a beach somewhere, but she definitely wasn't on vacation.

Unless she found it restful to hang with demons.

Yeah, the beings that appeared in my last round of sketches — the ones the blond was fighting off with her sword — looked a hell of a lot like demons ... big, dog-like demons with five-inch claws.

Demons created by my broken brain, destroyed by a golden-haired girl in red leather pants with a deadly sharp katana, then revived in charcoal and paper. Of course, the pants were rendered in shades of black in my sketches, but I'd always remember the blur of red as the blond danced across the gray beach in the moonlight. I'd always remember the demon claws at her throat. The shock of blood on the dark, wet sand. Her falling, the demons swarming, and the pain in my chest when I thought she wouldn't get up.

I'd thankfully only gotten glimpses of the demons, because that was more than enough.

I'd stopped questioning a long time ago why my mind showed me what it did, but I found the series difficult to work on ... draining, dark, and edgy. They would sell like crazy if I ever finished them. And I had to finish soon, if only for grocery money. Plus, once they were sold, the hallucinations shouldn't haunt my thoughts so much. But I could only handle working on refining the images for short periods of time.

I'd never seen anything as terrifying as what I saw in my mind those few days last fall. My broken brain had suddenly become adept at weaving complex, dark tales of demons, blood, and chaos. The hallucinations had never been as strong, before or since. Maybe I was wrong about my usual methods of exorcism being good enough to get me through the residual hauntings of the hallucinations. But the pills and the sketching were my only defenses, so they would have to do.

All of this, including the Brave and the new life I was seeking, would have to be enough, because I wasn't letting anything hurt me any more than it already did.

I could handle this much.

I was in and out of the pharmacy in fifteen minutes. Doing errands at night had always been a comfortable routine for me. It meant that fewer people were around, so I could move through the mundane bits of life quickly and efficiently. My tinted glasses still garnered stares from those who didn't know me, though.

What's-his-name Hoyt was hanging outside the front entrance of the Residence. I actually stopped in my tracks at the northeast corner of Hastings and Carrall Street, though the walk light was urging me forward. The streets weren't empty, but they were quiet. It was a Monday night, and Welfare Wednesday was over a week away. I stepped into the doorway of the empty store on the corner, careful to not disturb the nest of blankets and garbage there, and watched Hoyt across the street for a moment.

The Residence was housed in a revitalized section of the Downtown Eastside. An entire block of old brick buildings had been stripped back — only the facades were salvageable — and renovated into a bunch of expensive lofts and shops. The developer had been forced by the city to provide some lower-income housing, and had opted to lease this twenty-four-room apartment building to the ministry to help house older kids. I gathered it was a massive tax write-off. Or something like that. I didn't know or care about all the particulars.

Anyway, the point was, this was not really a neighborhood where people casually hung out smoking cigarettes with kids five or more years younger than them. Not that Hoyt appeared to be smoking anything, and the kids weren't just smoking cigarettes. Like I said, it was the supervisor's day off. But still, coming in smelling like pot was just asking to get kicked out. Most of us worked our asses off to get a room in the Residence. It seriously pissed me off that Jack, Elise, and Tim were risking their placements.

I quashed the impulse to stride across the street and tell them so, just as I always did. Keeping my mouth shut was my best defense against life.

A couple of twenty-somethings crossed by me, Starbucks coffees in hand and massive gray Gap knit cowls coiled around their necks.

Simon Fraser University housed its downtown campus two blocks west on the north side of West Hastings. The campus had been a part of the new development of the old Woodward's building a few years ago. The university ran a ton of night classes. I'd looked at the brochures more than once but had no idea what I should take after high school. I'd opted for the Brave instead.

Hoyt might be a university student, though he looked a bit old for it. That would totally explain him being here now and at the pizza place two days ago. Seeing him on West Broadway was probably just a weird coincidence. Maybe he worked around there. I was just being all weird and paranoid.

Still, ignoring the flashing red 'Don't Walk' signal, I jogged across the street and ducked into the alley without him noticing. Maybe the guy liked hanging out with underprivileged kids for some reason. He wouldn't be the first. He hadn't tried to preach to me about anything, but he might just have a long warm up.

I climbed into the Brave and locked the door behind me. I paused to push my boxes and suitcases farther back, until they were all tucked underneath the lime-green table of the dinette. I slid my portfolio on a slight angle between the table and the bench seat, though I wasn't too worried about anything moving around. I wasn't exactly a speed demon in this rig.

I climbed into the driver's seat and reached down to start the engine.

Someone rapped at my window.

I shrieked, and then bit my tongue attempting to tamp down on my extreme reaction.

Hoyt was standing next to the driver's-side window.

He smiled, chagrined. "Sorry about that." His voice was muffled by the window. "Didn't mean to scare you. Just wanted to say hi … again."

He made a rolling motion with his hand, indicating that I should lower the window.

I didn't.

I could taste blood. Not taking my eyes off Hoyt, I lifted my hand to my mouth. My fingers came away clean, so I hadn't bitten my lip badly enough to bleed. Just my tongue.

"Nice rig," Hoyt said, as if we were having a conversation and he hadn't just freaked me out in an empty dark alley. Well, I guess the delivery door of the Residence and its windows were well lit.

Even with the window and the entire metal-and-plastic side of the Brave technically between us, he was standing way, way too close to me. Gary had stood closer. He'd leaned right into the window, gestured past me toward the muffins in the passenger seat, and I hadn't even noticed his proximity.

There was something off about Hoyt, though.

"Thanks," I said. My heart was hammering in my chest, but I hoped it wasn't noticeable in my voice or face as I turned the key in the ignition.

"Going camping?" Hoyt asked over the sound of the engine.

"Nope," I answered.

I put the Brave in drive and rolled forward. I didn't want to run over his toes, but I wasn't interested in whatever he had going on.

He backed off, called something like "Have fun" after me, and thumped on the side of the RV as I pulled away.

As I paused to turn onto the street, I looked back at him through my sideview mirror.

Hoyt had moved to the center of the alley. He was holding his phone up as if he might be checking it for signal or texting … or like he was taking a picture of the back of the Brave.

I looked away, turned onto the street, and headed south for the border.

The jerk could try to recruit me long distance. Most likely he'd just focus on the easier targets at the Residence. He was probably some religious fanatic collecting brownie points for every soul he converted for his God.

Not that I had a problem with religion. Many people found comfort in it. I just had the feeling that most seriously religious people would stay far, far away if they knew I had two bottles of antipsychotics in my bag and another in my suitcase.

I shook off the residual creeps over Hoyt's alley ambush and forced my eyes to focus on the street ahead. The city was quiet as I cut through it back the way I'd already come. Only one more bridge, a tunnel, and an hour long stretch of highway and I'd be at the border.

CHAPTER FOUR

"How long will you be staying in the United States?" the border guard asked.

"I'm not sure," I answered. "A couple of weeks, maybe? It's a trial run. I might be back through tomorrow."

"Where are you headed?"

"Straight to the coast. First chance I get to turn off the highway. I've got RV sites all through Washington and Oregon memorized. But I might just stop and stay at the first place I find."

There hadn't even been a hint of a line by the time I pulled up to the Peace Arch border crossing, but I'd figured that would be the case. Ten o'clock on a Monday night was probably a weird time to travel.

I'd taken off my tinted glasses. It was too dark out to wear them while driving anyway. I put the registration papers for the Brave in my passport, then handed both to the border guard the second I pulled up to his booth.

He hadn't flinched at my eyes.

Bonus points for him.

I'd bought tinted contacts once, but never managed to force myself to use them. I didn't even like pulling down on the skin underneath my eye, let alone touching my eyeball.

The border guard was sandy-haired, in his mid-twenties, and had the heaviest American twang I'd ever heard. He eyed my papers and then stepped out from his booth to give the Brave a look of appraisal.

"She's in great condition," he said with a grin. A white plume of frozen breath accompanied his words, but he didn't seem cold underneath his thick, waterproof uniform jacket. I could see the edge of a gray-and-white striped hand-knit scarf zipped into his collar. Someone loved him.

"Mint," I said with an answering grin. I'd never smiled as much I had today in my entire life, but I loved this RV.

"1970s? Brave?"

"1975."

"Are you bringing any contraband into the country? Firearms? More than ten thousand dollars in cash?"

"No, sir."

"Fruit?"

"Just my drawing supplies and a cellphone with GPS."

He handed my passport back. "I'm going to ask you to pull over there …" — he indicated five or so parking stalls off to the left ahead of us — "… for inspection. Shouldn't take more than a minute. If you think you're going to come and go more than twice a year, I'd suggest a nexus pass."

"Thanks."

"Have a great trip."

He waved me through and I pulled over where he'd indicated. I wasn't surprised that a nineteen-year-old in an RV was getting double-checked heading into Washington State from British Columbia. I'd expected it.

I climbed out of the Brave without being prompted, then waited in the cold underneath the exceedingly bright overhead lights. I was the only one in the parking area, which was good because I hadn't exactly nailed the parking-within-the-lines thing. It wasn't raining yet, but I really should have grabbed a hat and my jacket. Thankfully, I had my used-to-be-black hoodie and my mittens.

The two-storey building next to me was a wall of steel and glass, at least on the parking lot side. A line of empty window counters, like the tellers at a bank, lined the far wall. A series of small offices, all of which also appeared to be empty, jutted off a corridor that ran the width of the building on the far right.

I was starting to wonder if I should go inside and take a seat in the pamphlet-flooded waiting area against the front windows when a customs officer wandered out from the depths of the building.

He spotted me, took in the Brave behind me, and then exited. A gust of warm air followed him through the glass doors. He smelled of burned coffee, but he smiled at me readily enough.

"I'll need to walk through," he said.

"I understand." I'd left the door to the Brave open, but was now regretting the heat loss. I didn't want to drain the reserve batteries by turning on the electric heat if I couldn't hook up somewhere tonight. But then, I had no plans to stop driving anytime soon, not even to sleep. I'd had enough sleep to last a good long while.

"Anything to declare?" the officer called over his shoulder as he entered the motorhome.

"No," I called after him.

I'd thought he might bring a dog with him, but I guess I didn't scream 'drug smuggler.'

"I'm opening these boxes," he called from inside.

"I understand," I repeated. "They aren't taped."

And that was that.

The customs officer was out of the Brave and inside pouring himself another mug of coffee, or so I imagined, within five minutes. But first, he handed me a brochure that detailed all the Washington State rest stops. I didn't tell him I had the major highways, roads, and free RV hook up locations memorized already.

I climbed back into the Brave and crossed into the United States of America. I was now as far away from my involuntarily-adoptive home as I'd ever been. And I wasn't about to look back.

I was only a few miles outside Blaine on Interstate 5 when the migraine hit. I managed to pull into the Custer rest stop before the hallucination took my eyesight, but it was an unusually close call. I got the Brave parked — badly — but thankfully there wasn't anyone else in the RV-designated area of the lot.

The pain followed its usual path up the back of my neck, over the top of my head, and settled like a fifty-pound weight on my forehead. A weight equipped with oscillating five-inch spikes shredding my frontal lobe.

I dropped the keys as I scrambled out of the driver's seat. I didn't stop to try to find them underneath my feet.

Suddenly sightless, I fell down the two carpeted steps into the kitchen area of the Brave. Thankfully, I didn't smack my head on any counter edges ... but maybe getting knocked out would have been better than the debilitating pain of the migraine.

Pure white light flooded my mind. A blistering wave of pain kept me on my hands and knees. I stifled a full-throated scream and clawed my fingers into the thick carpet in an attempt to hold myself steady. I choked on the next scream, throwing my head back with the pain as it seared through my brain.

I crawled, moving one hand, then one knee, through the torment my mind was inflicting on my body and psyche. Still completely blind to my actual surroundings, I slowly pulled myself forward. I just had to get to my bags before the hallucination took hold of me.

The white light in my mind faded into a mist, then resolved around a figure just as my fingers found and frantically grasped at my suitcase.

Oh, God.

I could see her.

Her golden curls were longer than before, now tumbling down between her shoulder blades. She was wearing a vibrant-colored cotton dress and flip-flops. I'd never seen her dressed like this before. She turned to look behind her.

I flinched. For a moment, she seemed to be looking directly at me, but she didn't see me. She saw someone over my head. A cocky smile spread across her face. She was holding her glowing jade-green knife in her hand.

I didn't dare turn.

I didn't want to see anymore.

I didn't want to see what she saw.

Without being able to see with my actual eyes, I found the zipper of my suitcase and opened it to dig through sweaters and jeans and underwear.

In my mind, the blond turned to look back into the … temple? She was standing in some sort of temple …

No. I refused to see.

A lightning strike of pain slashed through my head from the top of my spinal cord, just as I realized I was looking for my pills in the wrong place. I screamed, unable to stifle it this time and unable to continue my search.

I clutched my head between my hands, grabbing fistfuls of my hair as I curled up on the floor of the Brave to ride out the episode.

In my mind, the blond wasn't smiling anymore.

She glanced up. I looked with her. The ornate ceiling of the temple cracked. A deep fissure zigzagged through the carved stone.

My foot brushed against something. The raging migraine eased just enough that I could think.

My bag.

I had pills in my bag.

Fighting through the throbbing pain, I attempted to kick and manipulate the bag with my foot until I could just reach it with my fingers.

In my mind, the blond looked down at the ground. It heaved up and then fell beneath her. The stone splintered into multiple cracks at her feet. She spun to look back at whoever she'd been smiling at before. She was screaming something — obviously scared for the person I couldn't see, rather than for herself — but I couldn't hear the words. The hallucinations didn't always come with audio.

I managed to tug the bag closer until it was even with my hip. I dug my left hand into it, encountering the necklace from my mother before I found my pills. I must have forgotten to close the zipper after I'd pulled my passport out. The gold links were smooth and cool against my fingers. Somehow, the migraine eased further. The pain abated just enough for me to sit up and drag the bag into my lap.

With my mother's necklace grasped in my left hand, I found and opened the lid on the bottle of pills with my right. I dropped two in my mouth — twice my usual dose — and reminded myself not to chew or swallow them.

Clutching my mother's necklace to my chest and still completely blind to my actual surroundings, I lay back on the floor of the Brave and willed the pills to dissolve quickly. I didn't have enough saliva, though. I desperately needed the pills to dampen the misfiring receptors in my brain.

"Please, please," I whispered. I could feel tears of pain at the edge of my sightless eyes. The thick gold links of my mother's necklace dug into the flesh of my fingers, rubbing against the bones of my hand. I embraced this sharp sensation as the pills started to soften and spread through my mouth, triggering the taste of metal along the edges of my tongue. I tried to visualize the disintegrating pills flowing down my throat into my stomach, into my blood stream, then into my brain.

In my mind, the cracked ceiling of the temple caved in over the blond. No one could survive being crushed by that much stone.

"No!" I screamed.

Then, much more quickly than it had hit, the white-blindness of the hallucination was gone and I was left staring at the ceiling of the Brave by the dim light of my phone. I must have brushed the touch screen while digging around for my pills.

The migraine was simmering in the back of my brain, but the worst of the pain was gone.

I was surrounded by the sum total of my life — my clothing at my head, my bag at my side, and my mother's necklace in my hand. All cradled within the comforting confines of the Brave.

The light of the phone winked out.

I closed my eyes instead of continuing to stare into the darkness. The drowsiness that came with the pills swept over me, and I didn't fight it. I let the blackness settle over my beleaguered, broken brain.

Not bothering to drag myself farther back to the bed I wasn't sure I could lift myself into, I slept.

The hallucination haunted my dreams. Over and over again, I watched the blond get crushed by the massive stone ceiling. She hadn't even screamed. She simply covered her head and hunkered down, after which the hallucination would end and cycle back, from the blond's cocky smile to the caved-in ceiling. I saw it over and over again.

It had been many years since I'd asked why. Since I'd questioned why and what I hallucinated. But tonight, in my drugged sleep, I hoped. I wished.

I wished … but for nothing in particular, because this was life. This was my life. I was doing all I could do about it.

I'd sketch the hallucination tomorrow before I headed to the coast. Then it would be done. And I would have done all I could do to keep moving forward.

Completely groggy and with my mouth feeling like it was full of cotton balls, I picked myself off the floor two hours later. The interior of the Brave was pitch black. Without consciously making the decision to do so in the terror of the onset of the hallucination, I'd parked facing away from the rest stop's washrooms and info booth, both of which were fully lit. Even with the curtains wide open all along the sides and back of the Brave, I could barely see.

Waking like this was nothing new for me. In a sea of blackness, on a hard floor, and cold … I was so cold.

Whether I was lost in a blackout or a whiteout, I often had to rely on nothing but touch, sound, and taste.

I dragged my chilled-through-to-the-bone self through the contents of my suitcase, which I'd strewn all over the floor in my stupidity. I'd made sure I had my pills within easy reach all day. I should have taken a second one after the incident on the bus, but I didn't want to be dopey for my meeting with Carol. Also, I wasn't supposed to drive medicated.

And I'd wanted to drive. I just wanted to drive and drive.

At least I'd made it over the border.

I managed to sit at the table in the dinette area, only to realize I was brushing my hands across my cheeks and through my hair as if attempting to sweep away the clinging hazy bits of the hallucination. Just like a crazy person ... like the crazy person I was ...

No.

I wasn't going to sit here and wallow. I'd been an idiot to not know I'd need extra meds today, and now I'd taken care of that.

My stomach grumbled to remind me I hadn't eaten for hours. Actually, I hadn't eaten all day. Another stupid move. The meds never held as well on an empty stomach. And I had muffins sitting beside me the entire trip.

I pressed my hands onto the table and stood up to shakily cross to the sink. I'd actually turned the faucet before I remembered I needed to hook up for fresh water. Miraculously, though, cool water splashed into my hand. I slurped sips out of my palm while silently thanking Gary for filling the holding tank. The man was an angel. If things like angels actually existed.

I turned off the water, aware that I needed to conserve it, and ran my still-shaking wet hands through my hair. Then — still holding onto every available surface for support — I made my way forward to the basket of muffins in the front passenger seat.

I kneeled on the stair bump up between the driver and passenger seats and stuffed a raspberry oatmeal muffin into my mouth. Barely tasting what I was forcing myself to eat, I peered out into the blackness of the parking lot through the front windshield. I could just make out the midnight blue sky and a sprinkle of stars behind and above the tall evergreens that buffered the rest stop from the highway. As I watched and ate, I caught glimpses of passing headlights from cars as they zoomed by the tall trees. I imagined at least one driver was racing home from a late shift. She was probably already dreaming of her warm bed, and maybe there was someone waiting up for her.

It had started to rain, though maybe only moments before I'd woken. The drops were light enough that I couldn't hear them as they hit the windows.

As far as I could see in the dark, the parking lot was completely empty. Though that wasn't surprising, since it was the end of January and nowhere near a long weekend.

A deep chill ran up my spine, and for a blink, the hallucination I'd just endured hovered before me instead of the rain-splattered windshield. I shook my head to knock my brain around and dispel the hold of the drowsiness, managing to lose the ghost of the hallucination. But it was the cold burrowing through my hoodie and jeans — and grappling for a hold deep into my soul — that really countered the sedative effect of the meds.

This wasn't an auspicious start to my new life, but it wasn't anything I hadn't handled before.

I was lucky no one had heard me screaming. I needed to dig deeper into the off-the-grid RV sites guidebook I'd downloaded on my phone, so I could safely suffer in isolation. Though maybe it was a bad idea to let the hallucinations have their way. Because, unfortunately, I always needed food and people after an incident as bad as this last one had been.

By food, I meant more than a muffin.

By people, I meant reality.

Sometimes I got a wicked hangover from the hallucinations — the bad ones, at least. And they never quite let go of me. If I slipped into them too deeply, the edges between what was real and what was in my mind started to get very, very blurry.

Unfortunately, this aspect of my condition was the one drawback to the RV lifestyle that I'd been dreaming of since I was sixteen. I'd opened my Etsy shop with this dream in mind.

I couldn't lock myself away, alone, too deeply. Otherwise I'd get lost in my own head.

Again — normally — I wasn't stupid about managing my condition. This was why a cell phone and data package were worth the expense. As long as I didn't go too far off grid, I should be able to find people somewhere, any time of the day or night.

I snagged a second muffin, then headed back to my scattered belongings to grab my bag, phone, and a jacket. After a quick Google search for an all-night diner or coffee place — and happily discovering that the second muffin had apples and cinnamon in it — I was feeling up for a walk.

It had stopped raining for the moment, but the air was damp in a way that let me know the sky was getting ready to open up and really hammer down. I didn't mind the mist on my face. It woke me up a bit, actually.

It kept me focused on putting one foot in front of the other as I walked to the diner I'd googled. It was supposed to be just off the highway, a mile or so south of the Custer rest stop.

I didn't worry about walking alone at night, I'd done so my entire life. I had self-defense training, of course, and a small Swiss-Army knife somewhere in my bag, but I rarely needed it. In my experience, most loners out after midnight weren't there by choice or with nefarious intent.

Mist on my face always reminded me of the one and only time I'd been to the water slides. A group of volunteers that worked regularly with foster kids had organized a trip to Splashdown Park in Delta, which was about an hour south of Vancouver. I'd been thirteen years old — almost thirteen and a half.

I'd been having a good year living with a great foster family, who had four other foster kids in a range of ages. It was a long-term placement, because I'd already decided I didn't want to go through the matching and adoption process anymore. They had an orange tabby cat and one of the younger girls had hamsters. I didn't have to switch schools when I moved in with them, because there was a direct bus.

I was as close to content as I'd ever been, in a well-fed, well-exercised, and well-stimulated way.

Anyway, the early summer morning was chilly after we'd showered and started to climb the ridiculously long stairs to the top of the water slides, but it was sunny and promised to be warm soon. I was with a bunch of kids I'd known forever. I wasn't exactly part of the group, but none of us really were. We fit together, though. A couple of community program groups showed up behind us, but we didn't mix.

The blue plastic slides were slick, like I'd expected. The seams were a little abrasive on my shoulder blades as I went down, but I loved the feeling of the ride. The weightlessness. I just jumped off at the top and rode the freedom all the way down.

While lying in bed that night, I could still feel the movement. As if the repetition had carved pathways into my brain ... the twists, the turns, the speed. The moments that took my breath away, where I thought I might flip over the edge but then didn't.

And ... the mist in my face.

The sunlight had glinted off the water-slick plastic of the slide and made it difficult to see while I was riding down. My eyes were, as always, sensitive to the light. But I didn't mind being sightless ... then. Like I said, it was freeing somehow. Climbing the stairs and waiting in line for the next slide was almost excruciatingly boring, but the ride was worth it.

I must have been about a third of the way through my fifth or sixth ride down when the hallucination hit. Though I didn't know what was happening at the time. I'd reached one of the flatter straightaways, where the sun created a blast of white starbursts off the shallow rushing water on which I rode. I squinted my eyes like crazy against this onslaught, but was afraid to close them completely. Some part of me was still sure I was going to go off the edge, though I knew that was probably impossible.

When I whipped around the next turn, my eyesight didn't come back. All I could see was white light. The slide, the blue sky, and the other riders in the slides beside me were all gone in a wash of white.

I didn't panic.

I was riding the high of the day, the thrill of the ride, and it happened so quickly I didn't even think to freak out right away.

I could still feel the solid slide underneath me, the tiny bumps underneath my shoulder blades as I slid over the seams, and the mist in my face. So somehow I knew I was okay. My eyes were doing something weird — probably because of their light sensitivity — but it would be okay.

Then I saw the dark-haired man. The man who I've never seen out of a dark suit and crisp white dress shirt since — though that day, he was dressed head to toe in black, including his gloved hands. The man who would go on to star in my hallucinations for the next six years.

As I rode the water slide completely blind, in my mind I watched the man gaze reverently down at a crimson red stone necklace. It was displayed on a yellow-gold velvet pillow atop a pedestal. For years, I would fill sketchbook after sketchbook trying to capture the exact edges and shading of this amulet. The stone glowed softly. The chain was made of thick gold, and the links were individually etched with strange letters. I never managed to reproduce the markings in my drawings. Similar to how I never managed to read a book in a dream.

I had no sense of time or place — I never did in the delusions — but I wasn't on the water slide anymore. Or my mind wasn't, at least. I was in some sort of gallery, though I could only really see the area immediately around the dark-haired man. He lifted the amulet and placed it around his neck, then quickly skirted the velvet pillow-topped pedestal on which it had been displayed and made a beeline for a large, ornately carved gilded wooden door.

I caught a glimpse of thick stone walls as he exited into a hall. Tapestries, artwork, and a gold carpet that also looked like velvet ran the length of the corridor.

Someone shouted.

I tumbled off the edge of the slide into the end pool. I went under, completely disoriented, and accidentally swallowed water.

I remember thrashing, twisting in the water. I began to panic as I realized I couldn't breathe.

In my mind, the dark-haired man spun around to see whoever had shouted at him. He smiled, his wicked look full of satisfaction and pride. Then he brushed his fingers across the crimson stone of the amulet and disappeared.

Someone crashed into me, slamming both feet into my head. I hadn't properly cleared the area underneath the slide and the next rider landed on me.

Then I was being hauled out of the water and fussed over.

Once it was determined I would survive, I was yelled at for not following the safety guidelines, then banished to the bus for the rest of the trip.

None of that really mattered, though, because I still couldn't figure out what I'd seen or what had happened to my eyesight.

Hours later at home, while setting the table for my foster mom, I made the biggest mistake of my life.

I told her.

I was safe, comfortable, and warm. My foster mom had made potato salad for dinner. We were going to have barbecued burgers.

And I told her what I'd seen.

She listened. Too closely, though I didn't know that at the time. I just knew I'd had an odd experience, and that I had someone who cared about me to share it with.

She asked questions. The same questions many other people asked me many other times afterward. Turned out she was a nonpracticing psychologist, though, I didn't piece that together in the moment.

I went to bed feeling less unsettled, less concerned about the incident. I dreamed of riding the slides. I dreamed of the dark-haired man. I woke up with an appointment scheduled to see the family doctor.

Many meetings and many doctors later, I was diagnosed with an unknown psychotic disorder. Not schizophrenia, because that manifested with auditory hallucinations. My voices presented themselves only in video.

It also wasn't a brain tumor, and not epilepsy or any other seizure disorder — all of which were ruled out through multiple tests and MRIs.

I was crazy — pure and simple — according to the professionals. Well, they didn't put it quite like that, but that's what I heard and that's what I lived with.

I didn't stay at that particular foster home for long after that. Supposedly, my attitude changed. I withdrew and became unmanageable. I bounced around in a few emergency placements before the ministry got me into a home that specialized in troubled kids. I kept my head down and my mouth shut after that. But by then, I had a prescription, weekly shrink appointments, and a sheet on the fridge that I had to sign to prove I'd taken my meds. I wasn't the only name on the list.

Everyone always knew what was wrong with me, even strangers, from the moment they walked into that kitchen and saw the list. The foster community was a small one in Vancouver. Too many kids in care, of course, but we all knew each other. The lifers, at least.

When the mist hit my face now, I didn't think of the diagnosis or the pills. I thought about how the hallucination at the water slides was the only one that had ever manifested without pain, without the migraine, without the debilitating need to sleep and then draw afterward. I thought about how I hadn't even been scared until I was underneath the water.

I hadn't hated myself for being weak or broken. I'd felt clear and free that day.

Driving the Brave was a close second to the water slides — maybe even a better ride, because I got to stay dry, warm, and completely in control of my destination. No one was going to yank me out of the RV, label me, and then shove pills down my throat.

Happy nineteenth birthday to me.

CHAPTER FIVE

"WHAT ARE YOU?" a deep male voice asked, tentatively. "A witch?"

I started. As far as I'd known, I was the only customer in the roadside diner. I looked up from contemplating the full mug of very hot coffee before me — then kept looking up at least six-foot-three-inches of lanky frame and broad shoulders.

His skin was the color of brown-sugar caramels. I stiffened my spine and squared my own shoulders in an attempt to fill more of the booth I was occupying. My immediate impulse — as when approached by any stranger after one of my 'incidents' — was to burrow farther into the powder-blue vinyl seat. I wasn't a hundred-percent clear-headed yet.

"Did you just ask me if I was a witch?" I sneered at his square chin and chiseled jaw rather than look him in the eye.

Even through the haze that the hallucinations and pills always left behind, he was crazy-beautiful. I'd never seen anyone who looked like him — not even online, say in a romance novel meme or a movie.

Instead of crossing my arms protectively across my chest, I deliberately wrapped my hands around the coffee that I had no intention of drinking, but I figured would keep the waitress mollified while I decided whether to order a salad or veggie soup. My shrink had spoken a lot about confidence being rooted in body language ... or some other garbage I usually only half listened to. But in this case, after midnight in an empty diner on the edge of I-5 and with no one actually knowing where I was or when to expect me back, I wasn't interested in looking like some victim.

The guy shifted his feet. His hands were stuffed into the pockets of his worn jeans. His navy hoodie was soaking wet. He carried a large, overstuffed backpack slung over one shoulder like it weighed nothing.

The sky had opened up as I was walking to the diner. I'd sourced its location and hours of operation with the ever-helpful TripAdvisor app, after discovering its existence via Google. Despite knowing it was going to rain, I'd left the Brave in the rest stop parking lot. I'd straightened it so it was parked within the lines before I locked up. I didn't want to draw attention. But I was too far gone in the grip of the clozapine to actually drive. Though I was wishing that I'd thought to buy a bike and strap it to the back of the motorhome.

Anyway, I'd walked the entire one-point-two miles to the diner, the last quarter of that distance in the rain. TripAdvisor had asserted that the place was open nightly until 2:00 A.M., and the chalkboard sign in the window confirmed it.

By the raindrops that still glistened from his cheekbones, the guy had gotten caught in the downpour for longer than I had. I felt a terribly weird impulse to pull my sleeves down over my hands and dry the rain from his face. I gripped my mug harder, as if to stop my hands from reaching for him without my permission.

"I ... I ..." He stumbled over the words. "I thought with the tattoos ... and I scented ..."

"Are you crazy?" I resisted the urge to tug the sleeves of my hoodie down over my arms for a completely different reason now. "Because I have enough crazy already going on in my head. I don't need yours."

He hunched his shoulders as if the rain was still pouring down on him. I felt bad for snapping at him. For dumping my issues at his feet and expecting him to just deal or walk away.

Yeah, I expected him to just walk away now.

He didn't.

"No," he said. "I'm not crazy."

I risked a glance at his eyes. They were a startling blue-green — a deep aquamarine. I'd expected them to be brown by his skin tone. He was mixed race then, and more the gorgeous for it. Not that I could say the same ... for some reason, whatever-kind-of-Asian-I-was mixed with whatever-kind-of-Caucasian-I-was didn't come with the prettiest-bits-of-both-races results.

I returned my gaze to my coffee.

Silence stretched between us, but again he didn't leave. I could actually hear water dripping off him. He was probably creating a pool at his feet. The waitress would come back from the kitchen and have a mess to mop up.

"Can I buy you a piece of pie?" he asked.

"Can you afford it?"

"Just."

I nodded. I still needed to eat after all. "I like apple."

"With ice cream?"

"No."

He stepped to the long counter that divided the seating area from the kitchen, leaned past the powder-blue vinyl-topped stools bolted there, and called into the back through the half-open swing doors. "Um, hello?"

The waitress had served me coffee with minimal chatter immediately after I sat down. I appreciated the brief interaction, even though I'd come to the diner seeking human contact. She'd returned to texting and chatting quietly to whoever was in the kitchen. She was about the same age as me. I guess the graveyard shift fell to the youngest employee.

"Two pieces of apple pie, please," he called. "One with ice cream."

I heard her sigh. Then she poked her head out through the swing doors and saw him. She missed her apron pocket and dropped her phone on the floor instead. Yeah, even soaking wet and — judging by his worn clothing — downtrodden, he was that beautiful.

"Pie?" he asked again.

The waitress glanced toward me, still dumbstruck, and then nodded. I could feel her disbelief from where I sat, but she didn't hold my interest for more than a second.

I studied him while his back was turned. He was wearing black-and-white Converse runners that looked vaguely new. His hair was clipped short against his head. I wondered if it would be curly if it was longer. It was even darker than mine, and I dyed mine as black as I could get it. His accent was southern-U.S. of some kind, but I didn't know the distinct differences. He was in his early twenties at the most.

He turned back to the booth so quickly that he caught me looking at him.

I didn't look away this time. I'd said the thing about being crazy and he hadn't laughed like I was joking. He also hadn't walked away.

He smiled at me. Not at the waitress, who was scrambling on the floor for her phone now. It was an easygoing, playful smile. My stomach … squirmed … or flipped … curled. I'd never felt anything like it.

"Sit then," I said, more gruffly than I'd intended. But then I was covering for whatever was going on with my silly stomach.

He slid into the booth across from me, filling the other side as much as two smaller people would have.

I slid my coffee mug across the width of gray-speckled table. He pulled his hands out of his hoodie pockets, swallowed the mug with them, and lifted the still-warm coffee to his mouth.

He looked like he could crush the ceramic mug without even trying. But then maybe he'd be sorry about breaking it afterward.

He scared me stupid — stupid enough to offer him a seat and accept the pie.

"You've been walking … in the rain," I said, aware I sounded like an idiot stating the utterly banal.

He nodded. "Couple of hours. Since the last Greyhound stop."

I figured the bus ran anywhere and everywhere, as long as you were willing to wait for the next one. The only reason to get off and keep walking was because you'd run out of money. But I didn't mention it. That was his business, not mine.

He started to pass the coffee back across the table, but I shook my head. "I don't drink it."

He smiled. His teeth were startling white against his mocha skin. "Just needed a reason to sit, huh?"

I shrugged. No need to explain I was cold. Cold in a way that made it seem I'd never be warm. Cold in my core, and afraid that if I stayed alone, I'd sleep. Sleeping directly after an episode was one thing. But waking and then sleeping again meant the hallucinations would haunt my dreams in a more visceral way.

The waitress dropped off two pieces of pie and two forks. She put the one with the ice cream in front of me, then lingered to fill my coffee mug, which was now in front of him. She deliberately placed her hand next to his as she leaned on the table. Her nails were lacquered carnation pink.

He didn't take his eyes off me, nor did he lose the easy grin.

I didn't look away from him either.

"Thank you," he murmured.

"Yeah, okay," the waitress said, her tone tinged with disappointment. She wandered back to set the coffee pot in the machine.

He reached over and switched the plates.

"Warm," he said, pleased.

He took a bite, making sure to spear both ice cream and pie on his fork. Then he said, "I'm Beau."

"Rochelle."

I took a bite of the pie. It was warm. It was also too sweet and the crust was tough, but I could taste the apple. Apples always made me feel better somehow. More grounded.

"Is that French?" he asked.

"No," I answered. "Well, I'm not anyway."

"My sister's name is French," he said as he took another bite. He was going to finish his entire piece in three huge mouthfuls. "Claudette. But she's not, you know, like me."

I had no idea what he meant. Maybe that his sister wasn't mixed race?

"Isn't your name French? Beau?" I realized what I was saying before I said it, but continued despite my embarrassment. "As in, good looking?"

He looked up at me without answering. I felt like I was missing something in his 'not like me' comment. I had no idea what it could be, though — or why it would hang between us so tangibly.

His gaze fell to my piece of pie, or maybe to my hands. I didn't fiddle with my fork. He unnerved me, but it wasn't at all unpleasant.

"No," he said, with a definite shake of his head.

I'd forgotten what we were talking about.

Then he reached across the table and — barely touching me — turned my left hand over until the back rested on the table. With a touch so light that I felt only the shiver of its passing, he brushed his fingers across the black butterfly I had tattooed on the inside of my wrist.

"Rochelle," he murmured. "Who are you?"

My stomach flipped again. This time the feeling was accompanied by a rush of what was unmistakably desire. This was a thing I had heard many a teenaged roommate gush about ... endlessly. Though I'd never experienced the feeling myself, not even during my previous, brief sexual encounters.

I stared at the tattooed butterfly as he withdrew his hand. I was suddenly very pleased that I had chosen to keep it free of the barbed wire, which also started at my wrist and wound up my arm.

"You got somewhere to stay?" he asked.

"Always," I answered, glad my voice wasn't as shaky as my insides.

I took a second bite of my pie, already knowing I was going to invite him back to the Brave.

"Good," he said, and he meant it for me rather than himself. As if he was glad I wasn't living on the street, even though he'd only just met me.

"And you?" I asked. "Got somewhere to stay?"

"Never." He answered without concern, or sadness, or self-pity.

"That works," I said, not really knowing what I meant.

"Yep," he answered. Then he finished his pie.

"There should be lights," I said as I stumbled up the two steps into the Brave. "Somewhere in here."

We'd walked back to the rest stop parking lot without really discussing it, without Beau even asking where we were going. It had stopped raining by the time the waitress informed us that the diner was closing. I probably should have been concerned about bringing a stranger back to the Brave — especially a man of Beau's size — but I wasn't. I knew a predator when I saw one. Unfortunately, most foster kids were pretty savvy that way, pretty early on.

"I can see," he murmured behind me.

It was seriously pitch black in the interior of the motorhome, even with the exterior lights still illuminating the public washrooms behind us. Completely blind, I reached for the countertop I was fairly certain was a couple of steps off to the side. I stumbled over some of the clothing I'd left in the middle of the kitchen-area floor.

Beau grabbed me by the elbow, so that I only listed deeply to one side rather than doing the face plant I'd thought was coming my way. As soon as I had my footing, he let me go.

I hunkered down, still blind, and started gathering the items strewn across the floor and shoving them back into my suitcase underneath the kitchen table.

"You don't have to do that for me," he said.

"I'm not."

Even without being able to see him, I could feel how he completely filled the darkness behind me. Knowing that the interior height was approximately six-foot-five, I guessed that Beau could just stand up straight inside, maybe with a couple of inches clearance. Yes, I'd practically memorized the owner's manual while waiting to buy the Brave.

I heard him close and lock the exterior door. "You can park here overnight?"

"Yeah, but there's no water hookup or electricity, so I'm running off storage tanks and the battery."

A light flared behind me. He'd found a large flashlight somewhere, though how he'd seen it in the dark, I didn't know.

"Cool," he said, looking around with the light. "I'd like to check the engine for you tomorrow morning."

"Yeah," I said, straightening up after wrestling the suitcase back underneath the table. "You think you're staying until morning, hey?"

A slow grin spread across his face. "I'm not going anywhere until you kick me out," he said. "I think you'll find me useful."

"Can you cook?"

He laughed, low and deep. A curl of desire ignited in my belly. Again, though I'd never felt such a thing before, it was unmistakable.

"I can."

He set the still-lit flashlight on the counter, facing upward so it illuminated the ceiling. Then he dropped his backpack on the bench seat of the dinette and took a short, deliberate step toward me. "I can drive. I can fix the engine. I get paid well to fix engines, actually. I can carry heavy things for you."

"I don't really keep many heavy things around," I said, aware that this was the beginning of some sort of mating dance and relishing every minute of it. What someone who looked like him was doing in my RV, I had no idea. But I also felt no need to question it. Not right now, at least.

"You don't," Beau said with another measured step and another glance around. He was now only about two feet away from me, standing in front of the flashlight. Even though its light was directed at the ceiling, he was so big that he actually blocked it. "You've just moved in?"

"Yeah," I answered, really unable to say or think anything of substance anymore.

He reached over, and with a touch as light as he'd used in the diner, he brushed his fingers across my cheek. He tucked my hair behind my ear, feathered his fingers over the side of my head, and then caressed down my neck and across my collarbone.

I shivered, swaying slightly toward him.

He dropped his hand off the edge of my shoulder. He didn't move closer.

He was quiet … still and gentle. But I didn't think he was sad. Of course, I didn't know him well enough to know exactly what he was feeling. I pressed the palm of my right hand to the table, and the cool kiss of Formica on my skin steadied me.

"You're a mechanic?" I asked, prolonging the conversation a few seconds more.

He grinned. I liked him smiling, which was silly, because whether or not he was happy wasn't really my concern or within my power to affect.

"Born and raised."

"You can be born a mechanic?"

"Some things are in the blood."

"I wouldn't know," I said. "I don't know my parents."

"I wish I didn't," he said. Though again, there was no hint of self-pity in his statement. "But I think you might be surprised. There's power in blood ... your blood."

"I have no idea what you're talking about."

"I know. It doesn't matter now."

I stared at him for a long, long time, and he let me. Then I reached up and mimicked his own movements as I touched his cheek, ear, and neck. He closed his eyes and shuddered.

I dropped my hand, worried I'd done something wrong or weird. He caught it before it fell to my side, pressing it against his chest. He was super warm even through his hoodie.

He opened his eyes, and for a moment in the dim light, I could swear they were glowing green. My breath actually caught in my throat.

"You have the most amazing eyes," he whispered.

I believed him. So help me, I did. I believed that he thought my weird, colorless eyes were amazing. "I was just going to say the same thing to you."

"Were you?" he asked. "I doubt you ever say anything unless it's the perfectly correct thing to say in the moment. Perfectly thought out."

"You think you know me?"

"I think I'm very interested in knowing you."

"It's my birthday," I said. "Or it was yesterday, before midnight."

"Happy birthday."

"Thank you." I'd never been so happy to have someone say that, not once in the nineteen years I'd suffered birthdays. "Let's not sleep."

"Never again?"

"Never close our eyes on today," I said.

He responded by kneeling before me — to even up our height differences, I guessed, though now my lips were level with his forehead — and pulling me tight against his chest for a searing kiss.

I was serious about the searing part. His lips were hot against mine. I could feel the heat of his hands where they splayed across my lower back and my right hip, even through my jeans.

I lost my balance — specifically, I lost control of my knees. I swayed into him, reaching around to wrap my hands around the back of his head and neck. I deepened the kiss, opening my mouth and inviting him in. He obligingly pressed his tongue to mine.

I'd never wanted anyone as much as I wanted to be with him. My previous sexual encounters had been planned and executed for the experience. They'd never lasted more than one night ... both of them. I pushed away my instinct to crush this feeling, to dissect and judge it.

He pushed his hand up underneath the back of my hoodie and T-shirt, seeking the bare skin of my back.

I moaned into his mouth. He transferred his attention to my neck, and it was my turn to shudder at his touch. I felt like every nerve ending in my body was crying out to be stroked. I hadn't felt this ... this ... vital, alert, teeming ... not since before I'd started taking the drugs for the hallucinations. Maybe not ever.

He had my hoodie and T-shirt off in one smooth motion that I would have scoffed at if a silly roommate had recounted it. I reached for the zipper of his hoodie, but he knocked my hands away with a grin.

"You first," he said. "I want to see where all the tattoos go." He raised an eyebrow and asked coyly, "Here?" as he ran his fingers along the edge of my jeans.

I laughed. A deep, husky sound I don't think I'd ever made before. "I guess you'll have to see."

He took that as an invitation to divest me of my jeans, which of course it was.

"Nice panties," he said.

My black lace underwear matched my bra. I'd bought the set from a crazy-expensive place on Granville Street two weeks ago, for no reason other than I didn't actually own a bra. I'd been oddly pleased when the clerk had fitted me in a size 32 with a B cup.

Kissing me again, he reached between my legs, pushing aside the panties he so admired to slip a finger into me. I felt hot and almost embarrassingly wet.

I cried out, swayed into him again, and clutched at his shoulders to keep my balance.

He grunted, satisfied and turned on. This noise somehow only increased my pleasure. Heat lapped up from the gentle pressure of his finger through my lower belly and up across my chest.

My nipples hardened further, almost painfully.

I couldn't concentrate on kissing him anymore. I wasn't a hundred percent sure I was even supporting my own weight.

He lowered his mouth to press warm kisses to my breasts, somehow holding me upright and getting my bra loosened, but not off, at the same time. He kissed all around the sides and underneath my breasts, one and then the other. Other lovers had always just gone straight for my nipples. I didn't know the rest of my flesh was so extremely sensitive.

He sucked a nipple into his mouth and I stifled a scream.

"I can't," I cried. "I'm not sure …"

He paused. Everything.

"Oh, God. I didn't mean no."

He obliging started moving his fingers and mouth again.

I started laughing. I had no idea why I was doing it, or why I would laugh in this moment. He laughed with me, chuckling against my breast.

"I don't think I can stand up anymore," I said.

"I think you can," he said.

"I really don't think …"

My feet started tingling. The feeling moved up my legs and through my body in a rush of utter pleasure, and I bucked underneath his fingers as I orgasmed.

He didn't stop moving his fingers until I cried out and grabbed for his hand. I stood there with his hand pinned against me, and his cheek against my chest, panting through the burn of pleasure. I'd never panted before.

"Your turn?" I asked when I could think again.

"Condom?" he asked.

"In the suitcase. I think."

He pressed me against his chest with his right hand at my lower back, then lifted me up like that. Grasping the suitcase from underneath the dinette table in his left hand, he carried me to the bed at the back of the Brave. I wrapped my arms around his neck and sucked lightly on his earlobe.

He grunted — a simple sound so full of pleasure that it made me feel bold and free. He lowered me onto the bed, leaning over for a lingering kiss as he laid me out on my back.

I slipped backward, wriggling to pull off my panties and bra.

He didn't take his eyes off me as he kneeled to dig through the suitcase and find the couple of condoms I had in a ziplock bag, alongside my toothbrush and toothpaste.

He finally looked away to peer at the condoms in his hand. "Hmm," he said as he straightened to fill the space above and around me. "These might not fit."

I laughed at his silly, manly joke. Then, still grinning, I leaned back on my elbows and splayed my legs open daringly. Invitingly.

He moaned and took his clothing off so quickly that he looked like a dark blur. I was sorry to not get a better look at him before he climbed over me and pulled my hips up to meet his. But then every other useless thought fell out of my head.

He was right about the condoms, actually. But neither of us complained.

CHAPTER SIX

"YOU SHOULD WAKE UP AND EAT SOMETHING," Beau whispered in my ear. The brush of his warm breath sent shivers straight down to my nether regions. Oh, God, I was so in trouble with him. Too far gone already.

I'd been delaying getting up since he'd returned to the Brave with — by the smell — coffee and some kind of baked goods. I'd woken out of a deep, dreamless sleep. Normally, with the strength of the hallucinations that had hit me last night, I would have been haunted all evening. I'd forgotten to close any of the curtains. On any other day in late January on the West Coast, this wouldn't have been an issue. But this morning, the sun had made an appearance.

He'd kissed me before he left just after sunrise, then whispered, "I'll be back."

I had refused to open my eyes and acknowledge the new day — and the conversation sure to come with it. I'd fretted and ached the entire time he was gone, like some silly bimbo looking to be rescued or whatever. This weirdness had only increased when he returned. My anxiety ramped up instead of being relieved. I mean, who picked up some gorgeous guy from a roadside diner after midnight and hoped to keep him in the morning?

Deliberately keeping my eyes closed, I sat up in a tangle of bed sheets and swung my legs off the bed. Beau made some sort of huffing noise. I opened my eyes to find him staring at me from the kitchen.

"You ..." he said. His voice was pained or heavy with some sort of emotion I couldn't identify. The morning light made his dark aquamarine eyes stand out even more starkly against his brown skin. He swallowed.

Then he laughed and shook his head. "I guess I shouldn't use words like 'beautiful,' or 'perfection,' or tell you how much I ache for you even though I just had you a couple of hours ago?"

The words actually hurt as I heard and absorbed them. It was a pain that I wanted to hold and cherish, that I wanted to grab and never let go of.

I smiled, and in lieu of a verbal response, I rose, letting the sheets fall away from me. I stood before him naked, except for my tattoos. Only the peony underneath its bandage on my left shoulder was still hidden from his intent gaze. I'd never exposed myself to someone so deliberately before. I had no illusions about my own beauty, but I wasn't stupid enough to question him, to question this moment between us. I'd take whatever he was willing to give, as I'd always done. If it lasted another hour, I'd be okay. If it lasted a week, I might be not okay, but I'd survive. I always survived. I might as well relish something for the first time in my life.

A satisfied grin spread across his face. He leaned back against the tiny lime-green kitchen counter with his hands gripping the edge, gazing at me through almost-closed eyes. His T-shirt was so tight across his biceps that I was surprised it wasn't uncomfortable for him.

"You look like a cat relishing a pool of the rising sun," I said.

This startled him.

I padded toward him. He leaned forward and tugged the blinds closed across the window above the kitchen table. He could reach across the width of the Brave and still lean against the counter. He was that long. The idea of him in my space should utterly overwhelm me. He should be too big, too much. And yet he wasn't.

"Bathroom," I murmured.

"I'll be here," he said.

I slipped by him, ignoring my deep need to press myself against the long length of him, and stepped into the tiny washroom to use the facilities. I washed my hands. Gary or Tess had made sure the soap dispenser was full. I couldn't brush my hair or my teeth because I hadn't unpacked last night. I settled for a damp-finger hair combing and rinsing out my mouth multiple times.

I slipped back out of the bathroom to find that Beau had put chocolate croissants on plates and set the table. Completely aware that he was watching me again, I crossed back to the wardrobe at the left front of the bed where he'd tucked my suitcase last night. I'd never had anyone look at me like this. But then, I'd never given anyone the chance before.

I tugged on a pair of panties and a T-shirt.

He groaned with disappointment.

I giggled. Yes, I giggled like a girl and didn't even blush about it.

Then I pulled on my jeans and padded barefoot back to the kitchen table where he was now seated. He hadn't taken a single bite of his breakfast or a sip of coffee. He also looked wedged in behind the table. The Brave was almost too small to be fully functional for someone as big as him.

"It's good I bought the twenty-one footer, not the nineteen." I slipped into the bench seat of the dinette across from him.

He raised an eyebrow.

"You're too big for the RV," I said.

"I'm not. I think I fit here perfectly."

He didn't mean the motorhome. That painful emotion tugged at the top edge of my ribcage again. Second time around, and I realized it was supposed to be some sort of pleasure, but I wasn't sure why it hurt so much. I surveyed the breakfast he'd provided to distract myself.

"I don't drink coffee," I said.

"It isn't coffee," he answered. "I had them heat it, though."

I grasped the paper cup and lifted it to my nose to smell the hot liquid through the tiny hole in the plastic lid.

Apple.

He'd had the bakery heat up apple juice for me.

I shouldn't read too much into the action. There was no way he could possibly know what apple meant to me, just because I ordered apple pie last night. But still, my throat constricted, and when I tried to hold the emotion at bay, it flooded with a wave of heat through my face and neck.

I gasped when the tightness moved to my chest. I couldn't breathe. Oh, God. I think this was … happiness. Extreme, insane happiness. This didn't happen in real life.

"It's okay?" he asked.

"Yes," I choked out. I looked up from the hot apple juice in my hand to lock my gaze to his. His face was blurry through my unshed tears.

"Don't kick me out," he said.

"I won't."

He opened his mouth to ask me something else, but then didn't speak. His hands were splayed on either side of his plate, as if he was deliberately holding himself there.

I took a sip of the hot apple juice. At the same time, I reached my free hand across the table and placed it over his. It was an easy, natural gesture. I'd never touched another human in such a way before.

He closed his eyes, swallowing whatever else he wanted to say. Then he opened them and smiled at me.

I swear my heart skipped a beat. I had to stop staring at him. I could literally feel all the reason draining out of my brain. I just wanted to be utterly unreasonable with him, for as long as such irrationality could last.

I looked down at my croissant. He did the same.

I removed my hand from his. My skin instantly chilled from where it had been touching him. In fact, the Brave was rather chilly all round. I hadn't needed to turn on the heat with him sleeping beside me. The hot apple juice helped to warm me now.

We ate.

"Where are we going today?" he asked.

"Where have you come from?"

"Seattle."

"Why did you leave?"

"I don't like to stay where I'm not wanted."

"I doubt you could be anywhere and not be wanted … being so useful and all."

He laughed, then sobered quickly. "I don't like staying anywhere I'm not … anywhere I don't fit."

"Is your family in Seattle?"

"No. Southaven, Mississippi." Ah, that was the origin of his accent. "And you're from Vancouver, British Columbia, Canada."

"You can tell the city by my accent?"

"No, by your license plates … and registration papers."

"You've been snooping."

"You sleep deeply."

I laughed and passed him the last bite of my croissant. He popped it into his mouth with a wide grin.

"I was thinking of heading over to the coast today," I said.

"I'm game. But first I want to look at these." He tapped my art portfolio with his foot. He couldn't fully stretch his legs out underneath the table. The portfolio was leaning against the side of my seat. "You're an artist, yes?"

"I guess the portfolio gives me away."

"And the tattoos. They're your designs?"

I nodded. "I thought I was a deep sleeper. You could have looked without asking."

"You don't care about your glove box or the refrigerator, but I'd never touch your bag or your portfolio. They mean something to you. Will you let me look?"

"Yes. But after."

"After what?"

I nodded toward the white plastic bag on the counter beside the sink. It wasn't mine. "You bought more condoms, didn't you?"

He was out of his seat and lifting me out of mine before I registered that he'd moved. He'd also managed to snag the plastic bag. He carried me back to the bed.

"You are good at lifting heavy things," I whispered into his neck. I pressed a kiss just behind his ear, and I swore I could feel his blood rushing underneath my lips.

"There is nothing heavy about you, Rochelle."

He laid me back on the bed and tossed the plastic bag to one side as he tugged on my T-shirt. I knocked his hands away.

"You first this time."

He laughed. "At least close the drapes."

I glanced around. Outside, the parking lot was filling, though no one was parked directly beside us yet. I scrambled around in a half circle and tugged the garish orange-striped blinds closed.

He pulled his T-shirt off, revealing in the dimmed morning light exactly why it seemed so tight on him.

"All the heavy lifting pays off," I said.

"Unfortunately, I think it's genetics."

"Unfortunately?"

He shrugged.

I dropped the conversation part of the bedroom dance. I didn't want to be serious. I didn't want to talk about parents or lack of parents. I just wanted to be locked up together in the cozy confines of the Brave, creating our own version of the world … a microcosm of our own design.

I crawled forward and tugged on the button of his jeans. He leaned over and nuzzled my neck.

"No screaming this time," he said.

"I don't scream."

"Don't you?" he asked. "Well, I always rise to a challenge."

"Yes, you do," I murmured as I slipped my hand into his boxer shorts.

The new condoms fit just fine, but he should have bought more than one box.

We lay entwined together while the sounds of the rest stop parking lot filtered in through the windows and blinds. The occasional conversation, door slam, or remote lock trigger tugged me gradually back to reality.

My stomach rumbled. Beau chuckled softly. His left arm was wrapped around me, with his hand cupping my bare ass. My head was resting on his shoulder, and I'd been watching his chest rise and fall with what I thought were the deep breaths of sleep.

I opened my mouth and let the world intrude into our paradise. "I've never dozed with anyone before."

"No?" he murmured sleepily.

"No."

He didn't say the same, and I tamped down on my sudden urge to interrogate him about every sexual partner he'd ever had.

I wasn't stupid. Just because I didn't randomly take gorgeous men back to my RV didn't mean that someone as obviously sexually experienced as he was didn't do it all the time.

"Tell me about Southaven, Mississippi," I said instead, though I knew this wasn't a subject he wanted to expand on either. "This is my first time in the States."

"Yeah?"

"Yeah."

"And you don't have any family? There's no one like me in Vancouver?"

I laughed. "No, there's no one like you in Vancouver."

He laughed. "I didn't mean … if you mean you don't have a boyfriend, I'm glad to hear it."

Again, he didn't mention if he had any attachments … but by the bulging backpack and the way he'd shown up at the diner — via walking in the rain along the highway — it was easy to guess that he was leaving something behind.

So was I, though I'd planned my exodus.

He let go of my ass, and the skin there instantly goose bumped with the sudden chill. He ran his fingers along my arm.

"This is what I meant," he murmured. "You feel that, don't you?"

His touch left a tingling wake down my shoulder to my elbow.

"Yeah." I murmured my acknowledgment of the way he made me feel into the warm, smooth skin of his left pec.

"You've never met anyone else that you felt that … electricity with?"

"That's a rather personal question." I wasn't completely teasing.

"I don't mean …"

He didn't seem to know what exactly he was trying to say. Or maybe he'd fallen asleep again. I lifted my chin and snuck a glance at him. He grinned at me. His eyes were darker in the filtered light than I'd thought they were before.

"Your eyes change color," I said.

"Do they? What colors?"

"Bluer now, more green last night."

"More green last night," he repeated, as if he was trying to piece something together.

I was starting to get the feeling we weren't having the same conversation.

"And ... do your eyes change color?"

"I don't keep track," I answered, flippant and completely lying. Why was I lying?

"What else changes color?"

"Beau," I groaned, "I'm hungry. But I don't actually want to move, because then I'll be cold."

"These are serious complaints," he said. "Do you think we have enough water for a shower?"

"Maybe one." I grinned while I attempted to not faint over him using the word 'we' and me completely loving it.

"Then I suggest I carry you to the shower so you don't lose any heat. Then we'll bundle you up and go in search of more food."

"Sounds like a solid plan."

He swung his long legs off the bed while dragging me across his chest. I wrapped my arms and legs around him in a front-ways piggyback, quashing my rising concern over the ridiculous dependency I was building the second it rose in my thoughts. Then quashing the voice of my shrink, and her condemnation of false intimacy between youths in the foster system. Supposedly, we orphans attempted to build relationships with other foster kids too quickly, too intensely. And foster kids ultimately weren't equipped to handle the responsibility of their own lives, let alone the emotions and needs of others.

Not that I'd ever had the opportunity to build any relationships, really.

"We'll talk about Southaven and everything else later, right?" I asked Beau's neck as he carried me through the kitchen to the bathroom behind the driver's seat.

"Yeah," he answered. "And you seeing eyes change color, mine and yours. And electric shocks ... and your tattoos and art."

He took my weight in one arm while he unlatched the bathroom door.

I kept my mouth shut about him calling me on my lie. I did notice my own eyes change color, but I really, really didn't want to talk about the headaches, the hallucinations, and the meds. The migraines affected my eyes, but I guessed that his eye color only changed depending on what color of shirt he was wearing. No mystery there ... just one big complication.

One big complication that would see him out the door. Probably. Eventually. Even Carol had hit her panic button when I'd had an episode in front of her, and she'd read my file. Being told someone had a psychotic disorder was way, way different from witnessing it. But we had to talk about it eventually. The confined paradise of the Brave couldn't last. Could it?

"Not today," I said.

"Okay."

We weren't going to fit in the bathroom with me clinging to him, not unless I wanted to sit on the toilet. I lowered my feet onto the chilly vinyl floor and reluctantly peeled my body away from him. He stood half in the hall and half in the bathroom, keeping hold of me as he reached into the shower to turn on the water.

I pressed my lips to his shoulder, shivering slightly everywhere he wasn't touching. "I have to wash my new tattoo."

"Yeah? Time to take off the bandage?"

"It's nothing to get all excited about."

"It's a part of you." He grinned down at me.

That smile lit up his face and tugged at my heart. Literally. I once again quashed the warning that was carried to the forefront of my thoughts in my shrink's voice.

Except that, brushing off those concerns as stemming from my out-to-lunch shrink was just a facade. Just me putting all my fears into the imaginary mouth of someone else.

Beau touched my shoulders, prompting me to turn, so I did. I was happy to have an excuse to hide my face for a moment. He gently removed the bandage that covered the peony tattoo on my left shoulder.

At some point, the facade would have to crumble. If I didn't orchestrate the reveal, the hallucinations eventually would. I couldn't hide my broken brain from someone I was sleeping with. Beau would figure it out. It was better if I told him.

But not today.

We didn't fit in the shower together, but we had fun trying. When I came out all scrubbed clean and fresh faced, I found Beau looking at my sketches. My collection, such as it was, consisted of a dozen or so 24-by-36 charcoal sketches, along with a few smaller sketches that I kept for sentimental reasons. Well, as sentimental as I got. Most of the larger pieces were unfinished, or needed a few final touches so I could list them in my Etsy shop. Beau had two of the bigger sketches on the table, and the others propped up against the windows, counters, and cupboards. Surrounded by my unfinished and half-finished art, he was hunched over a sketch that depicted the golden-haired woman who'd been haunting my hallucinations since last spring.

I hesitated to close the space between us. My stomach was twisted in a knot from seeing him so arrayed and so intently focused.

"Did you see this?" he asked quietly.

"What do you mean?"

He turned and looked at me then, and I wanted to pick up a piece of charcoal to sketch him. There ... his eyes once again greener in the midmorning light, in that hunched, coiled posture. He was a massive presence over the tiny lime-green dinette table. Just him, surrounded by my charcoal-and-white art. Art within art.

But that was hugely cheesy. And I never drew real life, not ever.

"This woman with the knife. And here..." — he gestured to another sketch propped against the bench seat to his right — "... the dark-suited man with the amulet. Do you know them?"

"Of course I don't," I said, pushing by him to get dressed. "I make it all up."

"You didn't see the magic you've captured here?"

"Magic?" I scoffed. "That's a generous assessment. It's shading and smudging. It's fantasy. It sells, so I draw it. It's a tiny talent."

"The drawing is a tiny talent?" he asked.

"Sure."

"Did you take classes?"

"No more than you did, in school."

He nodded and returned his attention to the drawings, studying each one of them with heavy, super-serious focus. I dressed, hyperaware of him and his questions. My chest ached a little, as if somehow I'd lied to him with my answers. Lied about what I saw and didn't see. Though I knew what he'd meant, and so I hadn't lied, not really.

"I'm a guest here, in your home. I'm the one invading your space, asking questions." He spoke without looking at me as I zipped up my dark gray hoodie. "You can lie to me all you want, Rochelle. Just ... maybe ... you shouldn't be lying so much to yourself."

"Like you never lie to yourself?"

"I don't," he said, lifting his blazingly aquamarine eyes to mine. "But that doesn't mean I like all the truth either. This is no tiny talent."

"Thank you." I wasn't exactly sure that had been a compliment, but I didn't know what else to say. I really didn't want to talk about the sketches, because that would lead to the hallucinations and the sketching being part of my therapy. That was all a topic for tomorrow ... or the next day.

He smiled sadly. Then carefully, only touching the very edges, he packed all the sketches back into my portfolio case.

I turned away, feeling just as alone with him three feet away as I had two evenings ago. I started unpacking my meager belongings into the double wardrobe beside the bed. I barely filled two shelves with my clothes and a third with my drawing supplies. This left the other side of the shelves entirely empty. I didn't mention this to Beau. His backpack was still where he'd left it tucked on the far side of the bench seat in the dinette area.

He slid my portfolio along the floor until it just nudged my foot, then he leaned it back so it wouldn't fall forward. I nodded and reached down for it, then tucked it between the wardrobe and the bed.

The silence between us was making me sick. It shouldn't be this way. A hint of discord, and I was all choked and angsty? It didn't make any sense, not yet, maybe not ever.

This so wasn't me. I opened my mouth to say so, to rave and rally against the feelings coalescing all around my heart. My ever-steady, never-tested heart. But ... I didn't speak. I didn't question. I didn't know what he wanted from me. I didn't know why he was here. And I found I was deeply afraid to ask.

"I'll check the engine," Beau said. I could see without turning my head that his hands were stuffed in his pockets, as they'd been last night in the diner. He turned to the door.

"It's fine," I said.

"Still, I'd like to have a look."

He waited at the door for me to look up at him. Then he smiled.

I nodded and he ducked underneath the doorway to climb down and out of the RV. The Brave actually dipped and righted itself as he did so.

I picked up my portfolio. I put it down on the table, unzipped it, and flipped it open. The sketches inside fanned out, falling open to one of the dark-suited man staring out at me. His expression was serious, maybe even deadly. I shuddered at the look I'd captured in his eyes. He haunted my hallucinations, my nightmares, and my art. He scared me, even tamed and captured on the page.

I closed the portfolio and tucked it back between the wardrobe and the bed. It was too wide to fit in any of the cupboards.

Beau had let it drop, as if it wasn't more than a casual line of inquiry. And, of course, that's what it was. What else could he want to know? He'd asked if I saw magic. He meant metaphorically, and I was so terrified of him knowing about the hallucinations that I'd shut-down at the question. Now, he probably thought I was a moron. But would he have stuck around this long if that was the case? Would he be checking the engine?

I didn't get the impression that Beau was just looking for a ride, either in my bed or my RV. He'd been perfectly fine in the rain on the edge of the highway, all alone. And so had I.

I wandered forward to the cockpit, grinning when Beau looked around the hood through the windshield at me. He was insanely beautiful and completely surreal standing at the front of the Brave. Standing there as if he belonged, as if he'd never even thought of being anywhere else. This juxtaposition of reality and the unreal — the parking lot behind Beau and the engine hood between us, his looks and his choosing to be here — was mind-boggling.

It was more than looks, actually. It was belittling to label him so simply and off-handedly. He was present. Stable yet unencumbered. Soulful, for lack of a better word.

His answering smile told me that everything was just fine by him. He ducked back under the hood. Next, he'd be asking for the owner's manual, and I'd be just fine with that too. Preemptively, I pulled the manual out of the glove compartment and set it on the passenger seat.

Then I settled in the driver's seat and leaned forward to fiddle around with the CB radio.

I was accustomed to taking life minute by minute. I'd take Beau, and his questions, wherever he and they led.

CHAPTER SEVEN

"SHE DRIVES NICE," Beau pronounced about an hour into our drive. "Someone took good care of her."

He meant the Brave. He filled every inch of the passenger seat beside me, even with it slid as far back as possible. I kept my hands firmly at ten and two on the wheel — not because I was that conscientious of a driver, but because I wanted to reach across and hold his hand or arm … just touch him.

"Yes," I answered. "I'm pretty lucky."

He turned to look at me. His gaze actually warmed the skin of my right cheek and neck. "You're not the only one."

He didn't mean the Brave.

I didn't answer, but I couldn't stop myself from smiling.

We stopped for groceries in Tacoma, just outside Seattle, where Beau helped some random guy get his car started in the Walmart parking lot. I tried to not just stand there and stare like an idiot while his agile hands dug into the failing engine. Thankfully, the owner was happy chatting to Beau about cars rather than attempting to engage me with boring conversation about the weather. Or maybe talking about the weather with strangers was a Canadian thing?

Though even I could tell that the owner knew nothing about cars or engines, Beau was completely pleasant. He got the car running with a few tweaks.

Walmart was cool about motorhomes using their parking lots, even overnight. It was supposed to be a place to socialize with fellow RVers — trading tips, routes, recipes — but for me it was just an easy grocery store to get in and out of.

Totally unasked, the random guy pressed a fifty into Beau's hand. Not bad for fifteen minutes of his time.

"Nice," I said as we wandered into the store. "You are handy."

Beau snorted a laugh and then promptly blew the entire fifty on Oreo's, Coke, and beef jerky in a multitude of flavors. "Every good road trip needs beef jerky," he informed me, utterly serious.

"I'm not big on meat," I said.

Beau wagged his eyebrows at me suggestively, and I couldn't help but giggle for the second time in my life.

Beau drew attention in a way that would have terrified me. Except that the looks coming his way were admiring. Before I'd dyed my hair and opted for the tinted glasses, I'd gotten stared at in a completely different way. Beau seemed oblivious to the attention, though, and no one even glanced at me as I walked beside him. I could get used to that.

Not that Beau needed any additional items in the 'pro' side of the list in my head. The pros were already stacked.

We didn't hold hands, but we walked close enough to brush arms numerous times.

I grabbed whole wheat bread, mayo, cheese, and a head of lettuce. When we got back to the Brave, I made us sandwiches on the handy cutting board that covered the stainless steel sink. I cut the crusts off mine but not

Beau's. He'd already eaten the ones I rejected. I quartered his sandwiches, though, which he found terribly amusing.

He shared his Oreos and didn't ask to drive as we turned west off I-5 to cut out to the coast. I'd already figured out where I wanted to stay the night — Andersen's RV Park in Long Beach, Washington — and Beau seemed happy to go along with my plan. I opted for the standard site, which was thirty-two dollars during the fall/winter season, rather than the ocean site for forty. I figured that Beau and I wouldn't be spending a ton of time gazing at the ocean from the Brave. The free WiFi was definitely a bonus, though.

I spent the entire morning and afternoon — even through checking into the campsite, hooking up the RV, and walking the beach before heading into town on foot — in a pocket of bliss I didn't think was possible. I had no idea that this kind of euphoria was even real.

Other people — more ex-roommates — might have gushed about true love and soul mates, but I didn't even entertain those sorts of beliefs, not even now. I also didn't believe in fate, or love at first sight, or serendipity. I believed that hard work, not luck, paid off. Anything else required me giving up too much control.

I would walk each step as far as it would take me, and not worry — not for one moment — about the unknown beyond.

Hoyt was standing in front of the kiddie carousel, which was closed for the evening, or maybe the whole day. That picture was still as creepy as it sounded, though. Not to mention completely out of context, because he was supposed to be in Vancouver, British Columbia, not Long Beach, Washington. Not standing like a creep in front of a carousel.

A creep who was waiting for me?

The sun had held out all the way to the coast. We'd bought ice cream at Scoopers, walked the boardwalk, and watched the sun set ... well, until Beau's stomach started grumbling. Then, we cut up to Pacific, downtown Long Beach's main street. We passed the city hall and the pharmacy on one of only two major intersections while we debated eating out, either at Long Beach Tavern or Hungry Harbor Grill, or grabbing groceries and cooking. By the sound of Beau's stomach, I wasn't sure he could survive if we opted for the second option. Eating out was definitely a luxury, though. I'd already filled the Brave's gas tank once and it was practically empty again.

So, Hoyt.

Long Beach — all two blocks of it — was definitely a tourist destination. And why not? The beach was beautiful. The carousel and other rides and games were set up right in the middle of downtown.

None of this explained what Hoyt was doing here.

I stopped in my tracks so suddenly that Beau, who was holding my hand, almost wrenched my shoulder out of its socket when he continued forward. I spun around, putting my back to Hoyt and staring into a dress shop window. I could see his reflection. He was texting or playing a game on his phone. In the other hand, he was rolling the silver balls, or coins, or whatever they were, just as he had been in Vancouver. Maybe they were ball bearings. What did people use ball bearings for? Fishing? Mechanics?

Except this time, the glint coming off the silver was wrong somehow. If I were to draw this reflection, if I were to capture this in charcoal, what light would I use to reflect off whatever was in his palm? The sun was setting behind the building before me, which cast a deep shadow across the street where Hoyt stood. The streetlights hadn't flicked on yet. The kiddie rides were dark behind him. Yes, it was a super creepy scene. Almost creepy enough to be a hallucination, but without the white mist and the migraine.

"Something you like in here?" Beau asked, perplexed.

I glanced at the clothing displayed in the store window I appeared to be fixated on. If I hadn't been so freaked, I would have laughed. The colorful and matronly shop wasn't bent toward nineteen-year-olds who heavily favored black and were working on dual arm-sleeve tattoos.

"Do you see that guy?" I asked, nodding toward Hoyt's reflection in the window. I was afraid to voice the question, but I had to. With the strange lighting and him apparently following me to Long Beach, I was now scared that Hoyt was a figment of my imagination. That he'd never been real at all.

"Across the street?" Beau asked. His tone was darker than I'd ever heard it. "By the kiddie ride?"

"Yeah. Tall, skinny, unwashed?"

"Yep." Beau lifted his nose as if sniffing the sea air. "You know him?"

"No," I answered, as relief unfroze my limbs. I hadn't realized I'd been frozen at all. "But he wants to know me, and really shouldn't be here."

"I can talk to him. I can be very convincing."

Beau's suddenly dark protective side — and the possessiveness it hinted at — should have concerned me. Instead, it eased my worry further.

"Let's just go back to the campsite."

Beau's stomach rumbled.

"I can make you another sandwich."

"I have cookies," Beau said with a casual shrug. "We can go wherever you want, anytime."

He placed his hand on my back and steered me the way we'd come. But there was nothing casual about his body language. He felt stiff and wary, and he blocked me with his body as much as he could the entire time we were walking out of the village. I could feel tiny static shocks coming off his hand, even through the three layers of my jacket, hoodie, and T-shirt. Though that was obviously just my imagination. I felt badly about bothering Beau with my concerns, but really happy to be within his protective cocoon at this specific moment.

That was, until the hallucination crept up my spine and rolled over my head, to settle in as a pounding headache over and across my eyes.

Then I was just terrified of everything.

I was frightened and freaked about Hoyt's appearance. Pissed that I'd forgotten to take my pill this morning. And really terrified that Beau would leave me once he knew how broken I really was. If it was going to end between us, I really didn't want it to end like this. I didn't want the way he looked at me to change, from what might possibly be the beginnings of adoration to pity ... to revulsion.

I stumbled.

Beau caught me without question.

I tried — I really, really tried — to keep putting one foot in front of the other, to ignore the pain sitting like a two-hundred-pound weight on my head. I really tried to hide my infirmary from Beau, to hide the crazy I'd so flippantly mentioned to drive him away the moment we met.

I stumbled again.

Then, contrary to everything I was feeling, I started running.

I let go of Beau, pushing off him as I ran. My sneakered feet slapped on new pavement edging the main road from Long Beach to the campsite.

Before I got more than five steps, before Beau could even react, I went completely blind.

My eyesight was wiped in a wash of brilliant white light. It always happened this way, though never this quickly. But stranded nowhere near my pills or my sketchbook, this was going to be bad. So, so bad. I never went anywhere without my bag or my sketchbook. What had I been thinking? I'd been coasting in Beau's bubble.

Stupid, stupid.

"Rochelle?" Beau was concerned. His voice was near, right next to me, so he must be jogging behind me. He couldn't understand what was going on. He had no context with which to understand, because I hadn't warned him. And I didn't have the words — or the will through the pain — to help him understand.

I stumbled sideways onto the gravel edge of the road and twisted my ankle. Perhaps the road had turned, or perhaps my besieged, blind brain could no longer navigate a straight line. I cried out, flinging my hands forward as I fell.

I never hit the ground.

Beau scooped me up in his arms and I clung to him.

"My pills," I cried. "I need ..."

Pain lanced through my brain. The outline of a figure formed in the white mist of my minds' eye.

I screamed, then stifled my cry in the flesh of Beau's shoulder.

"I'll get you there," he said.

The wind lifted the hair that had fallen across my face when he grabbed me. There hadn't been any wind before.

Beau was running. Could anyone run that fast —

Pain exploded behind my eyes. The hallucination forced its way through the mist, feeling like it was tearing the flesh of my brain as it did so.

The figure resolved itself into the curly-haired golden-blond woman with the jade knife. Again, she was inexplicably dressed in a brightly colored sarong and tank top. She stood among the ruins of the temple, so she'd obviously survived the cave-in I'd witnessed in my last hallucination. The oranges and reds of her skirt blurred as she spun until I could see her face. She was screaming. Her blond curls were matted with blood, but I could see no wound on her. She was screaming at someone I couldn't see. Then she dropped the knife to thrust her hands out to someone she couldn't reach, and her scream was far more terrifying than anything I'd ever heard before.

This woman was confident and strong. She scared me with a laugh. She jested as she traded blows with the dark-suited man. But here ... here, she was losing someone.

Someone she loved was dying.

I threw my head back — momentarily breaking free of the hallucination as I did so — and screamed. I screamed for the woman. I freed her pain. It poured through me. I stiffened and then bucked in Beau's arms. I bit my tongue. My mouth filled with blood. The metallic taste flooded my senses, making me aware of my surroundings.

I opened my eyes.

Gravel crunched under Beau's feet. We were steps from the Brave. I could feel it more than see it. I could feel my sanctuary was near. Light still flared across the deep blue sky. Beau had gotten us back impossibly quick. Or, more likely, I'd lost a bunch of time.

"Goodness," a woman said. "Is she all right?" Her voice came from behind us, perhaps from the campsite across the way.

"No, worries, ma'am." Beau's voice rumbled in his chest when he spoke, vibrating against my ear. "Just a migraine."

"Ah, poor girl. You take care of her, then."

"I will."

Beau reached for the door, popping the lock rather than using the keys in my pocket.

"No," I moaned.

"I'll fix it," he said. "I'll fix it all." Then he practically ripped the door off the Brave to carry me inside.

The hallucination flooded my eyes again, but it didn't seem to be a repeat of the previous vision.

Usually, they repeated.

This was going to be bad. Maybe the worst it had ever been. God, I didn't want to go back to the hospital. If Beau checked me into a psych ward in the States, could I ever get out?

"No hospital, Beau," I managed to say, though I think my words were garbled by the pain in my head. "No hospital."

"Of course not," he said. "Never. I know how things work."

I didn't know what he meant, but I wasn't up for questions and answers.

He placed me on the bed.

In my mind, the blond woman, still in her red and orange sarong, reached down and lifted a body in her arms as if it weighed nothing. I'd never seen the woman she carried before. She had the most shockingly emerald-green-dyed hair. It was never, ever a good thing for me — for my hold on sanity — when new people appeared in my hallucinations.

"Oh, God no. Not more ..." I moaned it instead of screaming. I twisted my head until my face was buried in the nearest pillow. Beau's manly scent filled my senses, pushing the hallucination aside.

Beau was trying to press a bottle of pills into my hand.

"How many?" he asked. His voice was stressed and full of fear. His brush off of the woman from the neighboring campsite was apparently just a brilliant act.

I couldn't see his face. I couldn't see anything but the blinding whiteness. "Two," I managed to answer.

He pressed a glass of water into my hand and tried to prop me up.

"No ..." I pushed the water away, spilling it across my leg and onto the bed. The cool wetness soaked into my jeans and pulled me further from the clutches of the hallucination.

He pressed two pills into my palm and I popped them into my mouth. Once again, I willed myself to let them dissolve under my tongue rather than chew them in my terror.

Pain lanced through my head again. I fell backward onto the bed, arching up and writhing with the agony. But I refused to scream, refused to open my mouth and lose the pills.

Beau pressed his hands to me, one at my shoulder and one at the opposite hip. He was attempting to hold me down. I probably looked like I was having a seizure, and maybe I was ... except multiple MRIs had ruled out any brain tumors that could cause seizures. I'd held out hope for a brain tumor — for any explanation — for a long, long time.

I fought Beau off.

He let me go.

The pills dissolved across my tongue, flooding my mouth with their chalky taste.

"My bag," I gasped. "My sketchbook."

Beau turned away, only to return split seconds later to press my bag into my hands. Still blind, I dug inside and found a piece of charcoal.

"Your eyes," Beau murmured. The fear in his voice lanced through my chest like a blistering brand. "They're white. Glowing white."

I shook my head at him. I couldn't absorb anything but the feel of the charcoal in my fingers and the pages of the sketchbook open on my lap.

I hunched over to draw.

"Wait," Beau cried. "That's not a blank page."

"It doesn't matter."

Despite my reply, I felt him flip the pages for me.

"I need you to go. Please."

"You want me to leave?" he asked, his voice heavy with pain.

"Not like that," I managed to say, though I desperately just wanted to continue screaming. I wanted to scream and scream until the pills took the pain away.

"I understand," he said as he moved away. "I'll be outside."

It was going to get cold outside. The thought worried me even as I applied my charcoal to the paper. Then, still utterly blind, I drew whatever wanted to break loose from the prison of my brain.

"Is it that guy?" Beau asked, his voice so low that I barely heard it. He must have been standing in the doorway.

"Just go, please." I didn't bother to look up. I couldn't see him anyway. "Please. It will pass. It always passes."

The Brave shifted with his exit and I heard the door click shut. I thought he'd broken the lock. The lock and the latch were separate things, then. I tried to hold on to this piece of reality. But with Beau gone, the hallucination dug deeper into my mind and had its way.

The pills would kick in eventually, and the sketching should appease the hallucination during the in-between time.

I didn't hear or see anything else of the real world for a long while.

The Brave was moving. When I opened my eyes, it was pitch black, so I didn't bother trying to see anything. The drowsiness of the pills beckoned me back under and I didn't fight it. I could feel charcoal underneath my fingernails. I'd been drawing with both hands.

"Bad one," I murmured.

Then Beau was beside me, radiating warmth and comfort as he tucked the sheets down around me so tightly that I couldn't move. Which was fine, because I didn't want to move.

Who's driving? I tried to ask, but I couldn't form the words outside my head. It was a silly question anyway. I was just mixing up moments. Beau was obviously driving. I should be angry about that. That he was driving my freedom without asking permission first.

He didn't leave. He saw my crazy and he didn't leave.

Just give him a chance, Rochelle, a nasty voice countered in my mind. This was the voice that kept me down, that kept my eyes behind glasses and my tattooed arms covered so I didn't upset the normal people. This voice normally sounded like my shrink, but it sounded exactly like me now.

So I ignored it.

I was accustomed to ignoring things, after all ... like the way Beau's eyes changed color, or the static charges when we touched. I was good at boxing all those things and locking them away in my crazy crate, my broken brain.

It was morning, though I wasn't sure of the time. I was alone in the Brave, but Beau's backpack was still on the dinette's printed orange-and-brown bench seat. The RV was parked in a completely different campsite. Neither of the sites on either side of it were occupied. I could hear the ocean, but could only see trees through the windshield.

I was so, so cold. And disconnected. Terribly, disjointedly disconnected. Distanced from the anger I felt at Beau for driving the Brave without my permission. Distanced from the anger at him for dragging me somewhere I didn't know I wanted to be. And I didn't mean the campsite.

I pulled a second hoodie over the one I was already wearing, aware that it probably looked ridiculous. But also aware that this was my space, and it didn't matter what I looked like at all.

The door opened and the Brave shifted to accommodate Beau's weight as he climbed in. It was the third time I'd noticed. That was odd, wasn't it? He couldn't possibly be that heavy.

He saw me standing in the middle of the kitchen area and paused only halfway up the steps, one foot still on the ground behind him.

I crossed my arms and resolutely looked away. I'd already invited him in once. I didn't like repeating myself.

"Sorry," he said. "I had to go farther than I thought."

He held up a brown paper bag. There was nothing wary in his voice, though he wasn't smiling. He looked tired. I guessed that he hadn't slept yet.

I nodded to the table rather than him.

He shut the door behind him, locking it. So he'd fixed the lock.

He stepped forward to deliberately reach into my field of vision and place the Brave's keys on the table before me. I left them there without comment. He stepped back to the counter beside me.

He pulled a paper cup out of the bag, removed the plastic lid, and pressed it to my hands.

Warm apple juice.

I started crying. Like a child. Something I'd sworn off doing in front of people since before I was twelve.

Beau took the apple juice from me, placing it on the counter as he pulled me to him. I clung to him and sobbed into his neck, which I could reach only because he was now leaning against the table.

"Did you think I'd left?" he asked. "I'm not leaving. I told you already."

"No," I cried. "It's just that I like the apple juice so much it scares me."

He threw back his head and laughed so hard that his arms convulsed around me. They squeezed me and I lost my breath in a whoosh. That was okay. I didn't need to breathe around him.

I was beyond breathing.

I was beyond reason. But I had been for a very long time now.

"You're all wet," I said.

"It's raining."

"Are you cold?"

"No."

"I am. So cold."

He tried to pull me in even tighter, rubbing my arms a little too hard. But I pushed him away and reached down for the button of his jeans.

"You should eat something," he said. "I googled those meds."

If he had googled the meds, then he knew everything.

He knew it wasn't migraines. He knew about the psychotic disorder and he still stayed. He drove the Brave to get me away from whatever had triggered me. He fixed the lock and bought me breakfast. My broken brain hadn't scared him off.

I felt relieved instead of terrified. I'm not sure I'd ever felt the relief that was now coursing through my limbs.

I locked my gaze to his blue-green eyes and touched my lips to his in a whisper of a kiss. He relaxed. His shoulders actually dropped as he reached up to brush his fingertips across my cheek and over my ear, weaving his fingers into my hair.

"You should eat something," he repeated, but he wasn't as absolute about it as he had been.

"Later," I murmured as I tugged the front of his jeans open and reached inside his boxers.

He groaned.

"I'm so cold," I whispered, pressing a firmer kiss to his lips.

He tugged off my jeans and underwear as I continued to stroke and kiss him. Then he lifted me up, settling me against him until he was deep inside me. I was wrapped around him in a seated position with my legs crossed behind him on the table. I couldn't move very well like this, but I didn't have to. He wrapped his hands around my hips, darting his tongue in and out of my mouth. Matching this rhythm, he rocked me up and down on him.

I arched my back, instinctively pressing my hips to him on an angle that increased the friction.

I cried out. My orgasm lapped up and over me before I even knew it had begun. I'd never come during intercourse before.

He lifted me off the table and carried me to bed, still entwined. But then he pulled out as he lowered me down.

I cried out in the painful pleasure of having him exit. "Please."

"I'm not going anywhere, Rochelle," he whispered fiercely. "You won't even be able to make me go now."

He ripped open a condom and rolled it on. I scrambled backward so he could climb over me on the bed. He didn't fit widthwise on the double without bending his knees, but he didn't complain.

He thrust into me and I cried out from the insane sensitivity. I clung to him, riding the painful pleasure. He buried his face in my neck with a moan.

"Don't make me go," he whispered, then thrust again.

My brain was going to explode.

"Don't ever make me go," he repeated with another thrust.

"I won't ..." The words were torn out of me with a moan.

"Tell me again."

"I won't ever make you leave."

"Again."

"Beau, Beau," I cried. "My beautiful, beautiful Beau."

He came, arching back from me on his arms with only our hips connected for a moment. Then he collapsed forward.

"I'll fix it," he murmured against my collarbone. "Somehow. Together. We'll fix it."

I believed him, though I wasn't exactly sure what he was talking about. My illness wasn't something that could be fixed, not by modern or even alternative medicine. Not like Beau could fix an engine with a couple of turns of his capable hands.

My brain was broken.

I was broken in a way that couldn't be repaired. I could only endure. I really, really hoped that Beau staying meant he'd endure with me.

CHAPTER EIGHT

"The pills aren't good for you," he said. "I don't think you should take them anymore."

We had both slept after the mind-blowing, earth-shattering, life-reaffirming sex, but I shouldn't have. I'd dreamed of the latest hallucination and it made me edgy. Edgy enough to fight. I wasn't a fighter, though. I was a walk-awayer.

"Oh, so you're a head doctor now?"

"No, but ..." Beau hesitated. "I know people we could see."

"We?" I countered. "It's my head. You think I haven't seen everyone there is to see?"

"Not like that. Not those people," he said. His tone was completely nonconfrontational.

I'd gone to the bathroom and was now bringing his cold coffee and my cold juice back to bed with me. He was sprawled across the bed, absentmindedly rubbing the satin-bound edge of the felted, pink blankets between his fingers. His dark caramel skin looked amazing, even surrounded by the garish green, orange, and brown decor of the Brave. But then, I bet his skin looked good in or around any color.

"Not those same people," he repeated. His voice was remote, thoughtful.

"What people then?"

"I bought pastries," he said, instead of answering my question. He pointed behind me to the brown paper bag on the kitchen counter.

"Not in the bed."

"No?" he asked coyly. "What else am I not allowed to do in here?"

I narrowed my eyes at him, aware that he was distracting me and attempting to do an end run around the conversation.

"I still don't like the pills," he said, proving my point as he climbed out of bed. "They dampen you."

"That's what they're supposed to do."

He couldn't step by me in the narrow hall without knocking me aside, but he didn't need to. He simply reached his long arm over my head, snagged the paper bag on the counter, and carried it back to the bed.

"Hey," I exclaimed as I followed him.

"I'll wash the sheets," he said, lifting the edge of the blankets to invite me back in.

I didn't budge. I did glare.

"You said you were cold."

"That was before."

"Before what?" he asked, a slow grin spreading across his face.

I was getting accustomed to this look. He was like a cat with a mouse. A nice cat. A playful cat, rather than a murderous one. Though maybe such a beast didn't exist. I didn't know. I'd never had any sort of pet of my own.

I was hit once more with the need to sketch him. To forever capture him as he was now, sprawled across the too-small bed and clothed only in old blankets and sheets. But in color, not in charcoal on white paper. I never drew in color.

I climbed into bed instead.

He'd bought danish pastries this time.

When we finally admitted we needed to get out of bed again, it was way after dinner time. I still had no idea where the hell we were camped.

It was dark and drizzling outside. Beau had hooked up the Brave with fresh water and electricity.

"We should have bought more groceries," I said as I looked at the meager offerings in the fridge. A couple of slices of cheese, mayo, and the outside crusts of a loaf of bread weren't going to yield much nourishment.

"Let's get seafood for dinner," Beau said. "Right after I run."

"You need to run now?"

"Yeah, sorry. I know it's not great timing, but it's something I have to do every couple of days and I've delayed it too long." He spoke as he pulled a T-shirt on and retrieved a set of sweatpants from his backpack. "I'm going to cut through the forest along the beach. If you're starving, you don't have to wait on me. Bike the path into Lincoln and we'll meet at the restaurant."

"Bike the path? Lincoln? Restaurant?"

"Yeah." He tugged on a baseball cap with the Seattle Mariners Logo on it. "Lincoln City. We're parked at the Devil's Lake State Recreation Area."

I couldn't see any sign of a lake as I tugged my hoodie up over my head and followed Beau out of the Brave. We appeared to be parked in the middle of a forest. Though, I could hear the surf crashing behind me. Our campsite was buffered from the next one over by a thin line of evergreens.

"I was thinking Pier 101 for dinner," Beau said. "My treat." Then he lifted his chin to draw my attention to the rear of the Brave.

He'd bought me a bike. It was locked to the back of the Brave. Its frame was black, but its wheels, handles, wire basket, and seat were white. It was one of those modern bikes made to look old fashioned. I loved it instantly, completely irrationally. Yes, me. The girl who was pleased — even self-righteous — that all her clothing fit into one suitcase.

"This is too expensive. I thought you only had enough for the apple pie?"

"Cash," he said. "I hit the ATM. There's one in town."

"I can't —"

"Yeah, let's not do that." He cut me off with a deliberate and lingering kiss.

"You have to let me contribute," he added, just as I was about to melt into the lip lock.

Then he jogged away toward a dirt path and what I guessed was Devil's Lake. He turned around, jogging backward, to flash a grin and say, "Pier 101. Take that path to the highway." He pointed to his left, further through the campsite. "The restaurant is right off the highway. Blue awnings, gray shingles. It'll take you ten to fifteen minutes to bike there. Don't forget your phone in case you get lost." Then he disappeared into the trees.

In case I get lost? Then what? Beau didn't appear to own a phone. So I guess I was googling the restaurant if I couldn't find it.

It was still drizzling as I rode along the dirt path that Beau had indicated, but the tall evergreens on either side kept me dry until I cut over to the highway. My bag fit perfectly in the white wire basket hanging off the handle bars. Despite the lack of lighting along the path and highway, I could see fairly well because Beau had also attached a strobing bike light to the handle bar, along with a bell that had a black butterfly on it.

Just like my tattoo.

If I paused to think about it, I would be terrified of how far into Beau I was after only a couple of days.

So I didn't think about it.

I didn't see a specific sign, but I was fairly certain I was now on the coastal highway, because I could hear the pounding surf just on the other side of the trees. That helped me place Lincoln City firmly in Oregon. The maps I'd studied before heading across the border had shown a highway twisting all along the edge of the coast from Astoria at the tip of Oregon through to the California border. The map had also highlighted a plethora of campsites all along the coast highway, though most were seasonal.

I assumed that Beau had driven over the wide bridge that spanned the Columbia River, and then through Astoria to continue along the coast to Lincoln City. Just as I'd planned to. While sleeping off the last round of hallucinations, I'd missed a lot of what I really wanted to see. It took hours to drive that distance, especially in an RV.

I refused to pout about it further, even silently. Beau had done what he thought necessary for me at the time. We could always backtrack up the coast tomorrow morning so I could see what I'd missed. That might be silly, but this was my life now. I could be all the silly I wanted to be.

Cars and a few campers passed by intermittently as I peddled west. I stuck to the generous paved shoulder obviously meant for cyclists until I came to the edge of Lincoln City.

I didn't care about the rain dampening my hair or face, because the bike was perfect. Though, I was seriously glad there were only three gears to figure out. I hadn't had regular access to a bike since my pre-teens.

From what I could see in the dark, downtown Lincoln City ran all along the very edge of the Pacific Ocean. The beach stretched as far south as I could see. The pounding surf was high and strong. It was the kind of beach that surfers would flock to year round. It was definitely more of a town than a city, though. None of the buildings on the main street were over four-storeys, and those that were all appeared to be hotels. The shops and bakeries heavily favored antique white paint with cornflower blue doors, window trims, and awnings, obviously going for the quaint tourist dollars.

I instantly liked it. It wasn't artifice. It was a choice.

Everything was closed as I biked through town except for the pharmacy and Pier 101. The roof of the restaurant was blue metal, the same color as the awnings. But Beau had neglected to mention the huge orange-red crab painted on the blue-gray shingles that faced the main road. That might have helped with his navigational concerns.

I locked the bike up on one of the front patio pillars. Beau had bought some crazy-heavy-duty U-lock with a key. It was so cumbersome I was ready to start cursing in my struggle to get the bike secured. I wondered if he'd purchased the bike in Lincoln City, after he'd hooked up the Brave but before I'd woken. Or if he'd seen the store somewhere along the highway and stopped impulsively. If the store was in town, I'd have to go pick up a helmet in the morning.

Pier 101 actually hung about ten or fifteen feet over the beach below. The entire dining section was supported by pillars and concrete in the sand, though the surf didn't seem to come high enough up the beach to wet the pillars. Or at least, from what I could glimpse in the dark, it didn't tonight.

A short bar ran just off the right of the entrance along the parking-lot side of the building. A small gift-shop area sat behind and to the left of the host station. Keychains, magnetics, and personalized pencils didn't interest me much. Rochelle wasn't a common enough name to be printed on a generic souvenir.

It was quiet enough on a Wednesday night in January that getting a booth by the windows was not a problem. In fact, only three other tables were occupied, and the bar stools were all empty. Of course, it was a rather late for dinner.

The booth seats were cornflower blue vinyl. The windowsills were painted blue to match. And most of the seafood was deep-fried. Very American. I had a feeling Beau would love it. I was going to need to ask if the clam chowder had pork in it. Oh … and onion rings. I couldn't remember the last time I'd had onion rings.

The front door opened with a gust of air and heavy rain that indicated the wind had picked up since I arrived. The weather did change quickly on the West Coast. I lowered my five-page plastic menu and looked toward the door, expecting to greet Beau with a big smile.

He'd be wet from the rain, like he had been the first time I laid eyes on him …

It wasn't Beau.

A dark-haired, dark-suited man walked through the entrance with not a drop of rain on him. He scanned the room, then looked directly at me. He was carrying a black leather art portfolio that was a twin to mine in size, but of more expensive quality.

My heart stopped — literally.

I couldn't breathe.

Then, my pulse started hammering frantically in my chest, making up for the lost beats and then some.

The wind from before inexplicably rushed through the room, blowing my hair back, tingling across the exposed skin of my face and hands, and plugging my ears, as if the altitude had suddenly changed. Then the gust subsided as quickly as it had come.

"Can I help you?" the host asked. But she wasn't speaking to the dark-suited man, who strode by her as if she didn't exist, his gaze still locked to mine.

"Yeah," a man answered. "A seat at the bar there and a beer would do."

I tore my gaze away from the dark figure walking toward me to see Hoyt grinning at me as he moved toward the bar.

Hoyt from Vancouver. Hoyt who'd spoken to me in the alley behind the Residence. Hoyt who I'd seen in Long Beach.

Hoyt was here with the dark-suited man from my hallucinations.

"No headache," I whispered. "No white light. No warning."

Oh, God. I was hallucinating in the middle of the restaurant and … and … my hallucinations could see me, could move toward me as if to start a conversation. That was not good. That was a terrifying progression of my condition.

Desperate and trying to hide it — I had years of experience hiding the hallucinations — I reached for my bag. I'd grabbed it from the Brave because Beau had reminded me of the cell phone, but it also held my sketchbook.

The dark-suited man stopped beside my table. "Lovely view, even on a cloudy evening," he said as he gazed out at the pounding surf beyond the window. "Quaint town. Though it doesn't suit you at all." He had an accent. Not British but something close.

I ignored him as I placed my sketchbook on the table. I flipped it open to a blank page as I dug deeper into my bag for charcoal.

"Ah, you're going to sketch. Perfect," he said. "May I join you?"

I shook my head, too frantically for my own slipping sanity. I was letting him in. I was acknowledging him. I shouldn't acknowledge him, right?

Right?

I didn't know anything about my own brain anymore.

My hand closed around a bottle of my pills instead of the charcoal I was seeking. Brilliant. I was still riding the fumes of the last two I'd taken, but I would willingly overdose to get him out of my head.

I pulled the bottle out of my bag.

"Don't," he hissed, sliding into the booth seat across from me.

I popped the lid off the bottle.

He snatched it from me.

The pills flew into the air, scattering over the table, seat, and floor.

Oh, God, oh, God. How could he touch me? This was not happening. This couldn't be happening.

"I'm sorry," he said as he swept the pills on the table toward him. "I need you sharp. From Hoyt's recounting, these pills dampen your sight."

He lifted the portfolio he'd been carrying onto the table and unzipped it.

Just get up and leave. Just leave.

Hoyt might be part of the delusion, but Beau had chosen the restaurant.

And Beau was real.

So just get up and leave.

The dark-suited man opened the portfolio. It contained easily a dozen of my original sketches. Sketches that I'd sold through my Etsy shop. Sketches ranging back years that featured him or his amulet. It was odd to see how my style had refined and sharpened from the first few to the newer drawings of him and the golden-haired woman in the castle. These were from my hallucinations last fall.

"I had a difficult time acquiring some of these. Your fans are ardent," he said. "But I'm a collector. I'm rather good at it. Money always motivates, and money means nothing to me."

He paused to let me speak, to let me react.

I didn't.

"North America is not the best place for me to set foot these days," he continued. "But for you, Rochelle Hawthorne, I would risk more than this."

I locked my gaze to his. He smiled at me, closed-lipped and full of satisfaction.

"What did you call me?"

"Your name, of course. I'm Mot Blackwell, sorcerer, of Blackness Castle, Scotland."

"My name is Rochelle Saintpaul."

He snorted. "That's your human name. You're a Hawthorne. By your looks and your power, you could be none other."

I stared at him, mouth agape. All my fear was quashed for the moment by the information this man offered with utter confidence.

"I have questions for you." He swept his hand over the sketches in his portfolio. "And with you out of Vancouver, away from the reach of the Godfrey witches and Jade's magnificent senses and overblown righteousness, this seemed like the perfect time to ask them."

"I have no idea what you're talking about."

"No, of course you don't." His tone was smooth and cultured. "Please excuse me. Such things are not germane to our conversation."

"I'm not talking to you," I said. I glanced around the restaurant. No one was looking at us. The waitress hadn't returned to the table with the water I'd asked for.

"Oh, them?" he asked. "They can't see or hear us, Rochelle. Well, Hoyt can, but he's done his job. Rather well. Thankfully, he's as proficient at tracking spells as he is with his inspired curses. Though I understand you almost gave him the slip in your new home."

He smiled again, baring his teeth this time, but his eyes were dark, joyless pits.

Fear curled in my belly. Jesus, my mind was wicked. Brilliant but wicked. To have conjured someone so complex, as compelling and terrifying as him ... Blackwell. The name suited him perfectly. Mot Blackwell, the sorcerer of Blackness Castle, Scotland. It was as simple as a children's story. I had no idea why I hadn't named him until tonight. I'd been hallucinating him since I was thirteen, after all.

I started digging through my bag again. I knew I had a piece of charcoal. If I could just draw him, sitting like that across from me with the top button undone on his crisp white dress shirt. If I could capture his black hair and dark eyes, both darker than they'd ever seemed to me before. But then, he was usually accompanied by a wash of white light.

He sighed. "Your way then," he said.

He closed and carefully lifted the portfolio off the table to place it to the side of his booth seat.

He pulled a golden disk out of his pocket.

It looked like a spinning top. A child's toy, but cast in gold and dotted along the top edge with tiny stones that resembled the large stone on my mother's necklace.

"I will have my questions answered," he said. "You will tell me what you see. Why you draw what you draw. And what other futures lie within your mind."

He set the top on the table and gave it a spin, turning it into a blur of gold.

Then, with a flick from his fingers, it shot across the table to spin directly before me.

I lifted my hands away from it.

A bundle of pain formed at the base of my skull, a malignant pulse sitting just at the tip of my very top vertebra.

Oh, God. No.

Having him sitting before me, talking to me, was bad enough. I didn't need the pain or the headache retroactively as well.

White mist edged my vision. I grabbed my bag and lunged away from the table as the hallucination hit me harder and quicker than it ever had before.

I screamed, arching backward and then convulsing with the pain of it.

Blackwell was touching me. He shouldn't be touching me, but for a moment I couldn't remember why.

He shouldn't be able to touch me.

Electrical shocks ran up over my shoulders from where he grasped my upper arms. He settled me back onto the vinyl seat.

"What is it?" he hissed. "Are you in pain? There shouldn't be pain."

Unable to see with my own eyes, I scrambled away from him, pushing back into the booth. My spine dug into the low sill of the window frame — the window through which I'd just been gazing at the white surf crashing over the dark, sandy beach.

I tried to hang onto that image, and to the sharp pain of the wood grinding against my arched spine. The restaurant had to be real — even if Hoyt and Blackwell weren't — because Beau was meeting me here.

Then I was drowning.

No ... she was drowning. She just didn't know it yet. She was surrounded in every direction by blue ... crystal-clear sea-blue water ... her curls were floating all around her head in a halo of gold. She looked as if she was sleeping. Except she shouldn't be sleeping underwater.

She was drowning in my mind.

"Drowning," I cried. "Wake up!"

"Drowning?" Blackwell asked. "Me? Where? When?"

His tone was eager and edged in darkness, like the junkies I'd seen every day on the streets of the Downtown Eastside after I'd moved into the Residence. The ones who refused food. Who sneered when I tried to help.

"Not you," I said, not knowing why I was answering him. Just that I felt compelled to do so. "Blond, curls. Usually carries a green knife."

In my mind, the blond opened her indigo eyes. They were a deeper blue than the ocean surrounding her. She looked frantically around, little bubbles forming at the edges of her nostrils. Then she started to panic.

My heart rate ramped up until I thought I'd pass out. I was gripping the top edge of the booth with one hand and clutching my bag to my chest with the other.

"Jade Godfrey," Blackwell sneered. I could feel him lean closer across the table to whisper intently, "And what is the warrior's daughter after now?"

"Jade Godfrey," I whispered, accepting Blackwell's offering of the name without question. "Jade Godfrey is going to die."

Blackwell snorted. "Jade Godfrey is notoriously difficult to kill. Unless she has a thousand-pound weight tied to her leg, I doubt she'll be drowning anytime soon. Now, what is she holding? Besides the knife, the necklace, and the sword? What treasure has Jade risked drowning to collect?"

The necklace. How had I never noticed the necklace the blond — Jade — wore? It was a gold chain with what appeared to be at least a dozen wedding rings attached to it. She wore it wound three times around her neck.

I had a necklace too.

Instead of answering Blackwell, I thrust my hand into my bag and yanked out my mother's necklace. The pain in my head eased.

"What is this pretty thing?" Blackwell murmured. "Its magic doesn't belong to you."

I clutched the necklace against my chest and curled away from him.

Then the door to the restaurant crashed open. But it wasn't the wind that threw it.

I felt, rather than saw, Blackwell turn to look back over his shoulder.

"Not your business, man." It was Hoyt speaking, still somewhere off to the left.

"What are you doing?" a deep voice growled. I'd never heard anyone sound so fierce.

I opened my eyes, not realizing I'd had them screwed shut. The top was still spinning before me. Blackwell had turned to face the front door.

"Beau ..." I cried.

He was striding through the restaurant. His voice had pulled me out of the hallucination, though the headache was still shredding my brain.

Relief flooded across my chest and out through my limbs, freeing them, allowing me to move.

Then I saw Hoyt dogging Beau's heels.

"Back off, big guy," the skinny stalker said. He grabbed for Beau's arm.

Hoyt — who was a figment of my imagination — could touch Beau.

My stomach bottomed out.

Beau shook him off with no apparent effort, but Hoyt went flying as if he'd been thrown. He crashed against the empty table one back and to the left of mine.

"Hoyt," Blackwell called sharply. "We don't want any trouble."

Beau stepped up to the booth, and then swayed back as if buffeted by a wind that I couldn't feel. His eyes were fixed to the spinning top on the table, his beautiful face marred with a fierce frown. He reached for me and I flinched away from him, then he turned on Blackwell with a snarl.

"Who are you?" he asked. "And what is that?" He jabbed a finger toward the spinning top.

"Nothing," Blackwell answered, smoothly and completely in control. "A helping hand. Rochelle and I are just having a chat."

Beau lifted his gaze to me. His eyes were brilliantly green. Glowing, actually. He looked wild, feral. "Are you okay?" His voice was throaty, edged with a growl.

"You can see him?" I could hear the panic in my voice. If Beau could see what I could see then ... then ... he was part of the hallucination.

"Are you okay?" he asked again.

I shook my head. "No," I answered, again feeling strangely compelled to respond.

Beau frowned, and looked down at his hand. It was covered in orange-black fur, and clawed. He shook it, as if this motion would cause it to revert to its normal state. It didn't.

I moaned. What fresh hell was this? I couldn't handle anymore.

"I asked you what that device was!" Beau shouted. He turned toward Blackwell, then hunched over as if in pain.

"Control yourself, shifter," Blackwell said. "We don't need an incident here. I've laid distraction and barrier spells, but —"

"No sorcerer tells me what to do," Beau spat.

"I was unaware that Rochelle was under the protection of the pack," Blackwell said. "I meant no disrespect. I would have gone through proper channels —"

Beau smashed his clawed hand down on the spinning top, crushing it and cracking the table in two.

I screamed and scrambled up, going over the booth seat and onto the table behind me.

None of the other customers or the staff in the restaurant seemed to notice that anything unusual was going on.

Blackwell was standing three feet behind Beau, closer to the exit. I hadn't seen him move.

Beau reached down for the broken table and grabbed its edges. Then he wrenched it — steel bolted center leg and all — out of the floor. His face didn't look right. It was stretched and too angular.

"It's all in my head," I murmured. "All in my head."

Beau twisted as if to throw the table at Blackwell.

But Hoyt, who was now standing to the left of Beau — in front of the bar and between the row of booths across from the window — threw one of his ball bearings.

The silver sphere flashed, streaking the air between him and Beau in a low, arcing line.

I tried to scream, but couldn't form words. My broken brain was controlling the scene before me, but I obviously wasn't allowed to alter the events as they were unfolding.

The silver ball struck Beau.

He cried out and dropped the table. Stumbling back, he fell to one knee beside the table on which I was still standing.

"Stop it!" I screamed, wresting control of my throat and vocal cords from my malignant mind.

Blackwell stepped forward, but whether he was attacking Beau or trying to help, I had no idea.

Putting all my weight into the blow, I slapped him across the face. I nearly toppled off the table in order to do so.

The sorcerer flinched away, pressing his hand to his cheek.

All the bones in my left hand ached as I solidified my footing and pulled my arm back to hit him again.

Blackwell shook his head as if he was trying to clear it. Then, he looked at me, utterly shocked but not at all physically hurt. A wicked smile spread across his face. It was the most genuine emotion I'd seen from him yet.

"I'd listen to her, Hoyt. She packs quite a psychic punch," he said. "I don't think you would like it." He backed off another few feet, standing beside diners who continued to obliviously consume their desserts. He held his hands up, palms toward Beau and me.

Beau was hunched over, holding his chest and panting in pain beside me.

"The shifter is young," Blackwell said. "He simply got caught in the spell of the amplifier. I'm sure he will get himself under control. The pack frowns upon public displays." That last part was directed to Beau, not Hoyt, as if in some sort of warning.

Keeping his gaze locked on Beau, the self-proclaimed sorcerer stepped forward again and picked up the crushed golden top where it had fallen to the floor. He didn't look pleased as he tucked the ruined 'amplifier,' as he'd called it, into his pocket. At least I think that was what he'd been referring to.

Beau straightened with some effort. The front of his black T-shirt looked melted. The skin underneath was burned, dark reddish-pink and oozing.

I cried out.

He turned and looked at me. His face wasn't his own anymore. It was a fearsome blend of man and beast. His cheekbones were too broad. His forehead rounded into his nose. And his teeth ... he was double fanged, like a cat. A cat with three-inch incisors.

"I'm sorry," he said, the fangs hampering his speech. "I should have told you sooner." Then he turned his fiercely glowing green eyes on Hoyt. "Spellcurser," he spat.

Hoyt, still between the bar and the first row of tables, was rolling a couple more of his silver ball bearings in both hands. He grinned at Beau. "Sorry, cat," he said. "Didn't mean to hit you so hard."

Beau charged him, leaping up and over the booth in front of him. He moved so quickly that Hoyt barely had time to hit him with two more of the silver balls.

Beau shrieked in pain, the sound completely inhuman to my ears. He landed half off his feet but managed to backhand Hoyt into and over the bar as he collapsed.

The spellcurser, as Beau had called him, flew back into the glassware hanging above the bar, hitting the liquor bottles on the mirrored back wall. He dropped to the ground behind the bar in a rain of glass shards and alcohol.

Beau whirled around to face Blackwell, stumbling to his feet. He was badly burned, with layers of newly formed scar tissue and open wounds covering his chest, neck, and upper arms. Both of his hands were furred and clawed.

Blackwell had dark orbs of shadow somehow pooled in his hands. Yes, he was holding some sort of dark light like … magic.

Beau charged, leaping back over the bank of booths again.

He was slower this time. Badly wounded.

Blackwell threw the black orbs. The smoky light slammed into Beau in mid-leap, blasting him backward. He flew past me, through to the end of the restaurant. He crashed into two booths before he stopped, tearing the tables and the bench seats from the wall. He fell amid splinters of wood, cracked Formica, and crushed vinyl.

I heard shrieking. I realized it was me.

Now that I had started screaming, I wasn't going to stop.

I screamed and screamed as I scrambled off the table to stand in the aisle between Blackwell and Beau.

Beau, my beautiful Beau, wasn't stirring from among the wreckage of the booths.

I faced Blackwell, the sorcerer of Blackness Castle, Scotland, and screamed.

I screamed until my throat was raw.

Blackwell, who'd been reforming the black orbs of light in his hands, blanched. He dropped the spell. Yes, I'd figured out that I was hallucinating some sort of magic, just as Beau had told me when he looked at my sketches.

The sorcerer held his empty hands toward me in surrender.

"Rochelle, please," he coaxed. "This was not my intention. My doing —"

I squeezed my eyes shut, grabbed a fistful of my own hair, and pulled. I yanked so hard that my eyes watered.

"Get out, get out," I screamed. "I will rip you from my brain. I will tear you from my mind. I will shred you, destroy you with my thoughts, Mot Blackwell, sorcerer of Blackness Castle, Scotland."

I opened my eyes and locked my gaze to Blackwell's. "Do you believe me?"

He nodded.

Hoyt stumbled out from the bar and made his way toward Blackwell. His face and hands were badly cut.

A tiger, easily eleven feet in length landed silently on the still-upright table to my right. The table shouldn't have been able to support its weight, but it did. The tiger let loose a snarling growl that rattled the windows. Then it turned its glowing green eyes on me.

I wasn't afraid.

Hoyt, on the other hand, stumbled back behind Blackwell. "Jesus. A fucking tiger. That ain't good, boss."

"No, it isn't," Blackwell said grimly. Then he pulled a business card out of his inner suit pocket and placed it on the empty table beside him to the right. The people on his left had finished their desserts and were looking over the bill.

"You will need me, Rochelle Hawthorn," he said. "You will want to know what I know someday, and I will willingly trade. I'm a fair man. You could be formidable, but you're lost. You don't understand your power, and there are very few who could teach you. The pack will lock you in a gilded cage. They hoard their power. With me, you could live. With me, you could have a life and riches."

"Get out."

He nodded, reached back, and grasped Hoyt's arm.

The spellcurser cried out as if the bone was broken.

Then the sorcerer brushed his fingers across his chest and disappeared.

With a pop, my ears unplugged.

People started screaming. They looked around, taking in the destruction surrounding them as if waking from some dream. Then they jumped from their chairs and fled the restaurant, brushing by me as they did so.

The tiger seemed to frighten them most of all.

I ignored them, stepping through the rubble of the trashed tables toward the exit. The tiger that used to be Beau walked at my side.

I reached to pick up Blackwell's business card. As I did so, I realized that my mother's necklace was still tangled in my fingers, and I paused to feel the weight of the stone in my palm. Its touch steadied and calmed me further. I dropped the business card into the depths of my bag. Then I went outside to retrieve my bike.

Nothing was real anymore. I didn't have to worry about who was hurt or afraid. It was all in my head anyway. I was stuck in the hallucination.

Everything made sense now.

Beau.

The way I'd felt about him. Our instant connection.

That he stayed with me even in the blatant face of my crazy.

But ... the hot apple juice was a lie. A lie of love whispered in my ear by my evil, broken brain.

I could let it crush me. I could let it destroy me. I could try to break the hold of the hallucination. I could try to wake up.

Or I could stay with Beau.

I'd made a promise.

I wasn't going to be the one to leave.

I wasn't going to be the one to expose the lie.

I didn't love him any less for not being real. He was magic, conjured by me.

My magic.

He was mine.

CHAPTER NINE

"I'm sorry. I'm so sorry," Beau whispered. "I'll fix it. I'll protect you."

I woke.

Beau wasn't beside me, and I thought for a moment that I was waking out of a dream, or a hallucination. But I felt alert, aware, and oddly settled. A sure sign I'd forgotten to take my pill at some point. A warning sign.

The Brave was moving, and quickly — if lying in the back bed having just woken put me in any condition to judge. I was still dressed in my jeans and hoodie, but I was underneath the covers with my sneakers and socks off. Light leaked in around the edges of the brightly striped orange curtains.

I struggled to get loose of the tightly tucked blankets and sat up, tugging the blinds open above my head. The sun hadn't risen yet, but the sky was lightning ahead. We were driving along a paved road. Fields stretched away to either side. I couldn't see the ocean anymore. As I watched, we passed a massive field of grape vines. An orchard? A farm? Nope. By the sign that blurred past, I was looking at a winery.

The Brave was moving way too fast, easily exceeding the speed limit if I couldn't read the signs as they blurred past. I slipped off the bed and started toward the cockpit, realizing as I stepped through the kitchen area that none of this was actually happening.

Did I even own the Brave? Was I lying on the floor of the RV right now, hallucinating? Had I never actually recovered from the hallucination that hit the night I crossed the border? Maybe I'd never even gone to the diner where I thought I first met Beau.

Had I even left Vancouver? Or had I hallucinated the entire day of my birthday?

I could see Beau in the driver's seat, but I grabbed my bag from where it was sitting on the bench seat of the dinette instead of going to him. I unzipped the inner pocket and pulled out my mother's necklace. I stared down at the large, dull stone and the broken chain. What had the jeweler said? That it was worth fifty thousand dollars? How utterly absurd.

An eight-month-pregnant woman gets in a car accident in Vancouver and dies, giving birth but never waking up to give her own name? She carries a necklace worth fifty thousand dollars, but no ID. Every social worker who'd ever been assigned to me passed the necklace along with my file all these years.

Where had I broken with reality? At what point did I become so lost that —

"Rochelle?" Beau called from the cockpit. "You up?"

I loved the way he said my name. The way his accent claimed it, made it unique. I could admit that now. I could be fully head over heels for him. Just because he was in my head didn't mean he wasn't real to me.

I wasn't lost at all. I was completely found.

"Yes," I called forward as I tucked the necklace in my hoodie pocket and wandered up to the cockpit. Beau filled the driver's seat — his knees up too high on either side of the steering wheel, which he gripped fiercely.

He flicked his eyes up to the rearview mirror to look at me hovering over his shoulder. His eyes were bright green with no hint of blue now. They were bright, like they'd been when he morphed into a tiger in my dream last night. People's eyes didn't change like that, so that was just another confirmation that Beau was a hallucination. Even in human form, he wasn't real.

He'd been hurt last night, severely burned by Hoyt's curses, but I couldn't see any evidence of those terrible wounds on his face, neck, or hands now. I was glad to see he was unharmed, but the speed of his healing only reinforced the truth that my mind was generating everything I was seeing.

I kneeled on the carpeted stairs between the driver and passenger seats, wrapping an arm around the back of Beau's headrest to steady myself. The speedometer was steadily pointing at 70 miles an hour. I knew that was too taxing a pace for the Brave to keep up.

"You're driving awfully fast," I murmured as I laid my hand on Beau's arm. The muscles of his forearm were ropey with tension.

"She can take it," he said, as if he knew what I was thinking. "The road is straight through from here to Portland."

"Portland?"

"Yes." He flicked his eyes to the rearview mirror again.

I smiled at him, and for some reason this made his beautiful face contract with pain. He looked back to the road before him.

"I'm not a hallucination." His tone was a combination of anger, frustration, and sadness.

I smiled brighter, wider. "I never said you were."

"Last night. You told me everything last night."

"I don't remember saying anything like that." I continued smiling. My jaw and cheeks ached with it. I needed him to keep up the premise. I wasn't sure I could maintain the delusion if he started questioning it ... and by him, I meant me, because he was obviously part of me. Some part I'd desperately needed even if I hadn't known it consciously. I'd needed someone to love, and my broken brain had conjured Beau.

"I'm real, Rochelle," he said. "I'm real. Tell me I'm real."

"You're real," I said obligingly.

The steering wheel creaked underneath his hands.

"Beau!" I snapped.

He loosened his grip. "Sorry, sorry."

"I'll get you some cookies." I stood up to make my way back to the kitchen.

"I don't want any cookies!"

Ignoring him, I opened the bathroom door and escaped inside, wanting to wash my face and brush my teeth. Three empty pill bottles were rolling around in the sink.

I slammed the door back open. "How dare you!"

"They're bad for you," Beau replied. "Even the asshole sorcerer thought so."

"You don't control me, Beau ... Beau ..." I faltered. I didn't know his last name. If he was a figment of my imagination, shouldn't I know his last name?

"Beaumont Jamison. I get my name and skin color from my father, who's a petty-criminal spellcaster I've barely even met. And the shapeshifter gene from my mother, who suppresses her changes with alcohol and accepts weekly beatings from a man far weaker than her. A man who happens to be my sister's father, whose magic is only good for one thing. Being a fucking bully."

This was a lot of information all at once, some of which sounded pretty fanciful. But then, I knew I shouldn't underestimate the creativity of my broken mind.

"You can't rescue someone who doesn't want to be rescued," Beau said.

I wasn't sure if he was talking about his family or me. "It doesn't matter anymore," I whispered.

"It matters, Rochelle. You matter."

I retreated into the dinette area, digging my sketchbook out of my bag and crossing my legs on the bench seat. I found some charcoal and flipped to a blank page as I settled in. I hovered my left hand over the page, thinking of the events of last night … well, the last night that had occurred in my head. I always sketched after an overwhelming hallucination, and none of my delusions had ever been more overwhelming than last night.

But I was oddly calm. The sorcerer and the spell-curser, as Beau had called them, hadn't haunted my dreams. In fact, I didn't remember dreaming at all.

"Beau's tiger," I whispered as I stared at the blank page. The tiger that had walked by my side — defending me from the sorcerer despite whatever the spellcurser had thrown at it — was the second most beautiful thing I'd ever seen. Second only to Beau himself.

I would draw the tiger. Its wide-set, brilliant emerald-green eyes. The black and white markings that defined the shape of its broad, orange-furred face.

Nothing happened. The blank page stared back at me. I could always draw. I looked up and out the side window to sort out my thoughts, to focus. It didn't work.

"Why Portland?" I asked, loud enough for Beau to hear me.

"It's the territory of the West Coast North American Pack," Beau answered. "If the wolves don't rend me limb from limb the second they scent me on their territory, they might protect you from the sorcerer. Actually, I'm hoping they'll protect you even if they do kill me."

Fear soured my empty belly. I tried to brush it away with the assurance that this was my hallucination, and that I wouldn't let anything bad happen to Beau. Except … I'd let him get hurt last night, hadn't I?

"I don't understand." I whispered the words, but Beau somehow heard me.

"I know," he said. "I can explain, but I can't stop. Okay? You're very special, Rochelle. I wouldn't risk it, except the sorcerer said something about the pack, like he's afraid of them. And I don't know of any other Adepts nearby. Not anyone powerful enough to stand against that asshole."

"Adepts?"

"People with magic. That's what they call themselves. The ones who know what they are, at least."

"But they'll kill you?"

"I'm an outsider, and not a wolf. The dominant shapeshifter species are werewolves. They're very territorial. I'm a loner. A rogue, in their eyes. They don't get that. They kill what threatens them." Beau delivered this information with the same ease he seemed to apply to everything … everything but me.

"You love me," I said.

"You doubt me?"

"Not for a second. Not since I … I … saw you."

"You didn't create me, Rochelle." Beau's voice held its calm. "You don't even create your sketches. You draw what you see with your magic. Your Adept senses. That's what the pain, the headaches are, maybe. Your magic. I don't know what you see. The future, or the past? Or if you just read magic, decipher it? But the pack will find someone to help you."

I didn't answer as I stared at the blank page of the sketchbook in front of me. The bright emptiness of its white expanse was like a void obstructing the welcoming, comforting lime-green of the table. The table was supposed to fold into a second bed, but I hadn't tried it. Its Formica was a lighter green than Beau's eyes, and somehow nowhere near as bright.

"Rochelle, do you hear me?" Beau called. "Did you have the pain, the headache, last night?"

"Yes."

"But only after the sorcerer showed up and used that device on you, right? The one that made it impossible for me to stop my own transformation, even though I'd just run and had no need to change."

"The amplifier, he called it," I murmured.

"And what about with me? What about the night we met? You didn't have the terrible headache then."

My head was starting to ache now, but not in that way. This was like my mind was being overloaded. Like Beau was trying to stuff too much information into it. Trying to make me believe …

"Yes, I did," I said.

"You're lying."

"I'm not."

"I can smell it on you, Rochelle. Even if you don't know yourself."

"I had a vision right before we met. It hit me here in the Brave. I took some pills, and when I woke up, I went to the diner."

"When you woke up." Beau repeated my own words back at me.

"Except I didn't wake up!" I was screaming suddenly. "I'm just having hallucinations within
hallucinations."

"Rochelle —"

"No! No. Stop talking. Just stop."

I switched the charcoal into my right hand. I didn't
usually draw with my right hand, but I had to draw. I
had to.

Beau swerved the Brave off the paved road, taking it onto some gravel side road or driveway. I slid
across the vinyl seat, but managed to grab the table and
my sketchbook before both it and I tumbled onto the
kitchen floor.

Beau hit the brakes. I slammed forward into the
table, painfully crushing my lower ribcage against its
edge.

Beau undid his seat belt with a click. He shut off
the engine.

I scrambled to right myself and the notebook, then
pressed the charcoal to the paper before me. I pressed
and pressed, but didn't draw. The charcoal snapped in
my hand. I dropped the broken bits and scrubbed what
remained in my hand across the page.

"I can't draw," I cried. "Why can't I draw?"

Beau strode back to me, lifted me out of the seat,
and cradled me to his chest as if I weighed nothing.

"I can't draw," I repeated.

"I see," he said. His voice was thick with emotion,
fear mixed with concern. "I see."

"Why? Why?" I was getting hysterical. I couldn't
seem to stop myself. I kept everything so very carefully
controlled. It was how I functioned. Now the pills, the
sketching, and my mind were betraying me.

"Listen to me." Beau pressed his lips to my forehead as he whispered fiercely. "Listen to me. It's right in

front of you. I'm right in front of you. You see me, you feel me."

"Yes, yes. I feel you."

"Do you feel the visions, or whatever happens whenever you draw? Do you feel those things?"

"I feel pain."

"Do you feel pain when you look at me?"

I pushed away from him, so that I could see his eyes. He settled back against the table. I lifted my hand and traced the lines of his face — up his cheekbone, around his eye, and across the top of his eyebrow. I still had charcoal on my fingers and I left traces of it on him, even darker than his mocha skin.

He shuddered at my touch, then closed his eyes. He squeezed me to him.

"Too tight," I gasped.

He eased off on his hug. "Sorry," he whispered. "I … I … my mother …" He shook his head, changing his mind. "I've met other Adepts, other magical people. Mostly in big cities, where I don't like to be."

"No jungle in the city," I said.

He barked out a laugh, shaking his head. I continued to trace his face as he spoke. "Some of these Adepts, they don't know what they are … their magic is weak, just a hint of a scent. They're practically human, maybe gifted but not unusually so. But you … you …" His voice cracked. "I scented you from the highway. I tracked you to the diner. I saw you through the window."

He was silent for a moment, as if fighting with his emotions to find the words he wanted.

"I know it's crazy to feel this way about you," he said. "So quickly. That kind of love doesn't exist."

"Doesn't it?" I said.

"You think I'm in your head, Rochelle. That gives you some freedom, doesn't it? To embrace what you think is a fantasy?"

I nodded. I couldn't lie to him, not cradled in his arms. I knew he wasn't real.

"So where does that leave me? Seeing you through that diner window. Knowing I should keep walking, and yet going in to talk to you. Figuring out that somehow you had no idea what you were, what you are? Then touching you? Feeling the magic on your skin? Seeing the sketches? I thought I'd have time. I thought I could slowly make you understand. Then that damn sorcerer showed up to ruin everything … to ruin us."

"No …" I was crying suddenly, sobbing from the pain his words were causing.

"And you love me." Beau was crying now as well, shaking with it. "You love me, without question. Like no one has ever loved me. Not because of how I look, or what you think you can get me to do for you. And you think it's a lie. You think it's a lie."

"Not a lie. The love isn't a lie."

Beau wasn't listening. "It's killing me. Slowly, painfully."

I could see him force himself into some sort of control. I wiped the tears from his cheeks even as I let mine continue to stream down my face.

"I'll help you," he whispered. "As best as I can. Even if you come into your power, and realize you don't actually love the me who isn't in your head."

"That would never happen." I pressed my hands to either side of his face, forcing him to look into my eyes. "Never. I could never not love you."

He stared at me for a moment but didn't respond. I could feel him closing off, withdrawing. It suddenly felt like I was losing him.

"Beau," I whispered. "You say you can smell me lying. You say I'm lying to myself."

"Yes."

"Am I lying now? I love you. I do love the way you look —"

He laughed. It was a sound of pain and desperation.

"I love the way you make me feel," I said. "I love the way I am around you. I feel lonely when we're apart. I've never felt lonely in my life. I never fit with anyone before, never wanted anyone in my space. You make my heart race. You feel more real than anything ever has before. Do you understand? More real than anything."

I dropped my hands from his cheeks. He had charcoal smeared on one side of his extraordinary face. "I saw you in the diner. I couldn't breathe at the sight of you. And you're right. There was no pain, no white light, no desperate need to draw. When you touched me ... I knew I would never want you to leave. I couldn't believe you'd stay. I couldn't believe that ..."

I had to pause, knowing he didn't want to hear my doubts, didn't want to hear my justifications. "I love you, Beau. Do you hear ... smell ... the truth in my words?"

He nodded. Relief flooded through my pained heart and spread through my limbs.

"I don't want to go to this pack."

Beau's face hardened. "We're going."

"I don't want you to get hurt. I don't want to lose you."

"That sorcerer is the most powerful thing I've ever scented. Scary powerful. He thought I was pack. That's the only reason he walked away. He'll be back, but he won't be able to get anywhere near you. The pack will know witches. The pack will know someone who can help you ... with the pain, and understanding who you are."

"Beau —"

"No," he said. He set me on my feet and determinedly walked back to the cockpit, leaving me standing alone and chilled without his embrace.

"I thought … I thought there'd be make up sex." I hadn't even gotten to kiss him. I desperately wanted to be continually kissing him.

He turned to look back at me. He was hunched forward with one hand on the headrest, ready to climb down into the driver's seat.

"We weren't fighting."

"What was that, then?"

"That was moving forward."

I stared after him as he slipped into position and turned the key. He pulled the Brave onto the road. I swayed, bumping into the kitchen table as he cranked the wheel and executed a three-point turn to circle back to the highway.

"I could get you cookies," I finally said.

"That would be nice."

My sketchbook slid across the table and bumped against my hip. I stared down at the blank page. Then I closed it and tucked it back in my bag.

I opened up the cupboard above my head and retrieved Beau's second-to-last box of Oreos. Then I made my way up to the front and climbed into the passenger seat.

I felt Beau glance at me, but he didn't speak. I opened the Oreos and pulled out the plastic insert that held the black-and-white cookies in protected rows. As I palmed three to pass to Beau, I saw the butterfly tattoo on my inner wrist. The Oreos were a weird reflection of the black tattoos on my pale skin.

Beau held his hand out.

"You think I only draw the hallucinations."

"Visions, I think. But yes."

"You think I can't draw last night, can't draw you … the tiger, because you aren't a vision."

"Yes." Beau took the cookies I dropped into his waiting hand. He sounded exceedingly satisfied with my understanding.

"I draw the tattoos," I said. "They aren't from visions."

"Aren't they?"

The question hung between us. I didn't answer. I didn't want to be accused of lying. I knew the tattoos weren't from visions. Why would I hallucinate the butterfly? The barbed wire? The peony?

Still … I did have a hallucination — within this hallucination that Beau insisted was real life — last night. One that came with the migraine and the whiteout. One that Beau claimed the sorcerer had triggered somehow. One in which the blond woman was drowning. The blond woman who Blackwell had named Jade Godfrey. The woman I had seen facing off against the sorcerer more than once.

She'd been drowning, her golden curls floating around her head. Then she'd awoken, her eyes a deeper blue than the water surrounding her …

My left hand started tingling. I rubbed my fingers together, feeling the kiss of charcoal still on my skin.

"What are you thinking?" Beau whispered the question, but it still made me flinch.

I glanced at him, shaking my head. Denying the sudden urge I had to draw the woman in the water — not of her drowning, but of the moment she woke …

"Your eyes," Beau said. "Your eyes glow white. I've never seen magic work like that before. I've heard some witches can see magic in color, but I never have."

I clenched my hand into a fist, denying the itch to draw, denying Beau's words. I looked away, staring out my window at the farmland streaming by outside. I tried to not remember the orbs of dark light in Blackwell's hands, or the green glow of Beau's eyes, or the way the woman's hair in my hallucinations always glistened gold.

Beau grunted, satisfied.

"It can't be true," I whispered. "That would be even crazier than I already am."

Beau didn't answer, but he did press down on the gas pedal to take the Brave's speedometer back up to 70 miles an hour.

I didn't caution him. The Brave would only break down if my mind and my fantasy needed it to ... right?

Right?

CHAPTER TEN

"How do you know about this pack ... of shapeshifters ..." — I stumbled over the terminology Beau had used — "...that lives in Portland?"

"My mother told me." Beau didn't turn his gaze from the highway. He was intently watching the green-and-white roadside direction signs as they passed, though I didn't know if he was looking for a specific turn off. He was executing some plan he'd made while I was still sleeping, and wasn't being very forthcoming about the steps.

"What are you looking for? I can help." We'd cut east along Highway 18 until it turned into Highway 99, the farmland giving way to the outer boroughs of a city. Beau had driven all night to get us this close to Portland before the sun had fully risen.

"The turn off to Walmart."

"We're parking the Brave?"

"Yes."

"Because of something your mother told you?"

"She told me to stay far, far away from the pack, so I'm already ignoring the most important thing she ever taught me. It might be difficult to park the Brave downtown, and this will ... well, if we have to run, they won't know where we're running to ... hopefully."

Fear curled its way down my spine to pool in the small of my back. I'd never felt that before. I was so scared for Beau, though he didn't sound particularly fearful himself. I didn't understand why I was imagining any of this. I didn't know why I would ever want to put him in any kind of jeopardy, even within my mind.

"We won't have to run," I said, summoning up every ounce of confidence I could muster about an imaginary situation of which I seemed to have no control.

"We're running now."

"The dark-suited ... Blackwell, the sorcerer —"

"I know who he is. I was there."

I could hear the anger in his voice, but didn't understand it. "You're mad at me."

"No, I'm absolutely livid with myself. I never should have let you out of my sight. He might not have approached at all if I'd been there."

"If that's the case, then you wouldn't be worried about him returning."

Beau let out a frustrated breath. "I'm trying to do my best. What I think is best."

"I hadn't planned on coming to Portland," I said, trying to alleviate some tension by changing the subject. "I hear it's a lot like Vancouver."

"Don't play nice, Rochelle. I want you, not the fake you who's just pretending."

"What if the fake me is all I have now?"

"Look deeper."

I shut my mouth with a frustrated shake of my head. I wasn't sure I could give him what he wanted. I was worried that at any moment, I was going to wake up in some hospital, drugged as high as heaven and without Beau.

He found the highway exit he'd been looking for. Then with a couple of more turns, he had us parked on the far side of the Walmart parking lot. Except for two other RVs that dwarfed the twenty-one foot Brave, the massive lot was empty this far from the store.

"Are they even open this early?" I asked as I peered through the windshield at the biggest Walmart I'd ever seen.

"Yes." His tone was blunt, but not unkind. He removed his seat belt and crossed to the exterior door.

Obviously now was not the time for small talk, but I missed the easiness that Beau and I had ... before. Before I'd known this was all a massive delusion.

I followed him into the parking lot. It was chilly, so I tugged on my mittens.

Beau checked the contents of my bag, making sure I had my cell phone, sketchbook, and some money. Then he locked up the Brave and tucked the keys in the bag's inner zipper pocket. Still without saying a word, he placed the bag over my head and across my body, testing the strength of the strap as he did so, as if he was afraid someone might try to rip it off me.

"Beau ..."

He kissed me then. Pulling me into his arms and off my feet, pressing me back against the Brave in a lip lock full of need and passion.

I broke the embrace to wrap my arms around him, whispering fiercely into the warm skin of his neck. "I won't let anything happen to you. I won't let anyone hurt you."

"I know," he said, though his voice was choked with more emotion than acceptance. "I love you, Rochelle. I know everyone would think me crazy to say those words now, so early, and in this situation. But I want you to know."

I nodded, offering him a smile instead of simply mimicking his declaration.

He smiled back and then set me on my feet. "Right. Ready for an adventure?"

"With you, anytime," I answered.

"First we need bus tickets."

"Well, that's a bit of a boring start."

He laughed like he meant it this time. The sound eased the fear I still felt in the small of my back. The tension didn't completely diminish, but it eased enough to make it easier to walk next to him as he urged me toward the nearest bus stop.

"Where are we going?"

"A park. Near the river."

"You've been here before?"

"No, but we're looking for wolves. Wolves like to run, and they hunt near water."

We'd taken a bus into downtown Portland and were now standing on a railed streetcar, cutting through skyscrapers interspersed with restaurants and clothing stores. The streetcar was packed. It felt like the entire city was heading to work at the same time.

"So ... we'll be prey?"

"Yep. Let's just hope they don't come in numbers. I could maybe handle three if I had to, but not without them hurting me. Badly. Any more and we're in trouble."

"We're talking about people, right?"

"Sure," Beau said, turning a worried, tense gaze on me. "People like you and me."

"So, they'll ask questions. Listen to answers."

"Yeah, at some point they'll start asking questions." He looked away from me, out the streetcar window at the city shifting by us. Every line of his body was bristling with tension — or maybe with barely contained terror.

I left him alone with his thoughts. I didn't have any extra room in my head anyway.

Apparently — at least along these city streets — Portland had a larger homeless population than Vancouver did. I'd also never seen so many African-American people in one place before. Though I hadn't seen an Asian person since I'd left Vancouver. When we'd first climbed on the bus that stopped by the Walmart, I thought people were staring at me, but it was Beau who fascinated everyone. I don't think he noticed.

Twice, Beau had consulted maps he'd taken screenshots of and saved on my cell phone. Each time he tucked the phone back in my bag instead of keeping it.

I wanted to freak out, to demand we return to the Brave, but I'd already made the choice to follow him wherever he went. So instead, I curled both of my arms around his left arm and tried to just enjoy being here with him. Even if it was just going to be for this moment, as the streetcar switched tracks and pressed me against the length of him.

Beau was peering out the windows. Then, seeing something, he tugged me to the back doors and off the streetcar when it stopped. People pressed against us, blocking our exit and the path to the sidewalk. Portland definitely felt like a bigger city than Vancouver, though I think Greater Vancouver's total population — including its outlying cities — was higher. Beau tucked me behind him, twisted his shoulders, and everyone made way.

We hustled along the side of what I thought might be a luxury hotel in another skyscraper. The Marriott, according to the sign I barely had time to read. Then there was a park before us. It was narrow — really just a patch of grass that ran alongside a huge river — but it was pretty.

We jaywalked across the Southwest Natio Parkway, which was clogged with early morning traffic, to a path that cut down to the edge of the river. Here, a paved river walk ran parallel to the water in both directions. I could see an elevated expressway on the opposite side of the rushing water. I'd never seen a huge highway traveling over and around a city like that before, or so many bridges crossing a single river. From my vantage point, I counted five connecting the two sides of the city. The river was like a huge artery with overpasses and bridges for veins.

"That's a lot of bridges," I said.

Beau grunted, not completely listening. He was scanning the crowd anxiously in either direction. An older couple, obviously tourists by the paper brochures they were chatting over, stood up from a bench on the grass at the very edge of the river walk. As they wandered off, Beau and I took their place. He tugged me down to sit next to him, his arm slung over the back of the bench above my shoulders.

It wasn't as chilly here as in Vancouver, but even with my hoodie underneath my jacket, a hat, and my mittens, it wasn't really bench-sitting weather. Beau was wearing his usual plain T-shirt underneath his gray hoodie, which was unzipped about halfway. He should have been freezing but obviously wasn't.

"So ... we wait?" I asked.

"Yeah, we wait."

"There isn't a number we can call? An Adept hotline?"

Beau snorted, but his amusement was mostly for my benefit. I placed my hand on his thigh and caught his smile in my peripheral vision. I slid my hand a bit higher and he laughed huskily. Then he lifted my hand, turning my palm up to place a tender kiss in the center of it.

I sighed and tucked my head against his shoulder. Maybe no one would come. Maybe we could watch the sunset, then wander back to that Voodoo Doughnut place with the huge line outside of it that we'd passed on the streetcar a few blocks back.

Every muscle in Beau's body tensed.

I looked up to see him watching a woman as she sauntered toward us along the river walk. A few dozen feet behind her, the grass of the park ended right before an expensive-looking hotel hanging out over the river. Its discrete signage declared it to be the RiverPlace Hotel.

A couple of joggers outpaced the woman. Based on her casual body language, and if she hadn't been staring directly at Beau, I would have expected her to walk right past us.

Beau took a single glance around us, really quickly — as if he didn't want to take his eye off the woman for even a second. His grip across my shoulders tightened, but he'd dropped my hand the moment he spotted her.

I glanced around as well. A few people were jogging or biking along the river walk, but the park was mostly empty. Which wasn't surprising since it was still fairly early on a weekday morning.

The woman stopped a few feet before us. Then she also casually glanced around. She was a few inches taller than me — maybe five-foot-six without the purple wedge heels. Her hands were on her hips. She was wearing a violet-paisley print silk blouse over a tight dark-plum colored skirt that fell just above her knees. Her shoulder-length dark hair lifted lightly in the breeze.

That was it. No jacket, no scarf. I shivered just from looking at her. She didn't even bother glancing at me.

Beau didn't move. He was so tense that his arm across my shoulder felt like it was made of steel.

The woman didn't look even remotely dangerous. Not until she opened her purple-glossed lips and said, "What have we here, cat?" She spat the final word.

"I'm Beaumont Jamison. This is Rochelle Saintpaul."

"Your names mean nothing to me. Do you know whose territory this is?"

"Yes."

"And you dare enter it without proper introductions?"

Beau squirmed. His gaze was focused on the woman's shoulder. There wasn't an ounce of aggression in her body language, but her voice dripped with derision.

"You think you can wander around Portland without being spotted?" she hissed. "You think I like getting phone calls this early in the morning?"

"I don't know the proper way," Beau finally said. I felt so bad for him. I desperately wanted to help, but I had no idea what to say or who this woman could possibly be.

She barked out a laugh.

"Oh!" I said. "You're a werewolf."

The woman closed the space between us in a blur of purple. She dug her thumb into the spot where Beau's neck met his shoulder. He grunted in pain, but didn't immediately push her away.

Not thinking, I grabbed her wrist. "Don't touch him," I hissed.

Static electricity passed between us. The woman twisted out of my grasp and backed off a few steps. She shook her head as if clearing it. Then, glaring at me, she rubbed her wrist where I'd touched her.

"She doesn't mean any disrespect," Beau cried, and then modulated his tone. "She doesn't understand this world ... or her magic."

"What witch doesn't feel magic?" the woman sneered.

"She's not a witch."

The werewolf turned her dark eyes on me, her full lips still curled into a sneer. "You're not welcome here without an invitation."

"Then how do we get an invitation?" I asked.

My calm question seemed to put her further off balance. She frowned and then returned her gaze to Beau. "Why are you here?"

"Rochelle is being hunted."

"So you bring her to the pack?" The woman laughed.

"By a sorcerer."

The woman stilled. Every line of her face and body smoothed out to neutral. Then, looking at me again, she whispered. "What sorcerer?"

"Blackwell," I said.

A slow, scary grin spread across her lovely face. I could suddenly see the wolf underneath her skin — or at least her capacity to be a wolf.

Beau shuddered, looking resolutely at her feet. "Please —"

"Blackwell," she repeated. "Anything that sorcerer wants, I'm more than willing to keep from him."

Beau let out a breath of relief.

"I'm Lara," the woman said. "Follow me. Now."

She turned and walked away.

Beau stood to follow. I tried to hold him back. "But —"

He shook his head and touched his ear quickly. Lara was a dozen steps away now, but Beau seemed concerned she could still hear us. "We go. This is why we came here."

"Is it going to be okay?"

"I'm not sure yet."

Lara, still sporting her scary grin, turned to look back at us. It was my turn to shudder as another curl of fear twined down my spine. The werewolf's grin widened.

"Try to not be afraid," Beau whispered. He pressed his hand to the small of my back as we followed Lara.

"How do I do that?"

"Pretend," Beau said. "Now is a good time to pretend. Werewolves like the scent of fear. Any predator does."

That pronouncement didn't really help with the fear factor, but I trotted to keep up with Beau's long strides nonetheless.

I could pretend. I'd been pretending for a long time now.

Lara led us into the hotel. This was as upscale as I'd imagined it would be, given its downtown location and the river with a marina to one side. The doorman let us pass without a word and Lara cut across the lobby to the stairs with us dogging her footsteps.

The stairs led to an underground parking lot.

The lot held a huge black SUV, which Lara re-mote-triggered and climbed into with barely a glance at us. She was texting back and forth with someone.

Beau urged me into the back seat. I'd never been surrounded by so much soft, black leather in my life. I didn't like eating meat, and I certainly didn't like being surrounded by this much animal skin, but I wasn't going to fuss about it in front of a werewolf. Beau reached around me to grab my seat belt, but I slapped his hands away.

"I'm crazy, not a moron."

He chuckled but closed my door without comment. Then he climbed into the passenger seat in front of me.

I caught Lara's dark-eyed gaze in the rearview mirror. For a brief moment, I thought her eyes glowed green.

"What is she then?" Lara asked Beau while she kept her eyes on me in the mirror. "She smells like a witch."

Beau shrugged as he pulled on his seat belt. "I'm not sure. She sketches things. The sorcerer, specifically."

Lara laughed. "Oh, the narcissistic bastard must love that."

"She isn't bait."

"That's not for you to decide, kitten."

Beau tensed as if ready to say something else, but I interrupted.

"Who does make that decision?"

Lara shifted the SUV into reverse and backed out of the parking spot.

"The alpha."

"Alpha?" I asked.

"Head of the pack," Beau answered.

"Lord of the pack," Lara clarified.

"And the alpha doesn't like sorcerers?"

"No one likes Blackwell. He's a demon-calling murderer." The word 'murderer' came out as a long growl. "I'll gladly dance naked on his bloody, well-gnawed bones."

Well, that was a clear and horrifying image I wouldn't be getting out of my head anytime soon. And my mind most certainly didn't need more encouragement toward darkness.

"He had a spellcurser with him," Beau said.

Lara threw her head back and laughed. "Perfect. Hoyt and I have met."

She stopped the car on the parking lot entrance ramp, tugging the blouse away from her neck to reveal a coiled mass of fading scars.

Beau grunted, pushed his seat belt underneath his arm, and turned to her while lifting his hoodie and T-shirt.

I watched, jealousy seething in my stomach, as Lara eyed Beau's chest and ridged abs. I hadn't realized that he still bore angry-looking, half-healed burn marks from whatever Hoyt had thrown at him ... in my hallucination ... right?

Lara smiled, but not in her scary way. She reached over and lightly raked her violet-painted nails across Beau's muscled belly. He lowered the T-shirt, nodding at her solemnly.

She returned the nod, then pulled the SUV out of the parking lot and onto the street.

Something intimate had just happened between them. It made me uncomfortably, irrationally jealous. It also made it even more clear that I had no idea what was going on and no idea how to deal with any part of what my mind was throwing my way.

What if this was all real? What if the real insanity was the process of having denied it this long? What if

Blackwell, and Beau's burns, and Lara who was supposedly a wolf, were all real?

As Lara maneuvered the huge vehicle expertly through the city, I gripped the handhold over the window by my head — the SUV so tall that I could barely reach it. Then, remembering, I dug my hand into my hoodie pocket for my mother's necklace. It was stupid to have left it there. With the large stone and the thick chain coiled in the palm of my hand, I found I couldn't actually close my fingers around it.

Feeling more grounded, I looked up to see Lara watching me in the rearview mirror again. Her gaze was calculating and penetrating. When I managed to look away, I caught her frown on the edge of my vision.

Then she laughed, the tenor of which let me know that werewolves weren't at all like Beau's tiger. By that look and that laugh, they were ruthless predators. I didn't have to see Lara in animal form to know that. I knew predators. Growing up in the foster system had put me in front of more than one. Though I'd survived those encounters mostly unscathed, I couldn't say the same for some of my childhood friends ... well, childhood acquaintances.

"Is there a good tattoo parlor in Portland?" I asked.

"Of course," Lara replied. "Do you have a need?"

I lifted my eyes to meet her gaze in the mirror again. I thought about sketching a wolf paw and having it tattooed among the barbed wire on my left arm. I would draw the paw pierced through its soft pad with a single barb.

Pleased with this idea, I smiled.

This time Lara looked away. She didn't meet my gaze again.

Yeah, I knew how to deal with predators.

Don't be prey.

CHAPTER ELEVEN

LARA DROVE US A FEW BLOCKS through the city before turning left, after which we climbed a short, steep hill and entered a high-end neighborhood. The meticulous homes — mansions, really — ran the range from vintage to brand-new, or in some cases, still under construction. The area resembled the snobby British Properties in West Vancouver, except the hill wasn't a mountain and the water view was a river, not the ocean. Still, so close to downtown, I imagined this was prime real estate.

Ten minutes later, we pulled up to a sprawling, single-level modern home perched on the edge of the hill. Lara parked the SUV in front of what appeared to be a three-car garage. She climbed out without a glance or word to either of us.

Beau turned his dark aquamarine eyes to me in the back seat. "We'll figure this all out," he said. "You'll be safe here."

"Will you?"

He smiled, but the expression didn't hold any of his usual easygoing charm. "She came alone and didn't kill me on sight."

"We were in public."

"True." He stepped out of the SUV and crossed back to my door. He opened it but I didn't move. I didn't look at him.

"Passive resistance?" he asked, teasing.

"I was thinking about it."

"Need some help, kitten?" Lara called. She'd walked partway to the double front door. A short stone path broke off from the driveway and ran across the front lawn. A wide, tall hedge hid the house from the street. "I'd be happy to carry the not-a-witch."

She was standing with one hip cocked, and jangling her car keys in her left hand. Then she caught me looking and stopped. I'd never thought to use my weird, pale eyes to intimidate anyone before. Maybe eye contact was just a big deal for werewolves for some reason. I noticed that Beau didn't look at Lara directly either.

"You're nervous," I said to Lara. "Why?"

Lara lost the mocking smile and took an aggressive step toward me.

Beau stepped into the space within the open door, blocking my sight of the supposed werewolf as he reached across to undo my seat belt.

"I don't like that she's nervous," I whispered against his warm neck.

"She can hear you," he said, but it wasn't a warning, just information. "All shapeshifters have great hearing. And she's nervous because she's bringing an unknown Adept — you — into pack territory."

He stepped away from the car, holding his hand out to me. Then he very deliberately looked back at Lara. "Plus, I'm bigger than her."

Lara snorted, then bared her teeth. "I'm a pack enforcer, kitten. I could have killed you in the park without anyone looking at me twice."

"I'd see you," I said.

Lara flicked her gaze to me. I took Beau's hand and climbed out of the SUV. It was a long step down to the ground, but I held Lara's gaze the entire time.

"Don't play dominance games with me, not-a-witch." Lara sneered as she looked away.

Beau snorted, then stifled the laugh.

Lara pivoted, then walked stiff-backed to the front door.

"So, suddenly you believe? Believe that you can see ... something?" Beau asked. His tone was hushed.

"No," I said. "But you guys do. I was just always good at poker."

"Yeah, I imagine you are."

We followed Lara through the door and all conversation ceased.

I'd never seen a house like this before. It was all wood and glass and stone tile. The entranceway opened up around us, with hallways branching off in opposite directions from where we stood, leading to what I assumed were a crazy number of bedrooms and bathrooms. A massive kitchen with a huge granite island stood to the left. A dining room with a wooden trestle table that was easily ten feet long took up the middle. The living room sprawled to the right, ending in a massive stone fireplace that occupied the entirety of the far wall. Floor-to-ceiling windows overlooked the river and city below, where thousands of cars crawled over the bridges and the highway.

Two steps into the house, and I already felt like a grubby orphan. I never, ever wanted to feel this way.

"I don't want to be here," I said. My voice rang through the open space before me. I was surprised my words didn't echo back.

"I know," Beau answered. I could hear that he understood exactly what I meant, even though I wasn't all that articulate. His commiseration settled me for the moment, though.

Heels clicked on the wide-tiled granite floor, and I cranked my neck left to see another dark-haired woman crossing toward us. She was taller than Lara by a couple of inches — though that might have been due to the heels, which were so high I was surprised she could walk in them. She was dressed in a sleek business suit that seemed to drip with money, even though I knew nothing of such things. She even wore a choker of pearls underneath her cream silk collared blouse.

I scuffed my sneakered feet on the floor but stopped myself. I wasn't ashamed of being poor. I had worked for every cent in my pocket. Every cent in my gas tank. By the looks of her manicure and her perfectly smooth cascade of hair, this woman didn't even know the word 'work.'

"These are the interlopers?" she asked Lara. Her tone dripped with contempt.

No hint of a smile or sneer appeared anywhere on Lara's face now, as she stared resolutely at the woman's right shoulder. "Applicants, maybe."

Beau's shoulders stiffened as if he wanted to protest something, but he didn't speak or look up from the floor when the woman turned to him.

"Really?" she murmured. Then, with what sounded like deliberate clicks of her pointy heels, she slowly paced around us, all her attention on Beau. She was sizing him up, like he might be a cow or a pig at a fair. Or maybe like a potential owner would eye up a slave or a gladiator, like I'd seen in all those movies and TV shows about ancient Rome. Or maybe it was Greece?

She was looking like he was just muscle, cannon fodder … amusement.

I didn't like that look at all.

Beau didn't flinch, though his grip on my hand tightened momentarily.

The woman stopped behind us. Her gaze rested on our interlocked hands. She lifted her eyes and seemed surprised to find me turned to look at her over my shoulder. She frowned.

"The witch has no manners," she said, directing this comment to Lara.

"No understanding of protocol, I think," Lara answered. "She supposedly doesn't understand what she is. And she might not be a witch."

"Ha!" the woman snorted snottily. "She's a witch. No other Adept would ever be so stupid in the presence of a greater predator. You're just intimidated by the eyes, Lara."

Lara twisted her lips as if stopping herself from speaking, maybe ready to deny being intimidated by me. Or rather, by my eyes. Funny, I'd forgotten to put on my tinted glasses. I couldn't remember when I'd stopped wearing them.

"See witch?" the other woman asked. She bit down on the 'ch' in the word. "Lara and the cat here know their place. If I were you, I'd learn quickly." She leaned toward me and her nostrils actually flared. "What smells like a witch must be a witch."

It was comical enough that I almost laughed, except I didn't like the way Lara was deferring to her. I didn't like the fact that Beau hadn't spoken yet.

Satisfied in her assessment, she completed her circle around us until she was standing face-to-face with Beau again.

"Audrey Rothchild, beta of the West Coast North American pack, daughter of Edith Rothchild, lady of the Assembly."

"Do you know what that means?" I asked Beau.

"Just the beta part," he answered me. Then he lifted his head to address Audrey's right shoulder. "I'm Beaumont Jamison. This is Rochelle Saintpaul."

"Your names mean nothing to me."

"Yeah, we're getting that a lot," I said. "The sorcerer called me Hawthorne, if you like that better."

Audrey pinned me with her dark-eyed gaze. It wasn't a happy look. "Control your pet, cat," she said to Beau.

"You misunderstand our relationship," he answered.

Audrey bared her teeth at Beau. This wasn't a smile. He dropped his gaze, hunched his shoulders, and then stepped his left leg firmly and deliberately in front of me.

Audrey's nonsmile grew. She stepped back, kicked off her shoes, and spread her legs as far as her tailored skirt would allow. She was four inches shorter without the heels, and yet she had seemingly grown a hell of a lot more intimidating.

I pressed my hand to Beau's shoulder, not that I had any chance of holding him back if they were going to fight. Audrey was barely half his size, though. What person would attack another under those circumstances?

"I think you're missing the pertinent part of the girl's declaration, my beta." A male voice coated with steel called out from the far hall.

"What part?" Audrey snapped without looking behind her.

"The part ..." — the man continued as he strolled farther into the entranceway — "... about the sorcerer."

Audrey whipped her head around to look at the massive figure behind her.

A mountain of man stood in the tiled hall. He was barefoot, with his hands tucked into the front pockets of dark jeans and a blue T-shirt stretched across impossibly wide shoulders. He was just shy of six feet tall and appeared to be almost as wide. His sandy hair was short and untidy, his face chiseled out of pale granite.

I'd never been scared of anyone at first sight before. But this man scared me silly ... scared me stupid ... speechless ... breathless.

I froze like some deer or rabbit seconds from impending death. Unable to run, unable to drop his gaze, and unable to breathe. He scared me even more than the sorcerer had. At least I'd known Blackwell — had lived with him in my head for going on six years. I didn't know this man, though, which meant he might do anything, might be anything. And I wouldn't be able to stop him.

The man stared back at me. He hadn't even glanced at Beau.

Then he turned and set his inscrutable gaze on Audrey. The dark beauty withered under his look. "Missed that, did you?" he asked, his tone soft and deadly. "Perhaps you should be listening rather than staking your territory."

All the hair on my arms and legs lifted, even underneath my clothing. It felt as if I'd just brushed against a live wire with a very low current.

I hadn't noticed that Lara had bent her head sometime since the man entered, but I saw now as she turned it into an actual bow, putting one knee to the ground. Audrey did the same, though she kept her head upright.

Beau grunted. His shoulders dipped as if he'd just picked up something heavy. The man glanced at him for a moment, then his gaze shifted back to me.

He removed his hands from his pockets. Curling his toes on the floor as he walked, he stepped closer. Though still out of arm's reach, he was near enough that

I could distinguish his eye color as light brown. Topaz, actually.

Beau was trembling before me.

Audrey spoke from her kneeling position. "May I present Desmond Charles Llewelyn, Lord and Alpha of the West Coast North American pack, son of —"

Desmond halted her introduction midsentence with a flick of his fingers.

Beau trembling turned to shaking, still as if he was bearing some terrible weight I couldn't see. A bead of sweat ran down his temple. I looked to Desmond. He was still staring at me.

"It's easier if you don't fight it, fledgling," he said. His voice was soft, even, and deadly. "I won't hurt the girl."

Beau collapsed before me with a moan. His shoulders heaved as he filled his lungs with air like he'd been drowning seconds before. I touched his shoulder. He raised his hand to cover mine.

I looked up at Desmond. He was gazing at our linked hands.

"Beaumont. Beau?" he said. "I don't know your family, but we appear to share a distant lineage of some sort."

"Yes, sir," Beau answered, his voice heavy and pained.

I had no idea what Desmond meant by lineage. Beau, with his dark skin and light eyes, couldn't possibly look more different from this man.

"And what magic do you wield, witch?" Desmond asked me.

I raised my chin. "I'm not a witch."

"What are you then?"

I thought about this for a second, then answered, "Crazy. Though psychotic might be a better word choice."

Desmond smiled, a tight, thin-lipped expression that only hardened his face further. "I won't be fooled with, Rochelle," he said. "Shall I kill your protector to provoke a display from you?"

The question was somehow phrased without threat, without malice.

"She … she doesn't understand," Beau said.

I didn't like how scared he sounded. Something in Beau's fear freed me from my own. Ignoring Desmond, I wrapped my other hand around the back of Beau's neck. His skin was warm and sweaty. "Don't worry, Beau," I whispered to the back of his bowed head. "It's not real. I won't let anything bad happen to you. It's not real. Nothing's real but you and me."

Beau's hand convulsed on mine. "Rochelle, please," he whispered. "Please listen."

"She doesn't understand her power?" Desmond asked.

"No, and she can't control it," Beau said.

Desmond pinned me with his predator gaze again. I straightened my spine, though it was an effort.

"And a sorcerer wants this unknown power?" Desmond asked, his voice barely a whisper.

"He wants her drawings," Beau answered. "He wants what's in her head. What she sees."

"And you think I'm in your head?" Desmond asked me. "You think you can control me?"

I did my best to look defiant. "If I wasn't afraid of losing Beau. I could end this all, right here and now."

Desmond chuckled. "Has the fledgling not taught you that shapeshifters can smell a lie?"

Beau dropped his hands to the floor, and splayed them next to his feet. Readying himself for something I couldn't see coming. I'd never been so blind in my life, not while my eyes could still see.

Desmond glanced over at Audrey, who rose. Her sneer was firmly back in place.

"The girl's mental condition is a concern," he said.

Beau rolled his hands into fists while Audrey eyed me coolly. Then the beta nodded and said, "We can keep her contained."

"So I'm an idiot because I don't believe that shape-shifters, and werewolves, and sorcerers are real?" I snapped.

Suddenly Audrey was standing in front of me. I hadn't seen her move.

I felt her fingers brush my face even as Beau straightened, slamming his shoulders up underneath Audrey's extended arms and throwing himself against her.

His feet slipped on the stone floor as if he'd hit a brick wall instead of a woman half his size. Still, he knocked the air out of Audrey's lungs in a sharp expulsion of breath.

She clenched both hands to fists and slammed her forearms across Beau's back. Then, with her long hair sweeping swaths of blurred darkness across my vision, she pivoted around him as he fell forward. She grabbed his left arm as she moved, twisting it up behind his back.

Beau crashed forward onto his knees at Audrey's feet. She grabbed his head with her other hand and twisted it hard to the side, exposing his neck. The hold looked painful.

"Stop it," I screamed. I darted forward, only to slam face-first into the mountain known as Desmond. I fell back onto the granite floor so fast that I couldn't even get my hands out to break my fall. Pain reverberated up from my tailbone to the base of my neck and through my jaw.

"Yes," Desmond said. "Let the boy go, Audrey."

"He comes into your territory —"

"For help. For protection," Desmond said. He stepped over to Beau, who was straining against Audrey's hold. "Where else would you have him go?"

I rolled to my feet with my hands flat on the ground before me. I was ready to lunge forward, to claw out Audrey's eyes.

"He has no family —" Audrey started to say.

"Or he doesn't know his family," Lara interrupted. "In rare cases, the shapeshifter gene can pass through Adepts who —"

"How dare you interrupt me, enforcer," Audrey spat.

"Take your hands off him," I said. No. I growled.

They turned to look at me, surprised. Almost laughably so. But I wasn't laughing.

"Take your hands off him," I repeated. "Or I'll snuff you out."

Audrey did laugh. No one else, though. She glanced around. "Really? The witch is amusing —"

"Look closer," Desmond said.

Audrey stared at me, the derisive look fading from her face. "Her eyes ..."

"Smell the magic," Desmond muttered. "Akin to witch, but not witch. You have no idea what power crouches coiled on my floor before you, beta. You've tested the fledgling's strength. Now, can you neutralize him and stop the explosion simmering in an Adept of unknown power at the same time?"

Audrey opened her mouth as if to answer.

"And can you do all that without it catching Lara, to whom you owe protection? To whom you owe your wisdom and strength?"

Audrey snapped her mouth shut. She glared at me. Desmond was schooling her for some reason. I had no power to harm any of them, but they didn't have to know that.

"Can I snap your neck, fledgling?" Desmond asked Beau without taking his eyes off me. "Without you even seeing me move?"

"Yes," Beau answered.

"You understand your position in this house? In this city?"

"Yes, sir."

At some signal I didn't see from Desmond, Audrey let go of Beau. He turned his head to me, trying to smile.

"The eyes?" Desmond prompted.

Beau shook his head. "Some manifestation of her power. She gets headaches. She sketches."

"She sees," Desmond said. "A seer, perhaps. I never met one."

He looked questioningly at Audrey, who shook her head. Then he turned and looked at Lara.

"I don't know any seers," the purple-clad werewolf said. "But her touch has a nasty side effect, like having a sliver of your soul ripped from you." She rubbed her wrist where I'd touched her in the park.

Desmond turned to look at me.

I glowered at him. "I have no idea what she's talking about."

"The sorcerer?" he asked Lara, keeping his eyes on me.

A smile spread across the brunette's face. "Blackwell."

Desmond grunted in satisfaction, though he seemed to have been expecting to hear that name.

"Any power Blackwell wants …" Lara said.

"… we're happy to keep from him." Audrey finished Lara's thought.

"May I see your sketches, Rochelle Saintpaul?" Desmond asked. His request, and use of my name, was oddly formal.

I glanced at Beau, who was still kneeling by Audrey. Though he looked grim, he nodded.

"I don't have all of them here," I said.

"What you have will be fine." The alpha held out his hand toward me expectantly.

I tugged my sketchbook out of my bag, and begrudgingly passed it to him. I would have refused, if not for all the neck snapping talk and Audrey's apparent super-strength. I didn't like sharing unfinished work.

"It's not good for me to be without it," I said.

Desmond nodded, and holding it gingerly by the edges, he took the sketchbook from me. He flipped it open just as carefully, as if expecting it to bite him or something. He flipped a few more pages, then stopped at the sketch of the golden-haired woman's jade knife that I'd begun three days ago at the bus stop. He stared at this for a moment, then looked over at Audrey.

The beta angled her head to look at the page he held open, then she snorted and stepped away from Beau.

Desmond closed the sketchbook, and handed it back to me. "Come," he said as he crossed toward the kitchen. "I'll feed you. As is my privilege and obligation."

Beau gulped as if a life sentence had just been handed down with this offer of food. Then he straightened and held his hand out to me.

Audrey picked up her spiky-heeled shoes and walked away down the opposite hall from which she'd come. She didn't bother to glance at any of us as she left.

"I don't understand," I whispered to Beau as I took his hand.

"An alpha protects his pack. Food is part of the ceremony of his acceptance of me here, but ..." Beau faltered.

I hadn't meant the food thing specifically, but I waited for Beau to continue anyway. He glanced over at Desmond, who was looking into a restaurant-sized stainless steel fridge. Lara had taken a seat at the granite kitchen island with her back to us.

The front door was right behind us. Closed, but not locked as far as I could tell.

"We could be gone before..." I whispered.

Beau shook his head at me once, sharply. Then, resolute, he took my hand and tugged me toward the kitchen.

"Text Kandy," Desmond said to Lara as he closed the fridge, then opened the side-by-side freezer.

"Sure." Lara pulled her phone from her pocket. "Text Kandy what?"

"Where is the dowser?" he growled. His inscruta-bility was cracking. He was really, really unhappy about something.

The brunette raised an eyebrow at Desmond's re-quest, but then applied her thumbs to her phone. Beau patted the stool beside Lara for me, then took the next one over.

"The sorcerer had an accent?" Desmond asked Beau as he moved from the freezer to look in some upper cupboards. They appeared to be filled with noth-ing but power bars and Gatorade.

"Yeah," Beau said. "English, maybe."

"Scottish." Desmond sneered, though not at Beau.

I felt a little woozy, sitting perched on a kitchen stool while they discussed Blackwell as if he wasn't some figment of my ... construction. They all were, but I was losing sense of it. Losing footing, starting to forget it was a hallucination. Maybe I just wanted to forget. Though, if that was the case, why I kept reminding myself I didn't know.

Lara's phone pinged. "Bakery," she said, reading from her text message.

Bakery? What was that supposed to mean?

"Good," Desmond said. "Tell her to meet us here, now."

Lara texted. Desmond turned away from the cupboards. "When was the last time anyone cooked ... or shopped?"

"There's Chinese in the fridge."

"Not enough. The boy looks like he hasn't eaten in months, or slept."

Desmond and Lara stared at Beau. Beau stared at his lap, where he held my hand.

Lara's phone pinged. "Kandy says the dowser won't come through the caves, so they can't get here before tomorrow. Ah, something about a vision from YKW. Who's you-know-who?"

Desmond steepled his fingers on the granite island as he selected his words carefully. "Tell her," he said, "that the vision will never come to pass. I made sure of that myself."

Lara's thumbs flew across her phone.

"Visions?" I asked. "You know someone who has visions?"

Desmond crossed his arms and looked at me smugly. "Why? Do you?"

"No." I snapped. I wasn't interested in playing games with him.

Beau opened his mouth, looked at me, then snapped it shut.

Desmond huffed out a laugh. "It's difficult to be circumspect and also help someone who desperately needs it at the same time, fledgling."

"I know where my loyalty lies," Beau said, keeping his eyes firmly fixed to the granite counter.

Lara's phone pinged. "Kandy isn't going to mention the black witch ... not while the dowser is baking. She doesn't want her to ruin a batch."

Audrey padded back into the kitchen. She'd left her shoes somewhere else.

"Text," Desmond snarled. "Blackwell."

Lara did.

Her phone pinged. "They're coming."

"Kandy's been away from the pack for too long," Audrey muttered.

Desmond nodded.

"You think they'll bring cupcakes?" Lara asked, hopefully.

Desmond and Audrey both looked like cupcakes would be some sort of brilliant boon from heaven. This was a rather abrupt change from their previous seriousness.

"We can't actually ask ..." Audrey said.

"I could hint ..." Lara said.

They both looked at Desmond.

He sighed and shook his head unhappily. "We'll have to settle for pizza and hope the dowser doesn't hold grudges forever."

"Does anyone deliver this early?" Audrey asked, glancing over her shoulder at the time on the stove, which read 10:53 A.M.

Lara opened a contact page on her cell phone screen. "Sizzle Pie opens in eight minutes."

"Get the Heart Attack Man and the Good Luck in Jail," Desmond said.

"Rochelle doesn't eat meat," Beau blurted, as if he was confessing some terrible sin.

The three other shapeshifters turned to stare at me, completely aghast. Like I was condemning their religion or something.

"She's a vegetarian?" Lara asked, her tone implying I was some sort of leper or something.

Audrey snorted. "She's so a witch."

Desmond shook his head. "I have calls to make," he said to Audrey with a nod toward Beau and me. "There's Coke in the fridge."

She nodded and opened the fridge door.

Desmond left the kitchen, returning to wherever he'd come from.

"I have no idea what's going on," I said to Beau.

"Yeah," Audrey said as she slid cold cans of Coke across the island. "We get that."

Lara snorted.

Now was probably not the time to mention that I didn't drink pop either. Beau cracked his can as Lara ordered pizza. Audrey eyed me as I fiddled with the can in front of me, but she didn't force me to drink it.

"Canadians are supposed to be nice," Lara said, her tone hopeful. "So she might bring cupcakes." For a moment, I thought she was referring to me, and I didn't know how to respond to this statement.

Audrey grabbed a glass out of the cupboard above and beside the double stainless steel sink and filled it with water. "Desmond did what any good alpha would have done," she said. "But the dowser won't forgive him." She glanced pointedly at us, as if reminding Lara we were listening to their conversation.

"Well, the black witch killed a bunch of us first," Lara retorted.

Audrey placed the glass of water in front of me. Then she slid my pop closer to Beau, who'd already finished his first with a single gulp and a satisfied sigh.

I picked up the water and sipped it. I didn't drop my gaze from Audrey's. Something had shifted between us, between her and Beau, and I didn't get it. She was suddenly like a foster mom with her first assignment. Careful but hopeful. Eager but reserved.

The beta werewolf smiled. "Family comes first," she said to Lara. "No matter how evil they get."

"Yeah," Lara said. "I don't think the dowser's going to bring cupcakes." She hopped off her stool and crossed around the island to pull a handful of napkins out of a drawer. Then, as the still-smiling Audrey leaned back against the counter and crossed her arms, Lara started setting the trestle table behind us.

I sipped at my water as Beau cracked his second can of Coke.

"It's going to be okay," I whispered to him.

"Yeah," he said. But for the first time ever, I didn't believe him.

CHAPTER TWELVE

"THE DOWSER'S HERE," Lara said as she slammed open the bedroom door. "All hell is going to break loose now."

The brunette spun on her heel and exited the room in the same motion she'd used to enter. I'd never heard anyone so gleeful about pending hell-on-earth. The door ricocheted and slammed shut behind her, the doorstop protesting this abuse with a whine.

I turned to look at Beau. He was still sitting on the gold brocade chair next to the plush king-sized bed on which I was sprawled. The bed on which he'd refused to join me an hour and a half ago, when we'd been ordered to nap by Audrey. We hadn't talked, so I'd finally dozed lightly. I don't think Beau slept at all.

He sighed, rubbing his hand across his face and then over the back of his head. Then he locked his gaze to mine. "I can smell her magic from here. This dowser they're talking about. Some sort of witch, who smells way too powerful to be just a witch. Spicy, like Chinese food. And she's deep in the house. I'd bet way on the other side. I shouldn't be able to pick up that much scent through that many doors. Maybe a wolf could, but not me. Not even if I was in animal form."

A gleam of green slid across his eyes and then disappeared, leaving his breathtakingly dark aquamarine behind. He sounded scared. Way more scared than he'd been in response to coming to Portland in the first place.

"Maybe this was a bad idea," he continued. "I knew they'd be … protective. That they'd call in a witch …"

"But now?"

"Now … with the talk of killing and black witches … and … this power I can feel …" He shuddered and didn't continue.

"Yeah, I caught that too. The killing part. We could go out the window?"

Beau shook his head. "We're in deep now. We wouldn't be able to get out of Portland without them tracking us. Maybe if we split up. You grab a cab, head for the Brave —"

"No."

Beau laughed, then sobered quickly. "I'd find you, Rochelle. They'd have to kill me to keep me away."

I climbed off the bed but managed to get completely tangled in the overstuffed duvet while attempting to crawl into his lap. I fell forward instead. He caught me, chuckling. Together, we freed my legs and then I wrapped myself around him.

I grabbed his face, as cheesy as the gesture was, and plastered my lips to his. He kissed me back, showing none of the hesitation he'd showed when he refused to join me in the bed an hour or so ago.

"The window," I repeated after releasing his lower lip.

"This side of the house is on the hill," Beau murmured, continuing to press me with light kisses. "I could make the jump, but I'm not sure I could catch my balance with you in my arms. And a fall like that would hurt you. Maybe even kill you." This statement was paired with a bone-crushing hug. I didn't complain.

Lara cleared her throat behind me. Beau glanced up over my head. I took a moment to just gaze at his perfect bone structure. How I'd thought up someone like him … that it was even possible that someone like him existed …

"Yeah, I expected you to follow," Lara said. "Don't make me drag you. Not that I'd mind laying hands on you, pretty kitty. But the dowser would get all pissy about it, and I'm still hoping she brought treats."

Beau sighed, then stood with me in his arms. My feet dangled a good six inches from the thick carpet. He laid a blistering kiss on me, and still lip-locked, lowered me to the ground.

"Don't leave me," he whispered fiercely.

The idea was utterly preposterous. I laughed.

Beau let me go. Then, with his fingers twined through mine, we exited into the long hall after Lara.

Desmond's house was divided into two wings, like a castle would be. Audrey had shown us to a bedroom halfway along one of the wings. She was "claiming us" according to Beau. He had deduced that she was new to her beta position, which placed her just one step below Desmond in the pack hierarchy, and that we provided an opportunity for her to shore up supporters. I had no idea what he was talking about, but I liked listening to him.

The high white walls of the house were mostly un-adorned, with no crowns or moldings around the doors. Modern architecture, I guessed, but I really had no idea. The hall floors were dark hardwood, while the entrance-way and kitchen were dark granite tile. The windows of the living room were huge and didn't seem to have blinds, at least not on the view side of the house. I didn't know anything else about houses. Except that everything here — even the linens and the plates used for the pizza earlier — looked and felt really, really expensive.

Lara, who was walking ahead of us, wasn't wearing any shoes. She led us back to the entranceway, then through into the living room with its leather couches and square glass coffee table. Then, after lifting her nose to sniff the air, she turned back and grinned at me. "Treat time," she whispered.

Beau stumbled as we stepped from the entranceway granite onto the hardwood of the living room. He was looking toward the kitchen. His eyes were round suddenly, his mouth hanging open.

I followed his gaze across the dining room. A green-haired, slight-framed woman was leaning against the massive trestle dining table, balancing three pizzas boxes left over from our early lunch in one hand and eating a slice from the top one, which was open. She watched us as we entered.

"Emerald-green hair," I murmured. Why did she look familiar?

"Werewolf," Beau said, quiet and so, so scared. But it wasn't the green-haired werewolf he was scared of. He was looking past her into the kitchen.

Audrey, having lost her pearls and pulled her hair back, was leaning against the kitchen island and once again looking like she wanted to wring someone's neck. Desmond was wearing the same expression, though in his more inscrutable way, and leaning again the stainless steel fridge. Both of them were barefoot. Which was odd, wasn't it? The house wasn't cold, but it was January.

Lara skipped ahead of us, darting around the green-haired werewolf and the dining room table. I could now see the five bakery boxes piled on one side of the kitchen island.

And there, in the middle of all the werewolves, a blond woman was reaching up to pull a stack of side plates from the upper cupboard to the left of the sink. Her back was to me. Her golden curls cascaded down the back of her aqua-colored T-shirt. She was wearing jeans like everyone else except Audrey. Even Lara had changed into jeans. And yet there was something … something …

"Her eyes are blue," I whispered as we continued to cross the living room toward the kitchen. "Indigo blue."

"What?" Beau asked.

The green-haired girl frowned and placed the pizza boxes down on the table. She raised her nose and sniffed the air, exactly like a dog would. A green gleam rolled over her eyes, just as I'd seen Beau's eyes do.

Audrey turned her head to look at us but didn't move. She didn't uncross her folded arms, and I saw that she was actually clenching her own upper arms so tightly that she looked likely to put a permanent crease in her pristine, fitted suit jacket.

Desmond's gaze didn't move from the blond woman.

"Jade?" the green-haired werewolf prompted.

The blond woman turned, her hands full of side plates, and looked at me.

Her eyes were indigo blue. A darker blue than the ocean I'd watched her drowning in only hours ago … in my mind. I'd watched her drown in the hallucination that Beau said Blackwell had triggered. The hallucination that had manifested within this continuing, all-encompassing hallucination. Right?

"Jade Godfrey," I whispered.

She smiled at me. A blinding, white-toothed sunny smile meant to make me fall instantly in love with her.

"We haven't met," she said as the room began to dip and churn around me. "I'd never forget magic that tastes like yours."

Everything before and around me melted into blackness. As if a dark cloak had been thrown across my eyes, over my brain.

Black, not white.

I'd never fainted before.

I'd been drugged to sleep by pills and overwhelmed by the pain of my hallucinations, but I'd never fainted.

I saw no white light, no shroud of mist. I felt no pain, no migraine. I didn't desperately scramble for my charcoal and paper. I felt absolutely no need to sketch.

I just shut down. Fell down, actually.

I had a split second to mourn Beau. I was terribly sure that if I ever gained consciousness again, it would be without him. And what good would waking up be if I had to wake up without Beau?

A man and a woman were arguing.

As I fought my way through the dark blanket currently enveloping my mind, I identified the man as Desmond, alpha of the West Coast North American Pack. So that meant I was still in the fantasyland meticulously constructed by my broken brain. But that was okay, because I was also nestled in Beau's arms.

Actually, the man was the only one arguing. The woman, whoever she was, just wasn't backing down.

"Stop railing at Kandy, Desmond," another woman — Jade — snapped. "You'll only freak the girl out even more."

"The girl …" I could hear Desmond's sneer. "… only fainted when she saw you, dowser."

Jade laughed. The sound echoed through my cavernous mind, burrowing deep, reminding me of all the visions … oh, God, the visions. Of Jade and Blackwell. Of green knives and swords. Of demons and so, so much blood. Of tears and screaming … and Jade drowning.

I opened my eyes, fighting back the scream that rose in my chest. Beau's face swam into focus. He was smiling, or at least trying to. His blue-green eyes were wide with tension, but he held me tenderly.

"Here. This will make you feel better," Jade said.

I turned my head. I was nestled in Beau's lap. We were on the floor near the dining room table. I could see one of its legs at the edge of my peripheral vision.

Jade was squatting next to us, holding two plates. Each plate held a cupcake. One was chocolate with chocolate icing. One was chocolate with strawberry icing.

"Chocolate cake with a kick of cinnamon, nutmeg, and cloves, frosted with chocolate butter icing," Jade said. "*Sex in a Cup*. Switch the spices for cayenne pepper and it would perfectly match your boyfriend here."

She eyed Beau appreciatively. He swallowed and kept his eyes fixed to the cupcake.

Desmond swore somewhere behind us, unleashing a string of imaginative curses strung together with utter fury … and jealousy.

I sat up abruptly, smacking my head on Beau's chin. "Ow," I moaned.

Jade laughed, husky and low. Apparently, my jealousy amused her.

"I don't like chocolate," I snapped.

Every werewolf in the room snickered … except Desmond. Jade's smile widened. "You know that shapeshifters can smell a lie, don't you?"

"You aren't a shapeshifter."

"No, I'm not," Jade said. "I sense magic, and occasionally mold it. Sometimes I can tell if it's unbalanced or missing something. Your magic needs this." She held the second cupcake out to me. "Chocolate cake with strawberry buttercream. *Love in a Cup*. To soothe you, Rochelle Saintpaul."

I reached for the plate without even wanting to, as if compelled to do so. Compelled to accept her offering. It felt similar to how I'd been compelled to answer Blackwell's questions in the restaurant, but less … sharply.

Beau took the chocolate cupcake without a word, but he didn't eat it.

I stared at Jade over the cupcake, which — now that I held it so close — smelled intoxicatingly good. I wasn't a strawberry person either, but I itched to sink my teeth into this cupcake, to lick the icing off my fingers after consuming every crumb.

She stared at me. Dowser, Desmond had called her. But she wasn't looking at me … she was somehow looking beyond me. I dropped my gaze to the cupcake. I fought my desperate need to eat it.

"Your magic," she murmured, but she didn't follow through with the thought as she settled down crossed-legged before us. A gold necklace as thick as my mother's chain in my pocket was wound twice around her neck. I'd glimpsed this necklace for the first time last night in my hallucination, but now I could clearly see that the dozen or so wedding rings were soldered to the chain like charms. The necklace glowed with a soft blur that caused me to blink if I tried to focus on it. It swung forward as Jade moved, then settled back against her chest. She caught me looking at it and smiled.

"Eat," she said.

I felt Beau look up behind me. I followed his gaze to Desmond, who was now behind Jade, leaning back against the kitchen island with his arms crossed. The alpha was staring at the back of the dowser's head, as if he either wanted to wring her neck or drag her to his bed. Even I could see that emotion seething from him, and I was usually blind to such things.

Though since this was all in my head, maybe I was cheating.

It was all in my head, wasn't it?

"Eat," Jade repeated, but this command wasn't directed at Beau and me.

Desmond snarled, then reached to the side and plucked a cupcake out of the open pastry box. This one appeared to be lemon cake with lemon icing. He stuffed the cupcake into his mouth without removing the wrapper.

Beau, keeping his arms wrapped around me, carefully peeled the paper off his cupcake. I glanced around. Both Lara and Audrey were moaning as they consumed different types of cupcakes as well.

"The werewolves are all eating cupcakes," I said.

"Yeah," Jade said. "They do that. Though why we needed to stand on ceremony just now, I don't freaking know." This last part was directed at Desmond, though Jade didn't turn to look at him.

"The fledgling knows his place," Desmond said.

"Bully for you, Desmond," Jade said. "How could I forget that going around frightening people is your full-time gig?"

The alpha responded by angrily stuffing another cupcake in his mouth.

"She meant it's surreal," Beau said. "The werewolves eating cupcakes." It sounded like his mouth was full.

Jade looked at me. "Surreal?"

"You know, not real. Not really happening," Beau answered.

"Eat your cupcake, fledgling," Jade said. "Then we'll talk."

"Blackwell," Desmond snapped.

Jade's shoulders stiffened, but she didn't answer him.

I took a bite of the cupcake. Then I took another bite. It was the best-tasting cupcake I'd ever eaten, and I wasn't a fan of cake in general. The strawberry flavor exploded in my mouth, the chocolate cake was moist, and the cocoa was deep, dark, and delicious. And, yes, the cupcake was somehow soothing and invigorating at the same time. A hint of how being in love with Beau felt, though how that was possible I didn't know.

"You make cupcakes?" I asked around my third bite.

"I do," Jade answered. "I have a bakery in Vancouver, British Columbia."

"I'm from Vancouver ... or I used to be."

"Are you? My bakery, "Cake in a Cup," is on West Fourth Avenue. I'm surprised that we haven't met."

"That's not really my neighborhood."

"Perhaps it's better that we've only met now," Jade murmured, dropping her gaze from mine. "This last year wasn't a great one for Adepts in Vancouver." Her smile was suddenly forced, dulled with a sadness that was palpable.

I looked at her then. Closer than I had before. I saw the way gold glinted off her hair and off her necklace. I saw the deep indigo of her eyes.

I reached out for her even before I'd made the decision to do so.

Beau grabbed my wrist and held me back.

Jade looked at him. "Her magic is wild. Ungrounded. It swirls around her ... in a haze of white that tastes of apple. Sweet apple with a tart finish. Juicy, delicious. Picked from the tree perfectly ripe."

"Yes," Beau breathed. He was seemingly relieved by this statement, though he still held my arm at bay.

"She's not a witch?" Desmond asked.

"Not a witch," Jade answered. "She doesn't even share a base magic with witches. She smells fresh, green to you, yes? But not like grass, right?"

"But you know what she is," Desmond prompted. "You know why Blackwell wants her."

"Blackwell collects magic."

"So do you."

Tension ran through Jade's face and along her jaw line. I knew that look intimately. It was a look I'd seen many times in my mind. I knew it meant that Jade was tamping down on anger, tamping down on something she wanted to say. Something that didn't match the golden curls, or the indigo eyes, or the cupcakes. Jade Godfrey swam in a deep well of emotion, and she preferred to paddle around on the surface. But then, even if what I had seen of her life over the last eighteen months was only a construct of my broken mind and hadn't actually happened, I'd be afraid of diving into her world as well.

My hand, still held aloft by Beau, hovered a few inches from Jade's necklace. "You have a knife," I said. "A green knife."

"You've seen my knife?"

"Yes."

A low growl ran through the room. I wasn't sure if that reaction meant that this disclosure upset the werewolves or if it excited them. I didn't look away from Jade.

"You've seen me?" she asked.

"Yes."

The green-haired werewolf stepped up behind Jade. Her arms were crossed, her face serious.

"It's okay, Kandy," Jade said quietly. "Her magic isn't harmful. Not physically, anyway." Then to me, she said, "But you don't believe I'm real? I'm surreal, like the werewolves eating cupcakes? Because you've seen me ... visions of me?"

I nodded. Then my chest compressed as if I was holding back breath ... and tears ... and pain. I moaned, not understanding the sudden crushing ache.

"Let her go," Jade said.

Beau tightened his hold on me. I pressed my head back against his chest as the pain in my own chest expanded. It contained everything that I'd held at bay all these years. Years of visions ... of denial ... of coping ... of terror fought its way up into my throat. I felt stifled, but not by Beau's arms. I felt like I couldn't hold it all in anymore.

"Why, why," I managed to cry. "Why this ... now ..."

"Let her go," Jade repeated.

"He's not yours to command," Desmond said, his tone smug.

"I'm not here to play games," Jade snarled. "You called me. You said Blackwell. The girl is in pain. Her magic is smothering her, killing her maybe —"

Beau released my hand suddenly, making me realize that I'd been pressing forward against his grip. I closed the few inches between me and Jade.

My fingers brushed her necklace. An electric shock ran up my arm, leaving it momentarily numb.

"Oh," I gasped, exhaling some of the crushing chest pain. I yanked my hand back and shook it.

"The dowser is the most magical thing you'll ever come in contact with," the green-haired werewolf said. She sounded proud.

"I think you might be wrong there, Kandy," Jade murmured. "But then, I'm certainly no seer."

She held her hands out to me, palms up. I moved to place my hands in hers, but at the last second, she withdrew slightly.

"I don't want to see what you see," she said. "No one should see their own future. It's like having your soul shredded."

"It is," Lara murmured from somewhere off to my right.

"I don't know what you mean," I said. I'd been saying that a lot today.

Grimacing as if she'd just tasted something really rotten, Jade nodded, then took my hands. More electricity ran up my arms. I'd never felt anything like it before. It was more than licking a battery or accidentally brushing against a live wire. A hundred times more.

A golden wash of light clouded Jade's blue eyes.

I gasped. The tight coil in my chest loosened further.

"It's okay," Jade murmured. "It's okay. I can take a bit of the magic, ease the pressure off for you. That's what being a dowser means. Well, that's what being an alchemist means, but I don't want to confuse you further."

She pressed one of my hands into Beau's. Then she reached up and brushed her fingers over my cheeks, one at a time. They were wet.

I was crying. Silent tears were streaming down my face, and I'd had no idea.

I wasn't sure what was happening but I felt like I could breathe again. The pain in my chest had ebbed to a dull ache, and my throat wasn't as tight.

"It's okay," Jade repeated. "You aren't alone anymore."

"She's not alone. She has the pack," Audrey snapped. "They came to us for safe harbor and we accepted them."

"And then you called me," Jade said. "The fledgling needs training. A mentor."

"All things we plan to provide," Audrey said.

"Her magic is wild —"

"Then fix it," Desmond said.

"She's a person, not an object."

"Then what good are you, dowser?" the alpha growled.

"They call her warrior's daughter now," Kandy snapped.

"Watch your tone when you address your alpha," Audrey snarled. "Or I'll rip your tongue out."

"Enough," Jade shouted.

My ears popped, like they did after Blackwell disappeared from the restaurant.

The room stilled as if it might be waiting for an earthquake to roll through … or like the silence of dark clouds as they gathered before releasing the thunderstorm.

Jade leaned forward, reached into the pocket of my hoodie, and pulled out my mother's necklace. "The fledgling already holds an object of magic. One that I can use to help balance her power."

"My mother's necklace?" I asked.

"Is it?" Jade answered. "It's not attuned to you, but the magic is similar. Your mother gave it to you?"

"By dying, yes."

As she held the chain aloft and watched the large stone swing, Jade looked back at me. "You don't know your parents?"

I shook my head.

"Well, that explains it some." She looped the broken necklace around my head and shoulders.

"It's broken," I said. "It's broken like I'm broken."

"No one thinks you're broken." Jade turned to snarl over her shoulder at Desmond. "How dare you make her feel like she's broken!"

The corner of the island countertop snapped off in Desmond's hand.

Beau wrapped his arms around me. He was tense against my back, as if ready to carry me to safety. I still felt oddly relaxed.

Desmond looked down at the chunk of granite in his hand and swore.

Jade snorted.

Desmond chuckled and shook his head.

Beau relaxed his grip.

Jade turned her attention back to the necklace. "I assume your magic comes in waves when it manifests? In these visions?"

I shook my head, no.

"Yes," Beau answered.

"Beau," I protested.

"The visions come," he insisted. "They blind you, and then you draw."

I sighed but didn't argue.

"I can fix the necklace with that in mind," Jade said. "Like it's a satellite dish. Or ... maybe you're the dish, the necklace is the antenna, and the magic is the signal ... the energy that needs to be held, then dispersed."

"Brilliant," Audrey muttered. "A genius at work."

"Sarcasm isn't going to help, Audrey," Kandy said.

Audrey looked at Desmond, asking for permission to do something. He shook his head and she backed down.

"Anyway, that only matters to me," Jade said. "I'll fix it, then I can find you someone ... to talk to."

"The far seer?" Kandy murmured reverently.

"Yes, he will know someone who can help, at least," Jade said. "I might be able to tune the necklace to ease the burden, but Rochelle is going to have to learn to wield the magic or be constantly overwhelmed."

"He can come here," Audrey said.

"One doesn't usually order guardians about, Audrey," Jade said. "But you go right ahead and give it a try." She didn't lift her eyes from the necklace, still running her fingers along the length of it. I could feel more tiny shocks through my hoodie and T-shirt.

Desmond sighed heavily. "You think she's a seer then?"

"No. The magic isn't exactly the same," Jade said. "Of course, the only seer I know is also a guardian." Her tone was distant. Her eyes glowed softly gold.

I reached out and brushed my fingers across her cheek.

She smiled, but then said, "Don't show me. Don't show me what you've seen of me."

"How would I do that?" I asked.

Jade shook her head, and didn't answer me.

"A reader?" Desmond asked.

"No," Jade said. "Though I haven't met one personally. I think we'd all know if she could hear our thoughts."

"What then?" Audrey snapped.

"If I knew for sure, I'd say so." Jade dropped the necklace back against my chest.

"You've fixed it?" Beau asked.

"I believe so," Jade said. "Rochelle? Does it feel different now?"

The gleaming gold of the thick chain was heavy around my neck. The raw diamond hung between and just below my breasts, which might have been provocative if I hadn't been wearing an old hoodie. Though the stone and chain had been tarnished and dull before, they now caught and held slivers of light as I brushed my fingers over the necklace. The pain was completely gone from my chest and throat.

I nodded, in answer to Jade's question, and wrapped my hand around the diamond, fully believing — if only for this moment — that it was a gift of healing from my dead, unknown mother.

"It's tied to you now. To your magic," Jade said. "Whether you believe in it or not, magic comes to you … like electricity to a light or iron to a magnet, maybe. I hope this helps ease its effects."

"No more headaches?" Beau asked.

"She got headaches?"

"Yeah, when the visions came, I think," Beau answered. "Then she would draw."

"I don't know," Jade said. "Maybe if she was denying the magic …"

"Yeah, with pills."

"Ah. That might do it."

I looked for the broken link in the chain. The stretched one that had made it appear as if the necklace had been wrenched from my mother's neck, perhaps during the car accident. It was whole again.

"You can bend metal?" I asked.

"I can bend magic," Jade answered.

"And metal," Kandy added.

"Well, technically." Jade rose to her feet with a chuckle. She was wearing funky green shoes with about a three-inch heel. When she pivoted to look at Desmond, she was almost his height. "I'll take the fledgling with me."

"No," Desmond said. "She stays here. We'll protect her from the sorcerer."

"I'll take the boy, too. So she'll have her protector."

"The boy," Desmond growled, "came to us."

"Yeah," Jade said. "Funny that, hey? Because you don't seem to know him very well. What with him being family and all."

Beau's arms tightened around me, as if he was as wary of the shift in conversation as I was.

"Not all feline shifters are directly related, dowser," Desmond sneered.

Jade laughed, snarky and angry at the same time. "Look closer, oh high and mighty lord. His magic tastes exactly like yours, with a dash of cayenne. Or can't you see past the color of his skin?"

Desmond snarled.

"How dare you suggest —" Audrey began, but Desmond cut her off with a raised hand.

He glared at Jade. The dowser stood, hip-cocked and arms crossed, glaring back at him.

"He's a tiger too?" I whispered to Beau. I'd assumed Desmond was a werewolf.

"Cat of some kind," Beau whispered back.

"This is brilliant," I murmured. "Like a cool, not lame summer blockbuster with magic, and unrequited love, and everything. I don't know how I can be making this all up."

"You aren't," Beau said.

"It's not love," Jade snapped. "It's possession and power plays."

Desmond frowned. But he didn't correct her.

Jade sighed, then rolled her neck and rubbed it as if it ached. Desmond's expression softened, just a tiny bit. I seriously doubted that Jade noticed, though, because she'd turned to look back at me.

I realized that I'd been stroking my necklace. Embarrassed at the gesture, which felt a bit lewd, I stopped. Jade smiled at me like I was a cute toddler, and with a wave of her hand toward Beau and me — like she was offering us up as an example of something — she looked toward Desmond again.

He remained silent and stoic.

"I'm not going to bicker," Jade said.

Audrey snorted but Jade ignored her.

"I don't know her magic," Jade continued. "I can only guess it's connected to that of the far seer —"

"I don't give a shit about your guesses," Desmond interrupted.

"I don't give a shit about whether or not you give a shit about my guesses," Jade snarled. "You're not going to use her for bait —"

"Watch yourself, dowser," Audrey growled. "You don't tell anyone here what to do, least of all the alpha."

"Jesus, already," Kandy said. "Just stay out of it, Audrey."

"Is that an order, enforcer?"

"Yeah, whatever." Kandy flipped a finger in Audrey's direction.

Desmond had time to sigh — apparently equally frustrated with his beta and Jade and Kandy — but barely.

Audrey lunged across the room for Kandy.

Jade slid her foot forward on the dark hardwood, tripping the werewolf as she passed between the dowser and Desmond. After the way Audrey had taken Beau down, I really wouldn't have thought it possible for Jade to trip her so easily.

Then all hell broke loose.

Exactly what Lara had been hoping for ... along with the cupcakes. Which were, in fact, delicious.

CHAPTER THIRTEEN

EVERYTHING HAPPENED IN A BLUR of movement before me. I saw it all from the safety of Beau's arms as he picked me up, skirted the dining room table, and leaped over one of the leather couches. He placed me in front of the huge stone fireplace. I crouched behind him as he turned to create a barrier with his body between the chaos erupting in the room and me.

As I shifted to one side, I wrapped my arm around his thigh, watching the scene exploding before us with disbelief and more than a little excitement. It was like seeing a vision, but without the pain or the white light. Without the nagging need to draw what I was seeing.

Audrey, tripped by Jade, had fallen and slid face-first across the dining room floor toward Kandy. The green-haired werewolf leaped up and over her, laughing manically and landing surefooted and steady on the dining room table. Her eyes now matched the green of her hair.

Audrey twisted to the side, using the slick hardwood to her advantage as she spun — still on her ass in her tight skirt — to face the dining room table again. She rolled forward and shot to her feet without her hands touching the floor. She lunged for Jade, who was now her nearest opponent.

At the same time, Lara jumped on the table behind Kandy and wrapped her arms around the green-haired werewolf's neck. The two women grappled, falling sideways onto the massive wood table, which groaned in protest. The pizza boxes went flying, spilling slices all the way into the entranceway. Oddly, both women were laughing as they wrestled.

Desmond took one step toward Jade, who was watching Audrey come for her. Jade turned to see his approach seconds before Audrey barreled into his shoulder like a freight train going off its rails. And then hitting a massive concrete wall.

Audrey stumbled back, holding her nose. Blood spurted through her fingers. She backed off, as if Desmond getting in her way was a warning to wait.

"Really, Desmond?" Jade snapped. "You think just standing there is going to solve this one?"

"I'll move if you want me to, Jade," he growled. "At your bidding."

I wasn't sure if this was supposed to be an angry retort. Because it sounded a lot more like a come-on.

"I can't figure out if Desmond is totally pissed at Jade or really likes her," I whispered to Beau.

"Both," he whispered back.

"I could go for some popcorn."

Beau laughed, but kept a wary eye on the fight amping up before us.

Desmond lunged for the dowser.

Except Jade wasn't where she'd just been standing. She was behind Desmond, a few feet closer to the side of the kitchen island.

This disturbed me in ways I hadn't even fathomed yet. As in, I felt like my brain might start leaking fluid out my ears if I tried to understand what had just happened. "She didn't just like, teleport, did she?"

"Nah," Beau replied. "Moved crazy-fast, though."

I glanced over to see that Kandy was still wrestling with Lara. The green-haired werewolf appeared to be pinned with her back widthwise on the table, but then got her foot up between her and Lara. Then — still gripping Lara's upper arms — she somersaulted backward off the table and catapulted Lara over her head.

Lara flipped in the air, spun over the leather couch, and slammed back first onto the square glass coffee table.

Beau crouched down in a ball before me, shielding his face with his arms and me with his body. The shattered glass from the table sprayed everywhere, but only sprinkled over our sneakered feet. This reminded me that the shifters were all barefoot.

"They expected a fight," I murmured. "They didn't want their feet to slip on the tile or the hardwood."

"They always expect a fight," Beau responded. "But this is just a tussle. Dominance games."

Kandy landed on her feet facing the kitchen, then immediately spun to glare at Lara, who was lying in a pile of broken glass.

Lara sat up, laughing. More glass fell off her, tinkling as it hit the ruins of the coffee table underneath her. Her violet-paisley print silk blouse was shredded, but she didn't appear to be otherwise injured.

Audrey, her nose apparently healed but her cream blouse dotted with blood, went after Kandy.

"Tag teaming?" I asked Beau.

"Yeah, wolves do that," he answered. "They fight in pack formation. You take on one, you take on all of them."

Attacking from the side, Audrey barreled into the green-haired werewolf. Kandy twisted away at the last second, though, so that they hit the table instead of flying past it. The huge table lifted off the ground and then slammed back down into place. Kandy and Audrey fell to the side, grappling with each other as they rolled across the floor.

Lara leaped from the shattered remains of the coffee table and landed on the back of the couch. She perched there for a moment, watching the other two werewolves wrestle. Then — with a cackling laugh that was completely at odds with her outward pretty-in-purpleness — she launched herself at the pile that was Audrey and Kandy.

"Stop them, Desmond," Jade said. "They're ruining the furniture." She was actually eating a cupcake, leaning back against the kitchen island now.

"I can't stop them," he replied. "Not until Audrey has exerted her dominance. Her position as beta is —"

Kandy screamed. Her terrible howl made the hair stand up on the back of my neck and my stomach instantly queasy with empathic pain. Something cracked nastily.

Jade wasn't at the counter now. She was standing amid the tangle of limbs that was the werewolves. She reached into the mass and yanked Audrey back by her ponytail.

Audrey snarled. Her face rippled as her teeth grew into fangs.

Beau moaned, then looked resolutely at the floor before us.

Audrey reached wolf-clawed fingers up for Jade's hand and arm, but the dowser didn't seem to notice the werewolf's attempt to free herself at all. She was gazing at Kandy hunched in pain before her, her face etched with concern.

I remembered the vision glimpse I'd had of Kandy before seeing her here in the dining room. In the white wash of my hallucination, I remembered Jade screaming for someone she loved, then carrying the green-haired werewolf's body from the rubble of the temple, or wherever they'd been in my mind.

I moaned. Beau reached back and laced his fingers through mine. I shook off the echo of the hallucination at his touch.

Lara scrambled back from Kandy, keeping her body low to the ground. She paused a few feet away, her back to the front windows, panting and watching.

Kandy slowly rose. She was holding her shoulder.

Audrey was twisting and snarling, but still didn't seem able to break away where Jade held her by the base of her ponytail and nothing else. The dowser's arm was stretched out and down, which cranked Audrey's head back at a vicious angle. The beta werewolf continued to claw at Jade, but didn't leave a single scratch on her. To me, it looked like those claws could shred metal.

"It's my fight, Jade," Kandy spat.

"That arm isn't fully healed yet. And now she's —"

"My fight," Kandy growled.

"It's not a good idea to get between werewolves," Desmond said. "My werewolves." His voice was low, steady, and edged with a warning.

"Yeah?" Jade asked. "You think Audrey has any chance of laying a hand on me?"

"Unhand my beta, dowser," Desmond said.

"Is that an order?"

"A request."

"Screw you, Jade," Audrey growled. "I'd rather die than kneel at your feet."

"That can be arranged," Jade snarled. She twisted her arm up and around her head as she spun and then released Audrey, throwing her down and to the side so that the werewolf slid across the wood floor and spun to a stop at Desmond's feet. As she did so, she pushed the huge trestle table out of the way with what looked like just a brush of her fingers.

Then Jade stood — a warrior suddenly, in jeans and printed T-shirt — facing off against Desmond and surrounded by werewolves. She was holding a jade knife in her right hand.

My ears plugged.

"The knife," I whispered. The glowing green stone of the blade and hilt appeared more vibrant than it ever had in my hallucinations. It fit in Jade's hand as if it was a natural extension of her reach.

Any second now, the white light that preceded a hallucination would overwhelm my sight. Any second now.

"Now it's a fight." Though Desmond only whispered, his voice rippled around the room.

"You didn't have to do it." Jade's voice was low and filled with epic amounts of sorrow.

"I did," Desmond said.

"Oh, Jade," Kandy whispered. She squeezed her eyes shut in a grimace of regret. When she reopened them, they were no longer glowing green.

Desmond stepped forward. His hands were loose at his sides. Jade didn't move. He was maintaining his inscrutable expression, and I couldn't see the dowser's face. I couldn't tell what, if anything, was passing between them.

I pressed my hand to Beau's forearm. It felt like a twisted knot of muscle and bone.

Audrey rose behind her alpha. She looked worried, maybe even scared, for the first time since I'd met her. "Warrior's daughter," she said. Her tone was now measured, formal. "We have not communicated effectively."

"I'm not confused, Audrey," Jade said. "I know what he did." She slowly raised her knife and pointed it at Desmond's heart.

Some sort of energy washed around the room. It was similar to the wind that had accompanied Blackwell and the amplifier device he'd used in the restaurant.

"Magic," I whispered, as I straightened from my crouched position behind Beau. Goosebumps rose on my arms and legs.

Beau tried to stand beside me and failed. He was shaking, as were Lara and Kandy.

Jade laughed. "Nice try, Desmond. But I don't come to your heel."

All the tiny hairs on the back of my neck stood up.

Beau moaned.

I didn't understand what was happening, but I wasn't going to just stand here and watch Beau suffer. "Please stop," I cried. "Please. I don't know what you're fighting over, but … but … just stop."

Jade looked at me over her shoulder.

I tried to smile — to placate her somehow — but failed. The tension in the room was almost suffocating, but the weight of my mother's necklace was oddly soothing. I reached up to wrap my hand around the raw diamond.

Jade's eyes followed this gesture.

"If we can't have Paris," Desmond said. "At least we'll always have Blackwell."

It felt like Desmond was attempting a joke of some kind, to ease the tension between him and the dowser, but I didn't get the reference to Paris at all.

Jade sighed, which she seemed to do a lot. Then she slid the knife against her right thigh until it disappeared.

My ears popped.

"Cool," Beau said, as if he hadn't been shaking in pain seconds ago. "Invisible sheath."

I turned to stare at him. He laughed and shrugged his shoulders.

Jade crossed to Kandy and reached for her shoulder. Then with a practiced twist and a sharp yank, she snapped it back in place. Kandy yowled but stayed on her feet, though Jade might have been holding her. By the sound of the injury, I'd thought that the arm had been broken, not dislocated. And maybe it had. Maybe Jade had just straightened the bone so it could heal properly.

"Shapeshifters heal quickly?" I asked Beau.

"Yep, and some quicker than others. Depending on the strength of their magic. And their connection to their alpha and to each other."

"The pack shares magic?"

"Yes."

"But you don't have a pack?"

"No."

I stared at Beau. He didn't sound like he regretted anything, not even this, but my heart suddenly felt heavy for him.

Desmond rubbed his hands across his face, as if massaging tension out of his jaw. Then he made a bee-line for the boxes of cupcakes.

"I don't get the Paris reference," Jade whispered to the green-haired werewolf.

"*Casablanca*," Lara said, grinning ear-to-ear as she padded by them on her way to the kitchen. "He was trying to be romantic."

"We're not done, wolf," Audrey growled at Kandy.

"Audrey," Desmond said. "Not now. Too much tension isn't good for the fledglings."

Beau snorted derisively, but then shuffled his feet uncomfortably when Desmond looked at him sharply.

Kandy stepped by Jade, looking resigned as she dropped to one knee before Audrey. She then very deliberately tilted her head to the left, exposing the side of her throat.

Audrey smiled. Though her face had returned to normal after Jade released her, her white teeth were pointier than I'd thought they'd been before. Her dark hair was half out of its smooth ponytail now, a mass of waves all around the beta's head and shoulders as she reached down and wrapped her hand around Kandy's neck. Somehow her French-manicured fingernails made this gesture even more aggressive.

"I owe you a life," Kandy said.

"No, my wolf," Audrey replied. "Yours was always mine to save." Then she released Kandy, turning away and padding over to get a cupcake.

"Great," Jade groused. "Like she wasn't insufferable before."

Kandy rose and turned to smile at Jade. "I'm not leaving you."

Jade nodded, awkwardly and quickly. Then she turned to look back at Beau and me. As she moved, her golden hair blurred, streaking the air around her head.

"No," I whispered.

The feeling of an impending hallucination bloomed at the base of my spine.

I gasped as I rolled all the way up and onto the toes of my sneakered feet. The feeling rose without pain, flowing up my spine and then wrapping around my shoulders and neck.

"Oh my God …" I heard Jade whisper.

The hallucination crashed over my mind and whited out my eyes.

"Jesus," Desmond grunted.

Beau reached for me, his fingers brushing my arms. I threw my head back as the sensation of the hallucination flooded my chest, my arms, and my legs. I'd never felt it like this before.

It was as though I was filled with whiteness — somehow buoyed up with brilliant, white light.

"Don't touch her," Jade said.

"It's fine —" Beau began. Then he grunted as if the air had been knocked out of him.

"You don't know how you're affecting the magic," Jade continued. "It flows through her, unbidden. Almost as if it wants to communicate."

Audrey scoffed. "Magic doesn't work like that."

"Normally I'd agree."

The mist in my mind began to dissipate. I caught a glimpse of a paved road, then low buildings through the white haze. But I felt no pain and no terror. Not yet, anyway.

"You think she's a harbinger," Desmond said. "A messenger." He didn't sound like he was overly pleased with the idea of a so-called harbinger hanging out in his living room.

"Don't know. Never met one," Jade said. "Does she speak in riddles? Proclamations? Prophecy?"

"No," Beau said from somewhere far off to my right. "She draws."

"Probably not a harbinger, then."

"You're being deliberately obtuse, dowser," Desmond growled.

"It's not my place to name magic, Desmond Llewellyn. Not even at your lofty command."

Desmond snarled, but the conversation finally faded out. The white swirling mist filling my mind and body resolved, solidifying into shapes and outlines. A building stood before me still partly shrouded in the haze. I stepped forward, reaching into the whiteout.

"Watch the glass in front of you, fledgling." Jade's voice was faint, saying something else about being here, or being near, or something, but I didn't hear her.

I was within the vision.

I breathed in the white light. I consumed it.

It was me. It had always been me.

This was me.

I was standing in a parking lot. It appeared to be late afternoon or early evening. The sky was muted and gray, but I could easily see that the painted lines of the individual parking spots were faded and the pavement was cracked. Dead, frost-covered weeds were attempting to reclaim every rupture and edge. A barbershop to my right was empty, derelict. Its 'For Lease' sign had fallen to one side.

The red-white-and-blue barber pole was smashed as if someone had thrown a rock at it. Its broken glass littered the concrete step in front of the entrance. The edge of the concrete was eroded. I wondered how many footsteps it took to erode concrete like that. How many rain or snowstorms? Also, I thought the helical stripe of a barber's pole was supposed to be red and white, signifying bloody bandages wrapped around a pole. Because barbers had performed bloodlettings in the olden days.

Was that foreshadowing? Please don't let that be foreshadowing.

What had Desmond called me? A harbinger?

Please don't let me be a messenger of doom and destruction. Though, even as I made the silent wish, I was aware that it might be futile. My hallucinations up to this point certainly hadn't been filled with fluffy bunnies.

It was a deserted barbershop. An easy target for vandals, nothing else.

I was aware I was avoiding looking deeper, farther.

Everything was so clear, so defined. Usually, a haze of white permeated my hallucinations.

Visions.

Not hallucinations.

I was having a vision, but I didn't want to turn my head. I didn't want to see what the magic wanted me to see, if Jade was right about that part. If she was right about me being some sort of conduit for magic. Like a satellite dish or something.

I shifted my gaze from the cracked pavement before me, just a touch. I felt compelled to do so. I felt like it might be my purpose to do so.

I'd never had a purpose before.

Blood drops on the eroded concrete walk between the parking lot and the barbershop drew my attention. I followed them to a hand. Its fingers were splayed open.

Tangled within those fingers was the rose-gold chain of a necklace. My mother's necklace. My necklace.

I reached up to touch the heavy stone I still wore around my neck. It felt strange … it was vibrating, at a subtle frequency that maybe only I could feel. A muted version of all the other electrical charges I'd felt over the last few days.

Not electrical charges.

Magic.

Beau's magic, Blackwell's magic, and Jade's magic. Magic felt like different degrees of electricity to me.

Still, there was a problem I was steadily ignoring. A problem with the hand before me that was holding my necklace.

I was wearing my necklace.

As I breathed in to belay the panic I could feel churning in my gut at the sight of the blood trail leading to a limp hand, I became aware that I wasn't breathing the air of the parking lot. By the frost on the weeds, the air in the vision should be crisp. I was warm.

I looked beyond the hand.

Beau lay dead on the sidewalk next to the barbershop. His dark aquamarine eyes stared sightlessly at me. A trickle of blood ran from his mouth, though I could see no other mark on him. He wasn't breathing.

My chest constricted. I clutched at the stone hanging between my breasts, the necklace digging into the back of my neck.

Beau.

A black leather-gloved hand reached down and plucked the necklace from Beau's fingers. His hand rose as if fighting to retain its hold on the chain. Then it fell limp back onto the concrete sidewalk.

I tracked the movement of the gloved hand to see an arm that led to the dark-clothed shoulder of Blackwell.

The sorcerer looked at the necklace. He was wearing his usual suit-and-crisply-ironed-dress-shirt combo. The suit was dark navy blue. The thin scarf twined once around his neck was black. Probably cashmere.

Not that it mattered at all. Nothing mattered in this moment except Beau lying dead at the sorcerer's feet. Except Beau lying dead and holding my necklace.

Blackwell glanced around the parking lot. A swirling, dark orb of light was pooled in his left hand.

I wanted to scream — *Who are you looking for?* Except I already knew the answer.

The sorcerer was looking for me.

I tamped down on my panic, reminding myself that Beau was alive and only a few feet away from me, sitting in Desmond's living room right now.

I had to see more.

I followed Blackwell's gaze around the parking lot. At one time, the lot must have serviced a small strip mall of some sort. All the stores were empty, though, and falling into disrepair.

Where am I? Shouldn't I be at Beau's side?

Then I saw the wolves.

Three of them, large and gray, were standing fifty or so feet away on a strip of frosted grass between the parking lot and the main road. A sign listing the defunct businesses stood behind and above them. I lifted my eyes, trying to read the names there, but they were flipped upside down and right side in. I looked around, feeling on the edge of frantic now, for an address or some other clue to the location of the parking lot.

One of the wolves lifted its head and howled.

The sound pierced my brain painfully. I covered my ears and cringed.

In the distance, another wolf answered the call.

They were hunting.

Hunting Blackwell.

Had Beau been the bait?

I whirled around to look back at Blackwell as the wolves gathered their hind legs and leaped as one toward him. But he'd seen the predators. He was ready for them.

He threw a mass of his black-colored light at the wolves just as they passed over me.

It hit them in their chests and faces, their bodies still extended in anticipation of landing.

All three fell howling and writhing to the pavement. They snapped and scratched at Blackwell's black light as it twined around them like smoky rope.

Not black light. Magic.

Blackwell was gone. Just gone, as if he'd never been in the parking lot.

Beau was dead, only steps away from me. I reached for him.

The vision washed out of my mind in a blazing fury of white light.

I opened my eyes, not realizing I'd closed them.

I was back in Desmond's living room.

Beau was pinned to the ground in front of the windows by Audrey and Lara.

"Take your hands off him," I said. I'd never heard my voice sound so nasty.

Audrey and Lara looked over to Desmond, who I could see standing off to my left without turning my head from Beau. The alpha nodded. They loosened their hold and stepped away.

Beau straightened his back, but kept kneeling and holding my gaze. He started to speak but couldn't seem to vocalize any words. He swallowed, then tried again. "What did you see?"

I shook my head, denying the vision.

"She's going to need to draw," Beau said as he rose to his feet. "Her sketchbook is in the bedroom."

"It wasn't real," I said, but even I could hear the lie in my voice.

I'd seen Beau dead at Blackwell's feet.

"You'll draw." Beau was speaking but I wasn't listening. "You'll feel better."

I was looking for Jade. She was off to the side, leaning against the stone of the wide fireplace behind and to my left. Her arms were crossed and her eyes downcast. I stepped toward her and she flinched.

She flinched. All that power, all the electric magic I could feel rolling off her, and I made her flinch.

I stopped and waited.

She lifted her indigo eyes to mine, offering me a sad twist of her mouth as a smile.

"Who did you see me kill?" she asked. "Everyone?"

Kandy moaned. Desmond cleared his throat.

"No one," I answered.

Jade nodded, but I could tell she didn't believe me.

"Can you …" I faltered on the thought. Was I actually thinking this was all real? I could feel the painful urge to draw. It had started as an itch in the palm of my left hand, but now my fingers were convulsing with it. I clenched a fist and fought the feeling. "Do you believe in fate then? If I see it, is it fated to happen?"

"I don't know," Jade answered. "That's a big question."

"Tell us what you saw, fledgling," Desmond said. "And we'll try to help you sort it out."

I pressed my aching hand to my chest.

"It doesn't work like that," Beau said. "She needs to draw."

"What I know," Jade said, "is that I've only seen fate thwarted once. And maybe it's only been delayed. Maybe it's still to come."

Delayed. I'd take delayed.

"By who?" My question was a tense whisper of pain. The itch to draw was crawling up my left arm now.

"By one who sees everything."

"Like me?"

"No. Maybe. Maybe you with a thousand years of experience."

"What did he change?"

"Me," Jade answered. "He stopped me from … going back. Why, Rochelle?"

"I don't believe in fate or destiny."

Jade laughed. It wasn't a happy sound. "It believes in you."

I shook my head as I stepped by Jade to follow Beau back toward the bedroom.

"Who dies?" Jade asked.

I didn't look back. I didn't answer her. I couldn't answer her. I couldn't acknowledge what I'd seen. Not until I figured out what to do about it, and maybe not even then.

"Me?" Jade called out. "Desmond?"

"Eventually, I imagine," I answered.

"Well, it can't be that bad," Kandy said. "If she's flippant about it."

"We need a plan," Audrey said.

"We'll wait until she shares the drawings Beau is talking about," Jade said. "Then we'll know what we're dealing with."

I turned the corner into the hall. Though I could still hear them talking in the living room, I could no longer make out distinct words.

Beau reached back and twined his fingers through mine. His hand was warm, and so, so real. But all I could see was my necklace laced through his limp fingers, and his hand lying so terribly still on the gray, cracked concrete of the sidewalk.

"They're discussing setting a trap for Blackwell," he said. As we continued down the hall, Beau's head was canted as if he was still listening to their conversation. I couldn't hear anything now.

"With you as bait," I murmured.

"Well, I won't let them use you."

The fact that the others were even discussing the possibility of using Beau to draw out Blackwell only confirmed that what I'd seen was the future, perhaps the immediate future.

I stopped at the half-open door to the bedroom, turning toward Beau. The pain in my chest was entirely different now. It quite literally felt like someone had stabbed me in the heart with a dull knife.

I stared at his neck, focusing on the zippered opening of his hoodie and the edge of his faded T-shirt. I struggled to absorb this feeling, to move through it.

I couldn't bring myself to look up at him.

"Oh," he gasped. "Your hair." He reached out and separated a hank of my hair, pulling it delicately from the side of my head into my peripheral vision. By the slight tugging I could feel as Beau held it, I knew it was from the left side of my middle part. It was white. Not just streaked white or faded black, as if my hair dye had suddenly washed out. Beau held a full inch of white hair.

I shook my head. I couldn't deal with my hair right now. I didn't want to deal with it.

I reached out and clutched at Beau's hoodie. Then I literally climbed, one fistful of fabric after another, up his body to wrap my hands around the back of his neck. I pressed the length of my body against his and gazed up at him. He still towered over me. This close, he filled almost every last bit of my peripheral vision. His size and strength comforted me, even when it should terrify me.

I should have run the first time I laid eyes on him.

Instead, I'd wanted to lick the raindrops off his neck.

"What are you thinking?" he whispered. "The vision?"

I shook my head. The pain emanating from my left hand intensified, continuing to flood up my arm, over my shoulder, and into my neck.

He was so beautiful, so real to me. And he was going to be really, really dead.

I stretched up on my toes, pulling him down for a long, lingering kiss. He obliged me by wrapping his hands around my hips and lifting me the last couple of inches.

Then I said, "I need to be alone."

Beau nodded. "I'll be right out here."

"Okay."

He set me on my feet. I turned and walked into the bedroom, feeling like I was physically tearing myself away from him. It was like I had painful Velcro all over my body.

I pulled my sketchbook out of my bag and found a piece of charcoal. Then I stood by the bed and looked back at Beau out in the hall. He grinned at me, then started to pull the door closed.

"I'm thinking of a tiger paw." I said.

He paused, surprised. "You mean for a new tattoo?"

"Yeah."

"In the barbed wire?"

"No."

His grin widened. My aching heart thumped once, twice, against my breastbone.

"So you ... believe?" he asked.

"I believe."

He laughed huskily. Then he shut the door between us. The latch clicked.

I stared at the closed door, feeling the smooth paper of my sketchbook and dusty charcoal in my fingers. Feeling that I'd left my heart in the hall on the other side.

Then, propelled by a force I couldn't deny any longer — that I couldn't hope to control — I sat on the bed to draw.

Right now, that was all I could do. But later, I was going to thwart destiny.

CHAPTER FOURTEEN

I DREW AND DREW AND DREW.

I ran out of charcoal and found another piece buried in the bottom of my bag.

I ran out of paper and almost started marking up the walls. But instead, I stopped myself and went back to the beginning.

I flipped through everything I'd drawn. I shaded and smudged. I rounded and edged. I honed the black and white images until they matched the pictures in my head. I released the vision into the paper. I contained it there, bound in charcoal.

And still, I didn't know what I could do to stop it. I didn't know when it would happen. I didn't rationally know if it would ever happen. But I felt it, in my gut — a cold certainty as the vision unfolded, reappeared underneath my fingers. A certainty I'd never felt before. I'd seen a glimpse of the future. A future that wasn't within my power to create or control, because I was looking at sketches of a vision ... not a hallucination constructed by my broken brain.

I went back to the beginning, again and again and again.

The abandoned barbershop.

The cracked sidewalk.

The frosted weeds.

The drops of blood that formed a trail of pain even when rendered in black and white.

Drops leading to Beau's hand.

My necklace tangled in his limp fingers.

The necklace I swore I would now never remove. They'd have to kill me to get it off. And by 'they,' I meant everyone in this house. Everyone way, way stronger, faster, and smarter than I was — better educated in the ways of this magical world. They'd have to kill me to get the necklace, to place that necklace in Beau's hand, and to set a trap for Blackwell.

I looked at the images a third time, reliving the reconstructed vision as I flipped the pages of my sketchbook. Again, I paused on each one, refining the shadows, sharpening the edges, but there wasn't much left to do.

I was exhausted. Bone weary, as I always was after an incident. Except it wasn't the pills making me drowsy. It was the outpouring of magic.

My magic.

I believed. I believed every line, every curve.

I believed everything laid out before me in black and white. No color anywhere on the page. No color to confuse or beguile my senses. No color to soften the message, or to soothe the pain.

In black and white, I saw the emptiness of Beau's eyes … and the regret in Blackwell's. Yes, regret. Just a hint, but it was there. What did that mean?

A cool heart and level head would tell me that evidence was circumstantial at best — the sorcerer's presence in the parking lot, the pool of dark magic in his hand, Beau lying at his feet — but I believed that Blackwell had killed Beau. But had it been an accident? Had Beau attacked the sorcerer first? As he'd done in the restaurant?

I slowly flipped through the sketches again, now interpreting them and mining them for clues.

The frost on the weeds told me this might happen today or tomorrow, but in this part of the world, I didn't think it could be a month from now. It would be too warm for frost during the day then. The presence of the wolves – I was willing to wager that two of the three were Audrey and Lara – told me the scene was in or near Portland.

And Beau had been wearing the hoodie, T-shirt, and jeans he had on right now. True, Beau didn't have many changes of clothes, not that I'd seen. But I knew he couldn't wear this exact outfit for many more weeks without it falling apart at the seams.

I'd once worn a hoodie until it shredded at the elbows. An expensive dark gray wool hoodie with a soft, lighter gray cotton jersey lining, which had been a Christmas gift from my last foster family. I'd clumsily patched the elbows, and then worn it until it had holes in the pockets and underneath the arms. My social worker had pulled me aside moments before I interviewed for the room at the Residence. She'd forced an ugly, scratchy, pink-and-brown-striped sweater from the lost-and-found on me and taken the hoodie. It wasn't until after the interview that I found out she'd thrown it in the dumpster. I refused to climb in with the rest of the garbage to retrieve it. I refused to give it such significance. But I threw the pink-striped sweater in after it, and walked home wearing only a thin T-shirt.

It had been a comfy hoodie. That was all. I could buy a dozen like it. And I had, once I was on my own and earning money from my Etsy shop. It had taken two more interviews to secure the room at the Residence, and I was completely certain that what I'd worn for the first didn't make a lick of difference.

I was never handing over something precious to another person for safekeeping. No matter how trustworthy they seemed, or should be. Never, ever again.

Yes, I believed.

But I believed in me. I wasn't going to trust that anyone else would do what I would do to keep Beau safe.

I believed I could change the vision. That I could change the moment laid out in my sketchbook in black and white. I just needed to change one thing.

One little thing.

I needed to be the one in the parking lot.

Time lines and all that — according to any TV show or movie that I'd ever seen — were either supposed to be a delicate balance that could splinter off into infinite possibilities or a major, unalterable fixed point, right? I guessed there was physics involved, but I wasn't a scientist or a mathematician.

I saw the future. Well, I was pretty sure I saw the future.

And why would I have visions of the future if I couldn't change what I saw? That wouldn't be logical at all. Magic had to have some logic, right? It was some sort of energy, captured and used by certain people with certain genetic abilities ... right?

Jade had witnessed the future being thwarted — or delayed — so why couldn't I do the same?

It had to be me in the parking lot, not Beau.

That was the only thing that was within my power to change.

Because I couldn't change what Blackwell wanted.

He wanted me.

Or rather, he wanted what was in my head. He wanted what he thought I'd seen, and wanted it so much that he would risk the wrath of the pack. Either that or he thought he was capable of eluding them.

So, if I gave Blackwell what he wanted, then there'd be no logical reason for the vision to manifest.

I couldn't change the presence of the necklace, because I wore it. Because I obviously needed it. The lack of pain when the vision hit — along with the clarity I felt now — told me I desperately needed the necklace to retain my grip on this reality.

I was guessing at the actions and decisions that must have preceded this vision. Actions that I also couldn't change. I could surmise that Desmond had used Beau as bait — which they'd been discussing doing as I left the living room — because Beau carried my necklace. And I could surmise that the sorcerer had somehow been drawn to the necklace by noting the disappointed way Blackwell looked at the chain after he lifted it from Beau's hand. Maybe thinking its magic was mine? Hoyt had tracked my movement down the coast somehow. Maybe Blackwell could track the necklace in the same, or a similar, way?

All that added up for me to one thing. It needed to be me in the parking lot, not Beau. That was the simplest, most logical, way that I could approach the problem. I couldn't trust anyone else to place Beau's safety above their own desires, least of all him. I couldn't trust that Blackwell would be satisfied with anything but my presence.

I flipped back through the remainder of the sketchbook, which contained about six months of work. Nothing refined, though. I went to a larger medium when I really worked up a vision.

Yes, I'd had a vision. Not a hallucination. The thought was mind-boggling, and far too complicated to tackle right now. I couldn't think about anything other than Beau's life being in danger.

I reminded myself that I didn't believe in fate. Not even now. Not even after meeting Beau and the way I felt about him. Not even with the sketches of a vision I believed to be a glimpse of the future captured in my sketchbook. No force controlled what I chose to do or not do. Or what had happened to me in the past. I refused to believe that my actions were predetermined.

I was willing to do anything to alter the vision I'd collected and contained within my sketchbook.

Anything.

Even if that meant facing Blackwell on my own again. Even if that meant I sacrificed my freedom — or even my life — to give the sorcerer what he wanted.

Beau had found me in that diner. He bought me a piece of apple pie and rescued me from the living hell of my broken brain.

I'd believed I was broken.

For Beau, I'd act like I was whole.

I wouldn't live in this world — real or not — without him.

Beau was asleep in the hall.

By the clock on my cell phone it was only 3:27 P.M. The day had already felt epically longer than that, and I was pretty sure it was nowhere near finished.

I'd packed my sketchbook in my bag, double-checking that Blackwell's business card and my cell phone were both still there. I tucked my necklace behind the zipper of my hoodie, put my mittens in my pockets, and made sure my shoelaces were tightly tied.

Then I tried to climb out the window.

A window that was easily a twenty-foot drop, then a long roll down a steep, rocky hill.

Right. Beau had already ruled out that escape route.

So I slipped out into the hall instead. I was planning to use the excuse of needing the bathroom, while hoping that Beau forgot that the bedroom came with an en suite. I found him propped up against the wall opposite the door, asleep. Even sleeping, he looked exhausted.

All I had to do was get across the hall and into any room on the other side of the house. At least, that was the plan.

I very, very carefully closed the bedroom door behind me until I heard the latch click. Maybe they'd think I was still inside. Maybe I'd get just enough of a head start. I only needed to set foot in the parking lot. To see Blackwell see me. Once Blackwell had seen me, the vision had to change. It just had to. No matter how childish and ignorant my logic sounded to my own ears.

No matter that — according to Beau and my visions — the house was full of powerful people who supposedly knew what they were doing.

I couldn't show them the sketches. Because if I went to anyone, all they'd see was what they wanted. They wanted Blackwell. They wanted Blackwell so badly they were willing to be in the same room as each other, despite whatever circumstances had led to the rift between them. If I had the time, I could probably piece together those circumstances from the sketches in my book and the sketches waiting for me to finish them in my portfolio.

But I didn't have time.

Because they would find me. They would take the sketches and the necklace. They would use Beau as bait. He would go willingly. He would risk his life if he saw the possibility to save mine. I didn't understand the nuances, but he'd already risked his life by bringing me to Portland in the first place.

They would do all of this with the best intentions and under the guise of keeping me safe from Blackwell.

I knew this, because I'd already seen how it ended.

As long as I had the necklace and dealt with Blackwell myself, I believed I could change the future.

I had to stop staring at Beau and start moving. Just looking at him now, his head slumped to one side in heavy sleep, made my heart ache. If he opened his eyes and looked at me, I'd never be able to leave him.

I looked away, steeling myself for the next moment I had planned. I needed to execute that plan without dissolving into a pile of mush.

I took a single step that separated me from Beau. Very, very quietly, I placed the bundle I'd been crushing in my left hand next to Beau's open palm. I refused to acknowledge the similarities between this sight of Beau's hand, limp with sleep, and the vision of his hand, limp in death, that was burned into my mind and rendered in my sketchbook.

I desperately wanted to touch him. To run my fingers along the creases and hard ridges of his work-callused hand, to feel the warmth of his skin. But I didn't.

I straightened as soundlessly as I could. The bundle, which consisted of the Brave's keys rolled within a note I'd written, lay beside Beau's hand on the granite tile.

I'd planned on leaving the note behind in whatever room I managed to escape from, but this was better. He'd see it as soon as he woke. My gamble wouldn't play into the wrong hands.

I thought he'd understand the significance of the gift, even though with his mechanical skills, he probably didn't need the keys to drive the Brave. But if I was screwing up and wasn't going to make it back to him — if I couldn't have the RV, if I couldn't have Beau — at least he'd have what little comfort I could offer.

The note read:

I see meeting you at the Brave — Rochelle

I'd wanted to write something about love, but I'd never actually written the word deliberately before, and I wasn't sure I could pull it off without melting down now.

The note — and the lie I'd committed to paper — would hopefully help save Beau's life.

It took me ten steps to reach the powder room. My sneakers were well broken in, and as supple as rubber-soled shoes could be. They didn't squeak on the wooden floor, but I really should have taken them off and put them in my bag. Each of the ten steps I took along the hall was paired with a thump of my heart. I was worried that even that tiny sound would wake Beau.

I shut and locked the door to the guest bathroom behind me. The walls and ceiling were wallpapered, making it seem like I was standing inside a wrapped gift box or something. It was pretty, but I didn't spend one extra second looking at it after I ascertained that the frosted window opened.

Unfortunately, the window was also alarmed. I stared at the little white box sitting level with my nose on the windowsill, completely unobtrusively. It was in two halves, one attached to the sill and one attached to the window, and designed to separate and trigger when the window was opened.

If I had a pocket full of tools or a tiny bit of Beau's know-how, I might have been able to remove the alarm, or to trick it somehow. But I didn't. I was also really running out of time.

"What else are you going to do, Rochelle?" I whispered.

I had wolves to elude, a sorcerer to find, and Beau to save. I didn't have time for second guesses, or to worry about whether or not the future could be unmade at all. Causality, fate, and destiny were just too much to think about, ever. I could deal with what was in front of me at any given moment, acknowledge the results, and then move forward as best as I could.

I opened the window.

I had to strain upward on my tiptoes to push it out all the way, but it opened wide enough that I could fit through.

I didn't hear anything, but I didn't wait to see what kind of silent signal I might have triggered. I'd seen how fast the shifters could move, and I was fairly certain they could snap the lock on the bathroom door without even thinking about it.

And Jade ... Jade could move even faster. Too fast for even Desmond to track.

I climbed up on the pedestal sink. I stuck my head through the window while lying on my belly. The ground looked really far down, but thankfully the window was partially obstructed by a bush with broad leaves.

I swung one leg up and over the windowsill. I awkwardly lifted my upper body to follow. I hung there, clinging to the window frame, one leg in the bathroom and one leg out.

The lock on the door popped.

I froze at the sound. I should have dropped. I should have run, but I didn't. Instead, knowing it was too late to do any of those things, I just turned to see what awaited me on the other side of the bathroom door.

It swung open slowly, as if the person on the other side was slightly worried about disturbing me. I saw blond curls and a shoulder clad in a green T-shirt.

Jade.

The dowser rested her left shoulder against the doorframe, watching me. Then she hit me with a blazing smile that nearly blinded me with its wattage.

"The rhododendron outside makes for a soft landing," she whispered.

"Yeah?"

"Yeah." She lost the smile, then sighed. "Beau?"

She wasn't asking where he was. She'd probably seen him sleeping in the hall already. She was asking about the vision.

My eyes welled with tears that I struggled to hold at bay. I nodded because I couldn't speak.

Jade nodded back. She reached up and twined the fingers of her left hand through the wedding rings soldered onto her gold necklace as she cast her gaze down at the white-tiled floor.

"Please," I whispered.

Jade looked back at me. Her eyes were swimming with tears. "Family," she said. "I get it." Then she smiled again, but it was forced. A learned gesture. "I didn't lay any protection spells on the necklace. I'll do that next time we see each other."

"Okay." My hands were cramping from gripping the windowsill between my thighs.

"Be careful with Blackwell, if that's where you're going. He's an evil bastard, but if you have something he wants he'll deal fair and square. Though he won't lift a finger to stop someone else from hurting you."

"Okay."

"Hoyt is pure slime, but I doubt he'd set foot in Portland," Jade continued. "They'll both be concerned about the pack, so you have that in your favor. I can't tell you what to do, Rochelle. We only know the right path as it unfolds before us … I hope."

"What if Blackwell wants information on you?"

Jade's grin turned scary around the edges. "We all make deals with the devil. Blackwell and I will have our day in the field, and I will extract my pound of flesh."

A shiver ran up my spine, and I swallowed the fear that had risen to clog my throat. Jade Godfrey was not all sunshine and cupcakes.

She must have seen something on my face, because her expression softened. "Cut left. There's a gate through the hedge on that side," she said. "I'll distract Desmond, but he's difficult to rile up when I want him riled. And he'll only buy it for a couple of minutes at most. Damn shifters. They can smell a lie, you know. But you can always rely on them to protect your back in a fight, which is exactly where they'll be … right behind you."

She shut the door without another word. It stayed shut. Apparently, she'd popped the lock but not broken the latch. More magic, maybe. Or lots of experience sneaking out of bathroom windows.

I blinked three times, rapidly. I couldn't believe that Jade was just going to let me go.

Then I lost my grip and fell out the window. I hadn't intended to, but at least I was outside now.

I stood, not bothering to check my clothing for dirt or damage. I actively ignored the fact that my right arm wasn't a fan of the seven or so foot fall. I tried to close the window behind me, but I couldn't reach it. Then I realized how silly it was to try to hide my exit from people who turned into wolves.

I made a beeline for the gate in the tall hedge at the far corner of the lot. Thankfully, this direction also placed me as far away as I could get from the two identical SUVs that were now parked in the driveway of the house.

I didn't bother skirting along the house or attempting to sneak away. I ran exactly where Jade told me to go. The grass crunched underneath my feet. The day was obviously cooling.

Thankfully, the gate wasn't locked. I wasn't sure I had the upper body strength to scale it. The bathroom window had already been a challenge to my total lack of athleticism. Plus, my right arm still wasn't feeling great from the fall out of the window.

I cleared the gate and ran, not caring about my direction. I took the first left and then another right. I wasn't a runner. Even though I was heading downhill, taking the path of least resistance, my lungs protested immediately. My legs, however, were willing to continue.

I made it three blocks before I slowed.

I had to think. I had to plan, and quickly. The people back in the house weren't morons. They were wolves — in their animal form, at least. Except Desmond and Beau. Anyway, wolves tracked by scent, didn't they? Running wasn't going to help me get very far, not after they figured out that Jade was deliberately distracting them.

But that was assuming Jade was on my side and this wasn't some elaborate setup. These might be the exact steps I needed to take in order to fulfill, rather than thwart, the vision of Beau's death.

I pushed my doubts about the dowser aside. I'd been seeing her in my mind for over eighteen months. I knew her. I knew her pained laugh. I knew of the darkness she fought. The darkness that scared her into rash and silly actions, such as letting me go.

Jade would help me, right up to the moment my actions put someone she loved into jeopardy.

Then all bets would be off.

I needed a car. I saw a lot of them around me, along with a lot of very expensive houses, but I had no ability to just jack one. Though I was willing to bet that Beau would be able to.

I'd never posited so many wagers in my life.

I took another random turn. I was cold, and with each step I took farther away from Beau, I seemed to get colder. It was a silly thought, but that didn't change the feeling.

A bus blew by, so close that if had I'd been one more step to the left, it would have hit me.

I started to run again, before I'd even made the decision to do so.

The bus rolled on ahead of me.

Wolves couldn't track what they couldn't smell, right?

My sneakered feet hit the sidewalk with a slap, slap, slap.

Where was the damn bus stop? My lungs couldn't take this running abuse.

The bus wasn't going to stop.

Then its taillights flashed red.

I whooped like an idiot before I could stop myself, watching as the bus swerved to pull into a stop where a bunch of people were waiting for it.

I just had to get there before the last person in line climbed on. I pressed forward, my thighs burning and my right arm aching something terrible.

Three ... two ... one ...

Everyone was onboard.

I waited for the doors to close.

They didn't.

I waited for the bus to pull away.

It didn't.

The flash, flash, flash of its orange indicator light urged me to continue putting one numb foot in front of the other. I ran the length of the bus. I could see people sitting in the window seats on the very edge of my peripheral vision, but I doubted that any of them noticed me pass.

I grabbed the stair handle and heaved myself onto the first step.

"Thank you," I cried.

The driver nodded and closed the door behind me before I'd cleared the steps. Barely able to breathe, I stumbled to the closest seat and dug into my bag for change. I didn't know how much the ride even cost. I didn't even know where I was going.

The bus pulled away from the curb and into the street.

My fingers brushed coins in the depths of my bag.

I stood and dumped what I had through the slot of the coin meter. The coins tinkled down into the glass-enclosed hold area. The driver didn't even glance down before he pressed the lever to release them into the storage canister below.

"Thank you for stopping," I gushed with what breath I could muster.

The driver glanced at me and flinched.

I hadn't covered my eyes.

I almost turned away from his reaction. I almost slunk off into some back seat. Instead, I smiled.

He smiled back. "It's your lucky day."

"I hope so."

I turned to find a seat.

"Take your transfer."

A piece of printed paper was sticking up at the top of the meter. I grabbed it. "Right. Thanks."

"You're welcome."

Fighting the sway of the bus, I made it to a seat at the back. The bus wasn't full, but I barely noted the other commuters as I passed them. It was time to implement the final stages of my exceedingly basic — and undoubtedly flawed — plan.

I pulled my cell phone and Blackwell's card out of my bag.

I opened a text message and typed in the sorcerer's number, which I hoped was a cell phone. Then I typed.

Abandoned barbershop. Somewhere near Portland? Rochelle.

And then I waited. I watched the gray wash of the city as it blurred by the bus window. I didn't know where I was or where I was going, and yet it all looked the same as it had three days ago in a completely different city. The same as it would tomorrow ... unless I wasn't here. Unless I was surrounded by the bright lime-greens and burnt oranges of the interior of the Brave. Unless I was driving by the brilliant blue of the ocean, walking the variegated beiges of the beaches, and picnicking on the fallen, weather-bleached trees. My evenings would be marked by the pinky-reds of the sunsets, with Beau at my side.

I was so cold again. Even after all the running. Clammy, but cold.

My phone beeped. I read the text message as I thumbed the button to mute the phone.

> *I know it. I own it.*

I let out a breath I hadn't realized I'd been holding as I texted back.

I need an address.

> *I'll send you a map link.*

I'm on a bus now.

> *I'll send you the route numbers then.*

I'm coming alone.

I expected another message quickly, but ended up waiting long enough that my thoughts wandered. I started remembering, experiencing the vision again. I flinched when my phone buzzed in my hand.

> *You won't be alone for long.*

A link to a bus route map appeared in the next text bubble. Then:

> *I look forward to seeing you again, Rochelle Hawthorne.*

His use of my supposed birth name unsettled me, as I was sure it was supposed to. It also reminded me that there were things the sorcerer could tell me — knowledge he'd alluded to about my family. The idea of that was momentarily intoxicating.

But Beau was my family now.

I'd made it this far in life without knowing anything of my family, or my magic. I could continue without knowing who my mother was, without knowing if she was like me, and without knowing if she'd seen her own death. If she'd seen me, or any part of my life, before I'd even been born.

Still, the idea had bloomed and couldn't be completely denied. I didn't even know my mother's first name. I could at least ask that of the sorcerer without letting him know he had leverage.

Couldn't I?

I texted back.

I'll let you know when I get near.

I stared down at the series of text messages between Blackwell and me, then read through the conversation a second time. I was glad I didn't have a number for Beau, because I was fairly certain I would have used it then. As pitiful as the pre-love-at-first-sight me would have thought it, I already missed him. I was worried that if the next hour or so went horribly wrong — if I was actually as naive as I knew I was being — then all I would remember, and all that would be left to hold onto, was the vision of Beau's dulled blue-green eyes staring into nothingness.

I pushed the thought away and touched the map link in the text message Blackwell had sent. My browser opened, and I began to figure out where the hell I was and where the hell I needed to go.

CHAPTER FIFTEEN

THE GRAY OF THE DAY almost perfectly matched the gray of the well-worn sidewalk beneath my feet. It had only taken two more buses to get to within a few blocks of the abandoned barbershop I'd seen in my vision. I'd texted Blackwell as I cut right from the bus stop to walk the final ten or so minutes to the strip mall.

The cluster of empty shops felt like it was on the edge of nowhere. If I'd continued heading west on the main road for another couple of hours, I might have hit the coast again. Not that my sense of direction was that great. In Vancouver, I'd always had the North Shore Mountains to navigate by. This area outside Portland wasn't part of the city, but it also wasn't residential, industrial, or pure farmland. It made sense that the businesses ended up being unsustainable in this location.

As soon as I'd cut off from the main road, the traffic almost completely died. No one else was stupid enough to be out walking in the chilly late afternoon either. The sun was thinking about setting, not that I could see it behind the bank of low clouds to the west, but it wasn't dark enough to trigger the streetlights yet.

When I found the barbershop, I was really happy that I was already cold, so I could pretend I was utterly numb to the fact that I was walking into a vision. I crossed through the empty parking lot toward the broken barber's pole. As I'd already seen in my mind, the 'For Lease' sign was hanging slumped to one side. Weeds were growing through the edges and cracks of the pavement, and shards of the red, white, and blue barber pole littered the sidewalk beside the front door.

No blood trail, though. And no Beau. Not as far as I could see. But still, I felt slightly off here. Queasy. Out of time and place, maybe.

"You've made the right decision," Blackwell said as he appeared behind me.

I spun around. A light breeze stirred my hair and tingled against my cheeks as it brushed by me, then faded. More magic, I guessed.

"Together," the sorcerer added, "you and I will be very prosperous."

I could have seriously sworn that the parking lot had been empty moments before. But then, I'd been fixating on the empty, eroded sidewalk outside the barbershop where I'd seen Beau's dead body in the vision. Blackwell could have been standing behind me for any amount of time before speaking.

"I'm not going with you," I said.

"No?" he asked. His smile was tight-lipped but confident. "Are you pack bait, Rochelle?"

"Not intentionally."

"Then you wish to open a dialogue."

"I wish to end one."

He laughed. "That's not a bargain I wish to make. This is not a short-term type of relationship."

"I brought my sketchbook. I'll give it to you. I'll give you anything."

He stepped closer, though he was now scanning the area behind me and above my head.

"Why do you own this place?" I asked. Blackwell was wearing the same deep navy-blue suit and crisp white shirt I'd seen him in before, with the black cashmere scarf twined once around his neck. "You obviously don't need the money."

"It behooves me to maintain a presence in Portland."

I didn't know what 'behooves' meant, but I understood the implication. "In pack territory?"

Blackwell smiled. "I thought you didn't believe in such things, Rochelle."

I lifted my chin and met his dark gaze. I might have my hands stuffed in the pockets of my hoodie for warmth, but I wasn't going to cower in front of this man.

His gaze dropped to my neck. He looked at me thoughtfully, his head tilted to one side. Then he smiled broadly, revealing wide, straight teeth.

"You've met Jade Godfrey."

I didn't answer, though a curl of fear ran through my already queasy belly. I couldn't help lifting one hand to confirm — by touching it — that he'd glimpsed my mother's necklace at the edge of my hoodie.

"And she blessed you with a creation? A trinket, as she calls them?"

"You want my necklace?"

He laughed. "No. I can feel that your magic has settled. It's better for me that you have it. Though it's a treat to be so near something of Jade's creation without being stabbed by it."

He stepped closer. "I'd like to see it, though."

"But that won't be enough."

"Not nearly enough. But there's no reason for you to fear me, Rochelle. Our relationship can be mutually beneficial."

"I'm sure the pack and Jade Godfrey would love that."

He lost the smile. "Do they pull your strings? Should I be expecting an incursion at any minute?"

"No, and probably."

He laughed, then waited. He waited as if we had all evening. Except we didn't. I needed to somehow finish this transaction before Beau arrived. I was completely sure I was operating on borrowed time now. I had been since I left the bedroom at Desmond's.

I unzipped my hoodie until the zipper cleared the raw diamond hanging just below my breasts. There was no way I was going to take the necklace off. The chill of the relentlessly gray day cut through my thin T-shirt underneath.

Blackwell leaned forward. Catching my gaze, he raised an eyebrow along with a hand. I nodded, giving him permission to touch the necklace.

He pressed his fingertips to a section of chain that sat across my left collarbone. He shuddered almost imperceptibly, then closed his eyes as if savoring something. His dark eyelashes were so long they almost touched his high cheekbones, like a smudge of black velvet against his pale skin. His expression hinted at some intense, secret pleasure. Something almost sexual.

His touch should have felt dirty. Invasive. Except it had nothing to do with me.

"You have a thing for Jade Godfrey," I whispered.

Blackwell opened his eyes. For a second I thought they were blown-out black, edge to edge. I blinked and they were normal again. With the light of late afternoon behind him as he loomed over me, I'd probably just seen a shadow or something. Probably.

"Have you seen Jade and me, Rochelle Hawthorne? Beyond the sketches I already possess?" he asked quietly. Something terrible underlay the question. A thirst, a hunger — but for what, I had no idea.

I swallowed. Not finding my voice, I nodded.

Blackwell mimicked my nod, then took a step back from me while he once again scanned the parking lot.

"And does Jade Godfrey end me, seer?"

"Jade says I'm not a seer."

"Or you aren't like any seer the dowser has come into contact with previously. And the answer to my question?"

"Do you want her to kill you?"

He laughed. "There could be worse deaths. Jade is vengeful, but not malicious. But, no, that is not the path I would choose."

"I don't know. I'm pretty new at the understanding part of all of this."

Blackwell nodded. "Your inability to interpret is not an unexpected impasse. You won't come with me, Rochelle Hawthorne? I can offer comforts you've never known."

"I doubt it."

He reached into his suit pocket and withdrew what looked like a thin silver hairband without the plastic teeth on the inside curve. The half-circlet of metal was dotted with tiny raw diamonds, which I could apparently identify on sight now. The band was maybe an eighth of an inch wide and spanned five inches or so, though it was thin enough that it might bend wider.

"I acquired this magical artifact many years ago. A few months after my father died unexpectedly," Blackwell said. "I have used it twice before, though it didn't produce the results I'd hoped. You, Rochelle, are far more powerful than the other psychics I've discovered."

"What does it do?"

"What I hope it does, is to allow me to … see what you've seen. A shortcut to the sketches."

"Will it hurt me?"

"Will that stop you?"

"No."

"I didn't think so. But it shouldn't hurt you. Drain you perhaps."

"Will it take the visions?"

Blackwell laughed. "No. No one, no object, no person, can steal your magic … or rid you of the burden of it, if that was what you were hoping. An Adept with enough power could drain it, perhaps, or dampen it. But it will eventually come back. Some say even stronger than before. Such power does not easily walk this world though, Rochelle. I doubt you will ever meet any Adept capable of such a thing."

"What about the dowser? She is … electric."

"Indeed, she is," the sorcerer whispered. "Am I wrong? Have you seen differently?"

I looked deep into his dark eyes. I could see nothing there that told me anything more about this man than I already knew from the visions. Jade had named him as evil, but she didn't seem particularly careful about her word choices. He was ruthless, but I couldn't see evil in his eyes. He was a well — a deep, dark well. Similar to the dowser, actually, though she hid her emptiness while Blackwell fed his.

Jade's emptiness might actually be born of sorrow, I thought, while Blackwell's emptiness was born from some need I hoped to never understand. A perpetual need for more, maybe. My shrink would instantly label him with narcissistic personality disorder, but I wasn't a big believer in easily checked boxes. Labels were difficult to erase … or outrun.

"No," I finally answered. Knowing that if I was lying, that if Jade was capable of draining or stealing magic and I had seen it in some vision I only half remembered, then this device he held might give him access to that information. But I wasn't big enough, or strong enough, to protect Jade Godfrey and Beau at the same time. Plus, the dowser didn't seem overly concerned about what I revealed to Blackwell.

The image of Beau lying dead on the sidewalk not two feet from where I was now standing haunted my every step, my every choice. I couldn't worry about anything else right now.

Blackwell nodded. Then, with his fingertips pressed to either side of the half-circlet, he held it out a few inches from my forehead.

"Our bargain, Rochelle," he said. "You will show me what you can right now. You will continue to gift me with any sketches that I deem relevant. You will make yourself available when I call, and answer what questions you can when I do. You will not knowingly endanger my life. We will be friends."

"And my part?"

Blackwell inclined his head, prompting me to offer terms.

"You will never lay a hand on Beau," I said.

"I will not forfeit my life at his hands."

"You will avoid harming, allowing him to be harmed, or killing him at all costs."

"Of course. I'm not a murderer."

"You will swear."

"That's what we are doing, Rochelle. Forming a pact," Blackwell said. His patience was thinning. "What else? We do not have much time. The shifters are near."

I didn't know how he knew that the shifters were near, but the bubble of fear in my belly ramped up to a full boil.

"That's it."

Blackwell hissed and shook his head. "That's a fool's bargain. Easily broken by one powerful enough to do so."

"Could you break it?"

"No. Not if I agree to it."

"Is Jade Godfrey powerful enough?"

"If she isn't, it's only because she hasn't tried yet."

"You won't harm, allow to be harmed, or kill Beau. And unless I call, or accept your visit, you'll leave us alone. You'll pay for the sketches, plus shipping." Yes, shipping. Even in the face of a supposedly evil sorcerer, being hunted by werewolves, and trying to thwart destiny, I was still oddly practical.

"As I have always done."

"And …" — I faltered, knowing I should ask for something big here, something to balance his requests. "And you won't use me to hurt anyone else."

Blackwell raised an eyebrow. "That's a very loose term. I won't ask you to harm anyone. But again, I won't forfeit my life to do so."

"And if I show you your death?"

"I will not go quietly."

That was the point of this all, wasn't it? I couldn't ask him to be willing to die.

I nodded. "Okay. I'll let you put that hairband on me. I'll send you any sketches that feature you. I'll answer any questions you have, if I can. You won't harm or kill Beau. You'll leave us alone, unless we mutually set a time and place. You won't use me, or what I see, to deliberately hurt anyone, unless your life is in danger."

"You could ask for protection, Rochelle," he said. "I'm powerful enough to guard you against the majority of the Adept world. You could ask for money, riches. A home. A car. Jewels."

I shook my head.

Blackwell gazed at me as if I was some enigma.

Then he nodded. "I will emphasize my 'friends' clause. I will not knowingly endanger you. If you get in trouble — and you will get in trouble — I will help if it's in my power to do so. You're an investment, Rochelle Hawthorne. I'm taking great risks standing in this parking lot, on this continent. The Godfrey witches and the pack are sworn against me."

"Jade didn't want to see what I've seen. Why do you?"

"She thought you capable of showing her? Without an object such as this?"

I nodded, though I wasn't a hundred percent sure whether Jade thought that, or whether she just didn't want to chance it being a possibility.

Blackwell smiled, showing me his teeth. "Jade Godfrey is very young, and we are very different beasts. But beasts we both are."

I nodded again, not completely sure I hadn't just signed some sort of deal with the devil. Then I stepped forward into the half-circlet. For Beau, I would bargain with any devil, any evil. The cool metal expanded to slide around my forehead. Blackwell didn't remove his fingers.

He applied just enough pressure to the band at my temples to make me look up into his eyes. Then he whispered, "Keep eye contact, please. Show me, seer. Show me what you've seen."

"I don't know —"

The metal warmed against my forehead. My mind instantly flooded with the white light that usually accompanied a vision.

Blackwell grunted, satisfied.

I saw Beau lying dead on the ground, two feet ahead and to the right of me. I cried out and tried to reach for him.

"Not there, Rochelle," Blackwell said as he held my head firmly in place by the band. "It's all in your mind. Show me more, show me everything."

Images began moving through my mind. First, I saw the details I'd frantically drawn of the vision of Beau's death. The drops of blood on the concrete ... my necklace in Beau's limp fingers ... the look in Blackwell's eyes as he scanned the parking lot for me. The three wolves appearing, and Blackwell blasting them with his black orbs of light.

Blackwell grunted, surprised. "She said it was black," he murmured. I didn't understand what he meant, but I guessed that 'she' was Jade. Everything was apparently about Jade with Blackwell.

The recalled visions morphed in my mind. Snippets of past visions blurred by, including some bits that I wasn't sure I'd seen before — still images, moving moments. Most of them contained Jade. Only some contained Blackwell.

Jade drowning. Jade being crushed by the stone roof of the temple. Jade screaming for someone — someone she loved who I couldn't see ...

Then we were on the beach in the dark ... in the dreadfully dark darkness with monsters boiling out of a black ocean.

I jerked away. I desperately didn't want to relive this vision. This was the hallucination that had landed me in the hospital last fall. Since then, I hadn't even been able to finish and sell the sketches of the terror I'd seen on that gray beach after dark.

The terror that featured Jade in her red leather pants wielding a samurai sword.

Blackwell clamped his hands harder against my head, exerting more pressure than I thought possible with his fingertips alone. "Yes," he said. "Show me what happened in Tofino. Show me what happened to the black witch."

Dozens of dark-gray demons swarmed across the beach, their wicked claws at Jade's throat, blood and sand everywhere. Then the other monsters appeared. The first was a pale beast, fanged and clawed and red-eyed as it danced across the sand like the battle was some kind of demon-slaughtering beach party. This pale monster fought by Jade's side, standing over her as she fell, as she bled. It fought side by side with another monster — a seven-foot-tall terrifying mix of man and beast. The trio was surrounded by countless clawed and long-toothed monsters — an army of monsters, pitted against an army of hellspawn, with Jade Godfrey at their center.

I moaned. Was this the past or present I was now seeing? Had Jade Godfrey already led these monsters into battle? Or was this her future?

Blackwell laughed. "Those are your chosen protectors, Rochelle. Desmond Charles Llewellyn, the alpha of the West Coast North American Pack in beast form. And I do believe he's standing side-by-side with Kettil the Executioner, of the vampire Conclave. Also known as the good guys."

The idea that the monsters who fought at Jade's side actually existed — and that one of them was Desmond — horrified me. But I also knew what it was like to be maligned for being different. Blackwell's laughter bothered me.

"So I should trust you over them," I said. "Because you hide your monster beneath human skin?"

"No. You should trust me because I don't pretend to be anything different than what I am."

I wanted to argue — though I wasn't sure why I felt like defending people I didn't even know — except the vision was pulling me farther across the beach, dragging me to follow Jade. I dug my heels in. I leaned away, but I managed only to pull against Blackwell's hold, not affecting the vision in the least.

In my mind, sand hung suspended in the air. Jade was running before me, leaving everyone else behind her. I'd seen her move this fast in Desmond's kitchen only a few hours before. Well, I hadn't seen her actually move.

The dowser raised her sword above her head, leaping through crashing surf that would have cut me off at the knees.

I squeezed my eyes shut, as if that would shut out what was to come. I'd never seen a vision in so much detail before. Maybe Beau was right and the pills had been obstructing my magic.

"Open your eyes, Rochelle," Blackwell said. "Remember our bargain. You show me everything."

I opened my eyes, knowing that closing them did nothing to stop the vision anyway. My heart rate ramped up, beating painfully against my breastbone.

"Everything," I muttered, becoming overwhelmed with the deal I'd made. "That … is that even possible?"

The images began to flip rapidly, somehow timed with my heartbeat. They piled on top of each other, fighting to manifest so quickly that they appeared as still images now. It was as if I was rapidly flipping through my sketchbook. More sand, a glint of moonlight off Jade's sword, blood on a craggy rock. Then Jade falling, black light swirling around her —

"Slow down, seer," Blackwell said. He sounded as if he was in pain, but other than the heat of the band, the cold of the day, and my own emotions, I hadn't felt any discomfort yet. Not even a hint of a migraine.

Then the visions began to blur so much that I couldn't distinguish between them. I became dizzy, and then queasy, from this deluge. Suddenly, I wasn't going to be able to stay upright much longer.

I swayed forward, my knees buckling. I reached up to steady myself by grasping Blackwell's wrists. His fingertips were still pressed to either side of the half-circlet against my temples.

I felt a pulse of electricity similar to what I'd felt when touching Jade, but this time accompanied by searing heat that flared between my hands and Blackwell's wrists. Or maybe it came from him to me.

He hissed and jerked his arms away from my grasp, pulling the half-circlet off my forehead as he did so.

The metal hairband hit the pavement between us, but I heard this more than saw it. The whiteout of the visions made my actual sight hazy, though I could now make out the outline of the sorcerer and the parking lot behind him.

Blackwell was shaking his wrists.

"I'm sorry," I cried.

"I told you to slow down." The sorcerer's face was pained. "I should have been more careful, but you must listen —"

He looked up and behind me abruptly.

I turned to follow his gaze, but I couldn't see anything except the empty parking lot and the side road beyond. No cars had passed since Blackwell had appeared. I wondered if he'd set up one of those spells again, like the one that had stopped the people in the restaurant from seeing us.

The white haze was slowly dissipating from my eyesight, but I still felt dizzy. Drained, as Blackwell said I would.

"Remember our bargain, Rochelle," the sorcerer said, pulling my attention back to him.

He stooped to pick up the half-circlet. This movement shortened the sleeves of his suit and shirt. The skin of his wrists was an ugly, painful-looking puckered red, burned with the pattern of my fingers.

I gasped.

He tucked the half-circlet into his pocket. "Your new friends are here, but they'll never be able to protect you like I could."

I looked wildly around the parking lot. I was starting to shake, and my legs still weren't holding me upright properly.

Just as I was about to look back and question Blackwell about the burns, three wolves appeared on the grassy edge of the far side of the parking lot. They stood together, posed as if they'd just stepped out of my sketchbook and into the real world.

The darker wolf in the middle of the trio threw its head back and howled. The sound reverberated through the parking lot.

The hair on the back of my neck stood up. I felt an intense need to run — or to fall on my knees and expose my neck. I didn't do either.

If the wolves were here, then I'd failed to stop the vision. I looked around frantically for Beau.

Then I remembered the necklace where I still wore it. I slammed my hand against it so hard that the stone dug painfully into my breastbone and palm, even through my T-shirt and hoodie.

The wolves on either side of the dark gray wolf lowered their heads, flattened their ears, and bared their wicked teeth in a series of snarling, ferocious growls.

"Hunting at dusk in wolf form. I'm flattered," Blackwell said behind me. "But the shifters have made a mistake, as they always seem to do. As they will with you as well, Rochelle."

I kept my eyes glued to the wolves. "They found you, didn't they?"

"Indeed. But they came without the warrior's daughter." The sorcerer laughed. "I'm oddly disappointed."

"You're insane."

"Aren't we all?"

An answering howl sounded out somewhere off in the distance.

As if they'd been waiting for this signal, the wolves crouched down, ready to spring.

"Remember, Rochelle," Blackwell said.

"I'll remember," I answered, but I didn't take my eyes off the wolves. I should be running, fleeing. The farther I took the necklace from the parking lot of the barbershop, the better. But could shapeshifters distinguish between friend and foe in their animal forms? And even if they could — would I be considered a friend? Or would they chase me if I ran?

All three wolves leaped for me.

I screamed, ducking and covering my head as I felt them blow past me. The fur of the one on the left actually brushed my face. A fleeting glimpse of a purple-paisley pattern obscured my eyesight. I blinked and it was gone.

The three of them landed behind me.

I spun, expecting to see the vision unfold before me. Expecting to see Blackwell throwing his magic at the wolves. Expecting them to fall, and knowing now that I couldn't do anything about it. That maybe I'd been foolish to try. Maybe I'd brought the vision to reality by trying to thwart it.

Blackwell was gone.

Gone.

The wolf on the left — the one who'd brushed against me — let out a high-pitched yip of pain, then stumbled. It shook its head and pawed at the side of its face. Then it turned back in a blur of gray, lunging to snap its crazy-long teeth in my face.

I nearly wet my pants.

But I didn't move. There was no way I was going to move. Only prey ran.

It would be ironic to save Beau from Blackwell — which, at least for this moment, I seemed to have done — but then die in a wolf attack myself.

The darker wolf, who'd been in the middle of the formation and was obviously the leader, slammed its shoulder into the snarling one, throwing it onto the pavement. The lead wolf then gnashed its teeth viciously at the wolf lying on its side, who didn't move from its thrown position.

Satisfied, the lead wolf trotted away.

The other wolf righted itself, shook its head a second time, and then slunk away from me, all the while looking back resentfully as if I'd hurt it somehow.

The three wolves spread out across the parking lot, noses to the ground.

I lifted my hand to my cheek. I could still feel the trace sensation of the wolf's fur there. I remembered Blackwell's burned wrists. I wondered if I had hurt the wolf. I wondered what, if anything, I'd shown it in the brief moment it had touched me. Or had I just imagined the indignant look it gave me? Had I just imagined the glimpse of purple paisley? Purple was Lara's color of choice. Was Lara the wolf who brushed against me?

The wolves continued to ignore me as they systematically crisscrossed the parking lot. Gathering scents, I imagined. Clues to Blackwell's disappearance.

I knew how the sorcerer appeared and disappeared. I'd seen the day he found — no, stole — the amulet with the crimson stone he always wore. I always thought it had been a hallucination, but it wasn't. I thought that hallucination had marked the beginning of the years of torture my broken brain had doled out.

Except ... my brain wasn't broken. It had been a vision, not an overly active imagination. Not a hallucination.

I didn't have an unknown psychotic disorder.

I saw the future. Well, I assumed I saw the future. Though how, I had no idea. 'Magic' was what everyone had been suggesting, but that word — that concept — was generic enough that it didn't actually supply me with any true understanding. Was magic energy? The energy I felt as electricity when I touched Beau, Jade, and Blackwell? Energy from where?

And why me? What purpose did the visions have?

Was I a harbinger? A messenger? If so, whose messages was I relaying? And, again, why?

And — pushing aside thoughts that were too large to comprehend while standing in the middle of a deserted parking lot, freezing, dizzy and surrounded by wolves — what had I just agreed to with Blackwell?

The sorcerer collected things. Magical artifacts. I'd seen evidence of these devices three times now. The amulet, the amplifier in the restaurant, and the half-circlet that somehow gave him access to my visions.

He also collected people. He desperately wanted Jade Godfrey.

And he'd just collected me.

I stood there in the parking lot while the wolves did their tracking thing, awash in questions and piecing together what few answers I could. The white haze of the visions had lifted, though I was still chilled to the bone and drained. Really, really drained. I also kind of wished I'd retained more of the numbness, because my right arm was starting to throb again where I'd wretched it falling out of the bathroom window.

Despite feeling like crap, I really wasn't interested in standing around waiting anymore. I didn't think werewolves could talk in wolf form, but I imagined others would arrive soon.

Maybe they'd want answers, or maybe they'd be pissed with me. I didn't really care either way.

I didn't need all the answers to all of my huge questions to know where I wanted to be. Besides not wanting to be here anymore, I mean.

I also wasn't interested in testing the theory of whether or not I'd thwarted the vision or merely delayed it. I needed the necklace — and Beau — to be nowhere near this parking lot, ever.

So I turned and walked away. The wolves let me go with barely a glance. I guess they'd already proven I was easy to track.

Each step I took back to Beau was less shaky than the first.

CHAPTER SIXTEEN

I STARTED TO WALK BACK the way I'd come, but when it came time to turn up toward the bus stop, I kept walking. I figured the road I was on was parallel to the main road, so that I'd see the bus when it passed. Though it wasn't like I could sprint the block or more to catch it, so my logic was definitely flawed. Still, I didn't feel like changing directions.

I wondered where the werewolves had parked. I wondered if they changed shape in their cars. If they did, where did their clothes go? I couldn't remember what had happened to Beau's clothing when he turned into his tiger.

I wondered if the wolves could track Blackwell when he just disappeared like that. Could they track the magic of the amulet he wore?

I wondered if they were going to come after me.

But I couldn't get worked up about any of it. I was so tired, bone-tired, and yet I felt light.

I felt free. I felt ready.

The sun came out from behind the low cloud to warm my back with a kiss of heat just before it finished setting. I pulled my tinted glasses out of my bag and slid them over my sun-sensitive eyes. It was an automatic sort of gesture, because I didn't really need them.

A few cars sped by in both directions, but the bulk of the traffic stayed on the main road to my right. I passed a few houses with large front lawns as I walked. Not all the driveways were paved, and some of the porches needed paint.

My phone pinged, and I checked it to find a text message from Blackwell. I was really hoping it would be from Beau, even though he didn't have a phone.

> *I look forward to our next meeting, Rochelle.*

So the wolves hadn't gotten the sorcerer. I should be worried about that, shouldn't I? Did I want the shapeshifters to get Blackwell? I didn't even know what the sorcerer had done to them, or to Jade Godfrey. I didn't really want to know. I just wanted to be in the Brave with Beau.

I was going to buy Beau a phone. No, I was just never going to leave his side again. Then I didn't have to worry about being able to call him.

An old Chinese man was walking toward me. I would have sworn I could see the street empty for blocks ahead, but I hadn't noticed him until he was only about two houses away. Maybe he'd crossed onto the sidewalk from one of the driveways.

I could see that the guy was a character even fifty or so feet away from him. He was wearing a white dress and flip-flops. I was cold in my jeans and hoodie, so he must be freezing. But he was smiling away like the world was his playground.

Maybe he was crazy. I didn't mind crazy. I still wasn't completely sure I wasn't living in a fantasy world myself. I was still working through all that in my beleaguered mind.

He was about twenty feet in front of me now, grinning at me like we knew each other. I wondered if I'd ever seen a person as old as him before. Yet, he walked

... lightly. He wasn't gliding or anything, but there was something about him ... something more.

"We meet," he said when he was about ten feet away. I'd been about to step to the side to skirt around him. I'd already averted my eyes so to not accidentally engage whatever weirdness he might have going on in his head.

He reached out his hand, but not for me to shake. It was almost as if he expected to grab something.

I tripped. With my head cranked to the side to look at the old guy, I hadn't seen that the driveway I was crossing was cracked right down the middle. I twisted my ankle. I threw my hands forward as I realized I wasn't going to get my other foot underneath me in time. I fell.

My left elbow connected with the old guy's outstretched hand.

A jolt of electricity ran up my arm.

I got my other foot under me just as the shockwave hit my brain and everything went blurry. My legs went to jelly.

"Sorry, sorry," the old man said. His Asian accent was crazy-thick. He was holding me aloft, as if I wasn't only an inch or so shorter than him and probably just as heavy. He was sturdy underneath the old man skin.

I got my legs sorted back underneath me as I straightened. He let go.

I stared at him. For someone so old, his almost-white hair was thick and his back was straight. He was wearing a robe, not a dress as I'd assumed. It was long enough to hit the tops of his sandaled feet, mostly white with some simple gold embroidery at the edges of the cuffs and neckline.

"You caught me."

"Yes."

"You knew I was going to fall."

"Big crack in pavement."

"You gave me a shock when you touched me."

"Did I?"

He was grinning at me so heartily that I started to think I'd imagined the electric shock and the hazy vision.

I turned away. The sidewalk stretched endlessly in front of me. But I didn't keep walking.

Why was I walking down this road anyway? The bus would have had me back in Portland by now.

I looked back at the Asian man. He nodded his head, encouragingly.

"I'm Rochelle ... Hawthorne Saintpaul."

"Yes. Daughter of Jane Hawthorne, the Oracle of Philadelphia, and Kai Lei, a sorcerer of Hong Kong."

The bottom dropped out of my stomach. Or maybe that was what it felt like when a long-lost fragment of your life snapped into place.

"I'm Chi Wen," the old man continued, as I swayed before him like I was ready to drop in a faint. "Far seer of the guardian nine."

"Guardian of what?" I heard myself whisper, though I wasn't currently formulating any thoughts in my empty, empty mind.

"The world and all the magic within it." Chi Wen laughed as if his assertion wasn't exactly as insane as it sounded.

"You knew my parents?"

"No. I'm sorry, fledgling. I did not. Shall we continue to walk? I'm enjoying the feeling of the setting sun on my face."

Completely mute, I pivoted and followed after him in the direction I'd just come. We walked, me a step behind for a block or more.

At some point, I spoke. "There are wolves up ahead."

"Yes," he replied gleefully. "Interesting creatures. I will soon meet one who runs with the warrior's daughter — her hair intrigues me — but today is not that day."

Warrior's daughter ... Far seer ... guardian of all the magic in the world ... Jane the Oracle of Philadelphia ...

"Green hair. Kandy," I blurted. My voice was shaky. But then, so was I.

Chi Wen nodded but said nothing else.

"Jade Godfrey ..." I said. "She said she knew someone like me."

"She said she knew someone like me." Chi Wen repeated my sentence word for word, yet there was a correction of my phrasing in there somewhere. I didn't catch whatever he was emphasizing though. Maybe the 'me?' It might have been his accent, or it might have been my inherent unwillingness to be corrected.

We walked for a few more blocks. I could see the strip mall up ahead, but it wasn't close enough for me to distinguish the barbershop yet.

"So ... this is all real?"

Chi Wen took a deep breath, and slowly lifted his arms like wings to the sides. "You feel the air in your lungs, yes?"

"Yes."

"The stone underneath your feet?"

"Pavement, but yes."

Chi Wen stopped and gazed down at the ground for a moment. "Pavement," he said.

He didn't move.

A car passed us, then another.

I shuffled my feet. I wasn't sure if … maybe he'd gone to sleep? With his eyes open in a completely creepy fashion?

"You …" My voice cracked. I started again, speaking louder. "You were saying?"

Chi Wen began walking again without warning. I stumbled after him.

"I like the sun," he said. "Most dragons do not, except the warrior. Jade's father enjoys the beach."

Yeah, I didn't follow that segue. *What did he and Jade's father have to do with dragons? And wait, dragons were real now? Like fire-breathing, treasure-hoarding dragons with wings and scales and wickedly long claws?*

Chi Wen held his right hand to the side at hip height, palm up.

For a moment, I thought I was supposed to take it. Then I tripped again. I caught my fall this time, without his help. I'd never felt so clumsy in my life.

He withdrew his hand.

"You are weary," he said without turning his head. That was an easy enough assessment to make just by looking at me. "You were not ready for the sorcerer's request."

I was lagging behind, both in the conversation and the walk. I jogged a couple of steps to catch up to him. He was walking with his eyes closed. I opened my mouth to admonish him, as if he was some child. Then I snapped it shut.

He chuckled.

"I'm confused," I said.

"Yes."

"You're not helping."

"I am helping. You are not absorbing. Shall I speak slower?"

"God, no. You could pick up the pace."

"I do not believe you could follow if I were to walk faster."

I sighed. Then I walked into him as he pivoted to stop directly in front of me. It was like hitting a brick wall and bouncing off. I stumbled back but managed not to fall. I'd cracked my forehead against his, and along with a wallop of pain, I got that burst of electricity again.

Magic. That was what a hell of a lot of magic felt like.

"First lesson, for hasty fledgling," the old man said.

"I'm not hasty at all," I countered while I rubbed my sore forehead. "I'm steady. I'm focused."

"Hasty fledgling," he repeated. "What do you see when you look at me?"

"Old Chinese guy."

"Look closer."

"Wrinkles, kind of gnarly teeth."

His smile expanded. Then, so quickly that I didn't register the movement until he withdrew his hand, he tapped me lightly between the eyes. "You are using the wrong eye."

I frowned. I didn't like hokey crap. Just because I was willing to take the leap that magic actually existed, that didn't mean I was going to get all spiritual or metaphysical.

"And be truthful with yourself, fledgling."

That pissed me off further. I was always truthful to myself ... at least I always tried to be.

But I'd asked the questions. I wanted answers. So I'd jump through his hoops.

I looked at Chi Wen more closely. He stood about two feet away and was maybe an inch taller than me.

"White ... gold," I murmured. "All around you. Is that ... magic?"

The old man shrugged. "Aura reading. A basic skill that your kind should manifest early."

I gritted my teeth at the 'your kind' part of the statement. I had no idea if he was dissing me or not, and normally I wouldn't put up with that garbage. But I was slightly worried about the pavement-staring-thing happening again. He'd been about to tell me something that I thought might be important — like how I could figure out what was real and what wasn't real — when I'd distracted him by correcting his word choice. I wasn't going to derail him a second time.

"What do you see when you look at me?" I asked him.

His smile widened until it was almost impossibly large for his tiny face. This expression informed me that I didn't want to know the answer.

"What color?" I amended.

"White," he answered. "All around you, but especially in your eyes."

He could see through my tinted glasses. I knew that shouldn't have surprised me. But I was getting the feeling he could also see inside my head, and that freaked me out.

"I'm a seer?"

"An oracle by birth." I wasn't sure that was an entire answer, but I pressed forward with my initial line of questioning, hoping to keep him on track.

"Same as you?"

"No."

"You don't see the future?"

"I do."

"But we're not the same."

"No."

Could he be more frustratingly enigmatic? Probably not. Based on his choice of outfit and the ever-present smile, I had a feeling it was kind of his shtick.

"Why do I see what I see … Blackwell and Jade Godfrey. And not, like, anyone I know, or public figures, or whoever?"

"Magic sees magic, not the mundane," Chi Wen answered. "Perhaps the sorcerer and the warrior's daughter are the most powerful Adepts within your sphere. Or perhaps magic has its own reason, only to be revealed when it comes to pass."

Well, that cleared that up … like not at all.

"Can I see my own future?"

"No."

"Can you see my future?"

"Yes," he answered. Then he leaned into me and spoke very deliberately. "As you will see mine."

With that statement hanging in the air between us, he glanced to the left, down the road behind me. "Ah, here comes the boy. Good. I'm hungry, and you have cookies."

I followed his gaze up the road, away from the waning sunset toward Portland. "The boy who?"

Chi Wen, grinning mischievously now, rocked on his feet and didn't answer me.

As far as I could see, the road was empty in both directions.

Chi Wen tilted his head to one side as if listening to something.

"Suanmi, fire breather of the guardian nine, calls," he said. "Let's not answer her right away."

"Okay." I had no idea what he was talking about, but it seemed to make him happy so it was cool with me.

Then I saw the Brave barreling toward us. "Beau
…" His name came out as a sob that I quickly swallowed.

Chi Wen patted my shoulder and I tried to not
flinch from the touch of his magic. "You must be careful,
oracle," he said. His tone was epically serious suddenly.
"What you choose to change won't always change. And
when it does, the change is not necessarily what is best.
The sorcerer had no ill intent toward the boy, and the
pack underestimated you just long enough. Jade Godfrey's magic is powerful, but it is volatile and not solely
within her control. You were lucky."

"I'll take it."

Chi Wen nodded. "Luck is also capricious. It de-
mands a sacrifice. Magic moves where it will, not where
we wish it."

I swallowed down the ball of fear that had lodged
in my throat, as I nodded back at him.

The Brave pulled up next to us. I looked up. Beau
was grinning down at me from the open window, but his
smile looked strained. "Am I late?" he asked. "I got your
note, but I figured as long as I had the Brave, I could
come to you. I'm not so cool with the waiting."

"Have you eaten all the cookies?" Chi Wen called
out. He was shuffling around the front of the Brave to
the door on the street side.

Beau laughed and looked down at me questioningly. I couldn't stop gazing at him. Only the need to
also be touching him forced me to finally look away in
order to follow Chi Wen.

I climbed into the Brave to find the old man at the
kitchen table with my sketches already spread out before him and the bag of Oreos in his lap. Inexplicably,
he also had my sketchbook, which should have been in
my bag. I hadn't seen or felt him lift it off me.

"That's not disconcerting at all," I muttered as I
latched the door behind me.

"The old man moves fast," Beau said.

As I crossed toward him, I caught my reflection in the rearview mirror. For a split second, I didn't recognize myself. It could have been the thick white streak among the black mass of my hair, or the goofy grin spread across my face, but maybe it was just that I was seeing me. As I truly was, magic and all.

"Rochelle?" Beau asked. "Everything okay now?"

I didn't answer.

Instead, I climbed in his lap to plaster a kiss on him. My ass hit the horn, but I chose to ignore it.

We cut west out of Portland on Highway 26 and turned south at Highway 101 to stop in Cannon Beach and get a glimpse of the Haystack Rock in the moonlight. It was chilly and windy on the beach, but not so much in Beau's arms. Chi Wen had left us before we pulled to a full stop in the Tolovana Beach State Park parking lot. The old man had just wandered off and not returned, at least not yet.

I had a feeling I'd be seeing him again. Soon.

Beau and I had tumbled into bed right there in the parking lot, though we couldn't legally park overnight. My boyfriend seemed very eager to make sure that every inch of me had survived my meeting with Blackwell unscathed. I had, but I certainly wasn't going to stop Beau when he wanted to check a second time.

And, yeah. I said boyfriend. My first and only.

Who else was going to put up with a girlfriend who saw the future?

Beau didn't ask about the vision that made me sneak out of the house and meet with Blackwell. I guessed he could flip through my sketchbook for enlightenment, but I didn't think he'd do that without asking permission. I really hoped he didn't ask though, because I'm not sure I could ever say no to him. But seeing himself dead wouldn't be very good for his soul, would it?

I was pretty sure Beau was mad about me leaving without him, but I certainly wasn't going to mention it lying naked, sprawled across his chest, post-orgasm. In fact, part of me never wanted to move again.

"An oracle, huh?" Beau murmured into my neck as he traced the edges of the peony tattoo on my left shoulder. The newly inked tattoo was still a little sore, but he was careful not to touch it directly.

"Yeah, supposedly."

Silence fell between us again, and I really wanted to drift off into the bliss of a post-coital nap, but I felt … off. I didn't like having things unspoken between us. It was a new and, honestly, unwelcome sensation. I'd never needed to be okay with someone before. I didn't really like the idea of needing anything other than food, water, and some sort of shelter.

"How did you know where to find me?" I asked.

Beau sighed, like maybe he'd wanted the bliss to last a little longer as well. "Yeah, Audrey texted," he answered. "She told me that you were okay, and where to find you. I was waiting at the Brave." He half-rolled off the bed, fished around in the pockets of his hoodie that he'd tossed on the floor, and held up a brand-new looking iPhone.

"What does that mean?"

"That I had to kneel down to get out of the house, otherwise they weren't going to let me go."

"Like Kandy did?"

"No, she was already a member of the pack, that kneeling thing was just her acceptance of Audrey as beta. I guess Kandy had been against it for some reason."

"So ... you had to become a pack member?"

"No," he answered. He sounded steady and straightforward as always. "I didn't have to take an oath or anything, but I'm under obligation now because Audrey vouched for me. It means I'm on the pack leash, for a trial basis at least."

"And that's bad? Being tied to them?"

"Maybe. It goes both ways, though. They might not want me as much as I don't want them. But you ... they'll always want some sort of access to you. Everyone will, won't they? Even beyond the dowser, the old man, and the sorcerer."

"I don't think Jade will be seeking me out anytime soon," I said, but then brought the conversation back to the deal he'd made with the pack. "Being a pack member has benefits, like the healing thing you told me about?"

"Yeah."

Beau didn't elaborate and I didn't want to push any further into the fight I could feel looming now.

"Then I guess we both made deals to protect the other today," I finally said.

"Yeah? With Blackwell?"

"Yeah. Does that make us even?"

Beau laughed, quietly. "I took you to the pack full well knowing what could happen, Rochelle. I don't regret one second of it. I'd do anything for you."

Emotion welled in my chest and I pressed my face into Beau's shoulder, hard, as if that would help me control an explosion of tears or declaration of undying love. He grunted, and ran his fingers up and down my spine to soothe me. I'd never had anyone say, or even act like, they'd do anything for me before. So, yeah, I guess we were on even footing in that regard, because I already knew I'd throw myself in the path of a runaway train for Beau. Though, if I thought about it too much, the path that now connected me to Blackwell and Jade Godfrey could prove much more destructive than that of a single train.

"You left me." Beau spoke so quietly I almost didn't hear his specific words. "I wasn't sure you wanted me to follow."

"Not today," I said. "Any other day, but not today."

He nodded.

"Let's see how far the pack leash stretches," I said.

"I'm game. North or south?"

"South, for a bit, I think."

"No more leaving, Rochelle," he said. "Not even for my own good."

"I'm not going to promise that, Beau," I replied. "You have to trust me. The old man said I was lucky this time, but that luck was capricious."

Beau lifted my left hand to his mouth and pressed a kiss to the black butterfly tattoo on my inner wrist. "I'll follow your luck anywhere. Then I'll fight and survive at your side if it runs out."

"When it runs out. It's always when, not if."

"Yeah, it is."

"To that I'm willing to swear, then. Me and you, beyond luck," I whispered. Then, I pulled the covers over my head as I climbed on top of Beau for the second time. He wrapped his hands around my hips, as I leaned over to press a tender kiss to his mouth.

Three days ago, I wouldn't have been capable of being tender, because that would have meant opening myself up to the betrayal and heartbreak that people left in their wakes when they walked away. But for Beau, I'd try anything once.

I had everything that mattered within my reach. Every single step forward was mine to take.

And that was more than I'd ever thought possible.

Acknowledgements

With thanks to:

My story & line editor

Scott Fitzgerald Gray

My proof reader

Leiah Cooper

My beta readers

Heather Lewis, Heidi Tengsdal, and Karen Turkal

For their continual encouragement, feedback, & general advice

Joanne, Linda, & Alison, for character background, for fact

checking, & advice

Nick Russell, for everything RV related

For her Art

Irene Langholm

Elizabeth Mackey

MEGHAN CIANA DOIDGE is an award-winning writer based out of Vancouver, British Columbia, Canada. She has a penchant for bloody love stories, superheroes, and the supernatural. She also has a thing for chocolate, potatoes, and sock yarn.

Novels

After The Virus
Spirit Binder
Time Walker
Cupcakes, Trinkets, and Other Deadly Magic (Dowser 1)
Trinkets, Treasures, and Other Bloody Magic (Dowser 2)
Treasures, Demons, and Other Black Magic (Dowser 3)
I See Me (Oracle 1)

Novellas/Shorts

Love Lies Bleeding
The Graveyard Kiss

For giveaways, news, and glimpses of upcoming stories, please connect with Meghan on her:

Personal blog, www.madebymeghan.ca
Twitter, @mcdoidge
And/or Facebook, Meghan Ciana Doidge

Please also consider leaving an honest review at your point of sale outlet

Time to stock up on chocolate.

You're going to need it.

Dowser Series · Book 1

CUPCAKES, TRINKETS, and other DEADLY MAGIC

MEGHAN CIANA DOIDGE

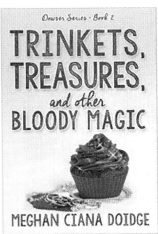

Dowser Series · Book 2

TRINKETS, TREASURES, and other BLOODY MAGIC

MEGHAN CIANA DOIDGE

Dowser Series · Book 3

TREASURES, DEMONS, and other BLACK MAGIC

MEGHAN CIANA DOIDGE

45112766R00163

Made in the USA
Charleston, SC
12 August 2015